C000193378

THE
DIVIDE

from Frome & Wells

from Frome

from Frome

Chapman...

Corsley Heath

"NOT SO LONG AGO, LET IT NOT BE FORGOTTEN,

Bradley Ho.

Kilmington

from Bruton & Castle Cary

104   102   100   The...   98

Stour Head Ho   Mere

100

from Wincaunton   a

Leals Ho.

K.

D O R S E

Shaftsbury

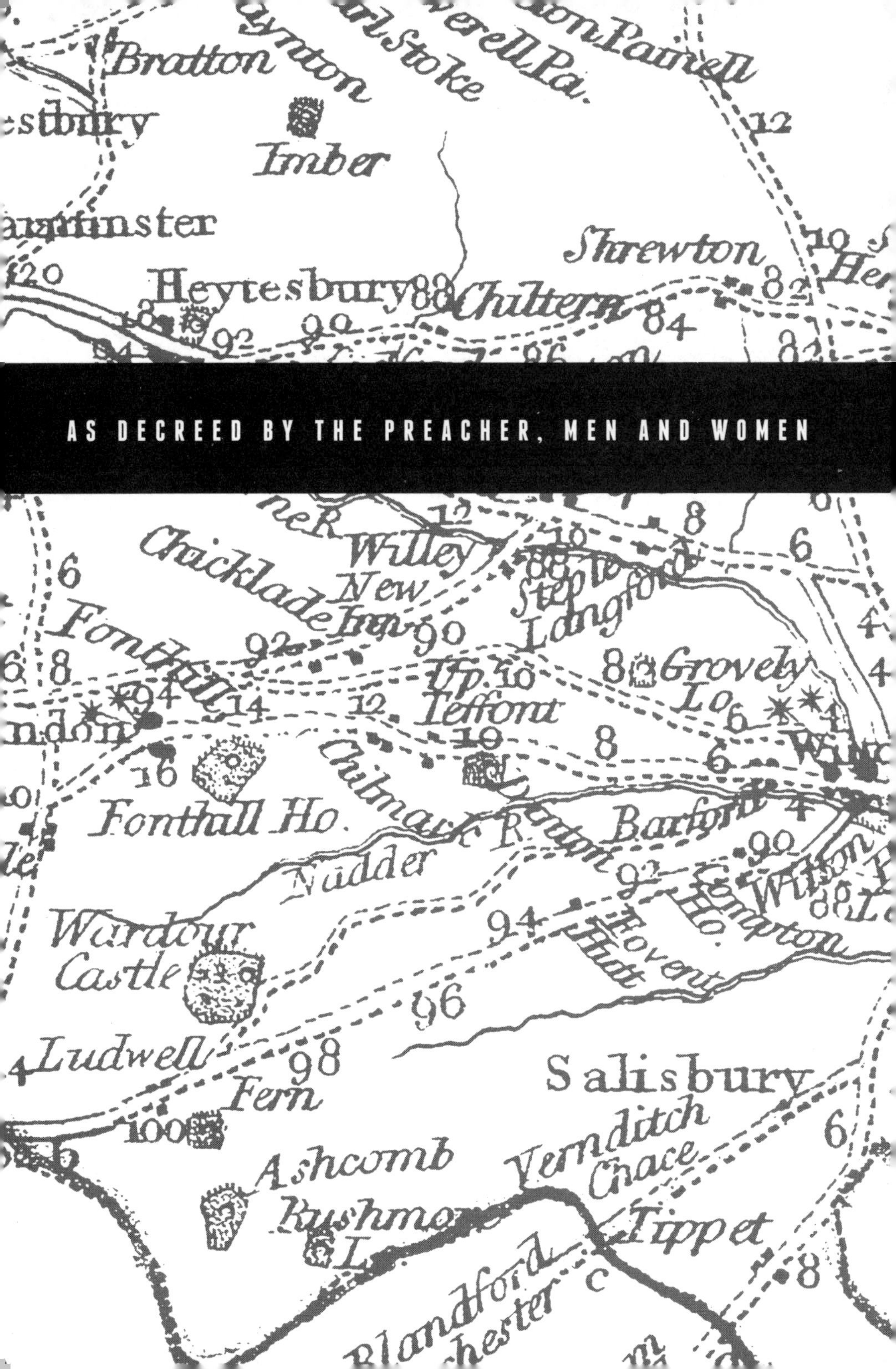

AS DECREED BY THE PREACHER, MEN AND WOMEN

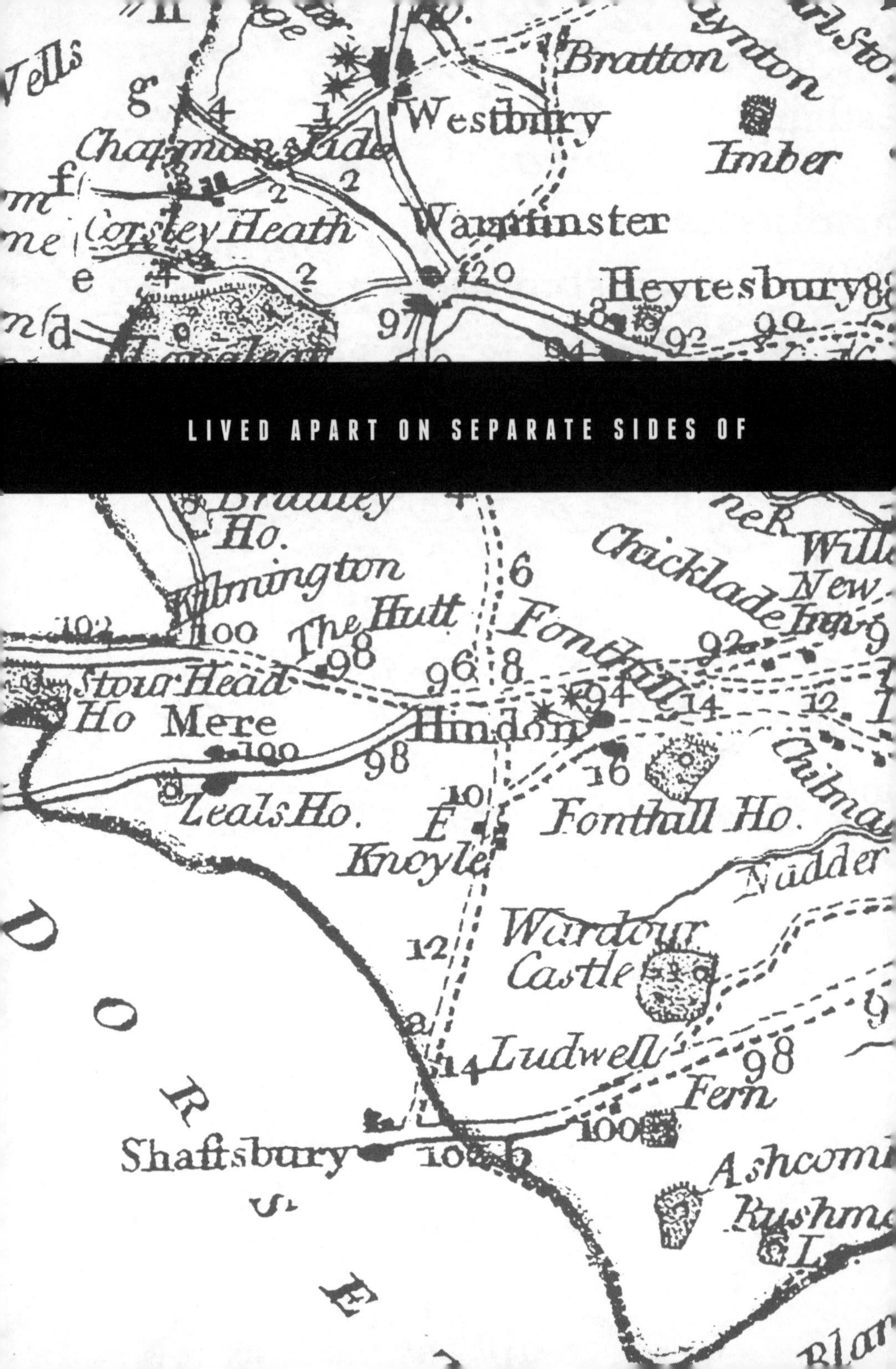

LIVED APART ON SEPARATE SIDES OF

THE DIVIDE IN SEGREGATED ISOLATION."

to Andover &
Basingstoke–the
London Rd.

to London by Weyhill
& Andover

to L

74   to London thro
         Stockbridge

76

Thruxton
To

Dean Ho.

Brickworth
White
Parish
Landford
Ho.
10

each
Ho.
12   to Southampton

to Southampton
thro Rumsey

shire

For Heth, Kath & Simon
for their undivided support
and for Rob Shearman
without whom …

THE DIVIDE

ALAN AYCKBOURN

Published in August 2019 by PS Publishing Ltd
by arrangement with the author.
All rights reserved by the author.

FIRST PS EDITION

ISBN
978-1-78636-446-3 (Signed edition)
978-1-78636-447-0 (Unsigned edition)

Cover and book design by Pedro Marques.

Printed in England by the T.J. International
on Vancouver Cream Bookwove 80 gsm stock.

PS Publishing Ltd
Grosvenor House
1 New Road
Hornsea, HU18 1PG
England
editor@pspublishing.co.uk
WWW.PSPUBLISHING.CO.UK

THE DIVIDE

Being so closely involved with the events leading up to the fall of the Divide, I have been asked on countless occasions to write down my experiences leading up to that momentous event. Till now, I have always declined. I had two reasons for doing so. The first was that, on a professional level, my reputation, such as it is, has been based till now as a successful writer of popular fiction. Not only was I hesitant to attempt a factual account of real events but I was anxious lest they be mistaken, especially by the young, as creations of my own imagination. This period in our history is far too important to be relegated to the realms of myth for recent generations who never experienced them at first hand. We are often too ready to dismiss or conveniently forget such uncomfortable or inconvenient chapters in our history. My second reason for refusing was, on a personal level, though long in the past the events are still too clear for us who lived through them for the pain they caused to be entirely softened by time, most especially for my Mother. Although we both lived through them together, I somehow felt she, a loving parent and partner, bore the brunt of events far worse than I, an immature fourteen-year-old. But my Mother died a few weeks ago. It was thankfully a peaceful passing, in her own bed as she would have wanted. She'd reached a good age and her family were all there, myself, her daughter, her devoted son-in-law and her three beloved grandchildren, Fayla, Japeth and Jilli, to say our farewells to Mama.

First, some apologies. What follows is less a straight narrative and more a montage gathered from various sources, mostly from my own diary from the age of eight upwards. I've edited this as little as possible, attempting to avoid the obvious trap of trying to improve, through misguided hindsight, the outpourings of an immature girl battling the usual agonies of adolescence. Some entries I was tempted to remove to spare my blushes. Particularly my embarrassing 'sub Brontë' period in which I appear to have been completely carried away! Nonetheless I hope my diary will capture at least some of the flavour of how it was to live and grow up, as a child, during the final years of The Preacher's regime, in an isolated, strictly puritanical all-female society entirely segregated from men. The inhabitants meekly underwent a form of endless penance on behalf of their sex for sins long past and wrongs long forgotten. The image in our Village Square of The Men's Memorial with its ten thousand names of those who died from The Plague will remain with me for ever. It stood dominating everything, a massive granite reminder to all us Women, of our responsibility for that appalling loss of life. We were a society ruled by guilt which we were seldom allowed to forget. Four times a year, spring, summer, autumn and winter, came those Days of Reflection, when the entire Village would fall silent for twenty-four hours, whilst each of us jointly acknowledged her responsibility for the past. I suppose my view of events is slightly skewed by the fact that my mother's partner, my Mapa as she was known, was devoutly Orthodox. As children, during our early years especially, my brother and I were brought up strictly according to the rules laid down by The Preacher.

As to The Preacher himself (or herself, we were never quite sure), we were encouraged to believe that he/she was immortal and still lived. But I think many of us abandoned that belief along with Father Christmas (who was most definitely frowned upon!) Evidence, following the fall of the Divide, suggests that the original Preacher died many years earlier (some reports say from a sexually transmitted disease!) and was replaced by a committee of two, initially men but later on of both sexes in an attempt to maintain the status quo established by The Preacher and the legacy he left in his *Book of Certitude*, the Bible we were all meant to live by.

There were, needless to say, powerful factions of society, particularly on the Male side, with a considerable vested interest to maintain it. But when has it ever been otherwise?

The other major source I have drawn from is my own brother, Elihu's diary. He was a slightly less conscientious diarist than I, being a boy he became preoccupied with Other Things.

In the case of both our respective diaries, I have used their original system of dating that is the PD (Post Divide) method we lived under at that time. I never quite understood why our lives were run on this system, rather than the previous Anno Domini version. Possibly it was intended to make our lives feel greyer still, without days of the week or calendar months. Just numbers and seasons. It certainly gave our existence a sense of remorseless monotony and so perhaps achieved its intention.

Other documents I've gathered from here, there and everywhere and must especially thank Talyed Chilzer, the former Chair of South Sarum Village Council for access to previously restricted documents including the trial transcripts. I have also included material from the archive of the now defunct *North Sarum Journal*. My reason for this was I was aware that I had otherwise included very little relating to conditions North of the Divide during that period. It was a region, of course, from which I, as a Woman, was excluded. By including samples of correspondence from its lively letters column plus a rather enlightened (certainly for the period) leading article, I hope to redress this imbalance somewhat. My grateful thanks also to the *Journal*'s Archivist, Simeon Mappletrose. Lastly, without apologies, I occasionally quote from The Prophet's *Book of Certitude*, a thick tome we were instructed to read every morning and night but rarely did.

By rights, I ought to dedicate this book to the memory of the lovers, Elihu and Giella, who more than any other single individual were instrumental in bringing down The Divide. But their praises have already been sung by many and countless legends have already been written about them both and even this book is really about them so I'm sure they will forgive me, wherever they are, if I dedicate this book to the least sung hero, my dearest late Mama, Chayza, who was there throughout and indomitably survived it all. This is for her.

Soween Clay-Flyn
April 2154

3

Part I
GROWING PAINS

"WE LEARN that in the beginning God created Man. And that from Man He also created Woman. And although we are told that God created Man in His own image, Woman was created separately, not in the image of God but as a part of Man, since she was created out of him. Woman was therefore intended to assist and serve Man and to bear his children. That was God's intention.

AT THE START, Men and Women were content to abide by this, faithfully following their God-given roles, each of them serving the other. Whilst Man toiled all day to support them, the Woman was content to stay home to care for his house, his children and his welfare. Unselfishly. Her natural role was to put herself second to her Man and to her family, remaining constantly faithful.

BUT AS TIME PASSED Woman grew restless and was no longer content to remain at home and devote herself to her family. Instead she yearned to leave the home, dissatisfied with the role God had allotted her. She questioned why she should stay home whilst Man went out to work? In this way she deliberately flouted God's wishes. But she cunningly prevailed upon Man, as she had done since the Beginning, and persuaded him that she too should abandon their home in order to work and She further prevailed upon him that he should sometimes stay home, thus contravening the laws laid down by God in the beginning. Once free of the house,

Woman grew powerful and more strident. Whilst Man, because he was weak, yielded to her wishes, granting her yet more freedom. But soon the balance between them became so unstable that neither Man nor Woman was content, neither fulfilling the task for which they had been designed. It was as if in olden times the servants had suddenly risen from below, driving the masters downstairs to serve them. As if the cart had suddenly demanded that it lead the horse. For just as Woman's weakness lies in her covert ambition to achieve supremacy over Man, so it is Man's weakness to succumb to her. For Woman by her nature is cunning and manipulative, much as the Serpent before her. Man's nature is open and trusting and vulnerable to her sly machinations, like Adam was before him.

AND GOD BECAME ANGRY when He saw this and resolved to destroy them. He sent down a powerful and terrible Plague which destroyed millions, both Men and Women. But then God grew merciful and relented and the Plague altered so that now only the Men were Vulnerable whilst the Women, though they still carried its poisonous seeds within them, became immune. So the Men continued to die and, seeing the Women were infecting them, they first sought shelter from them in fear, shutting themselves away. But the Women continued to hunt out Men to satisfy their carnal desires, so the Men, in self protection, began to slaughter them. And the Women responded and did likewise until there developed a terrible war between them and humankind was reduced to a mere handful.

AND THERE AROSE AMONG THEM one they called The Preacher who called for sanity and a return to the original wishes of God, imploring both sides to confess the folly of their ways. And The Preacher drew a line between them and ordered the Men to live to the North and the Women to the South. And he decreed that this line was hereafter to be called the Divide. He ruled that no Man, unless he was protected, should go South of this Divide and no unshielded Woman should step North of it. Thus Men and Women from that time on did not meet face-to-face except when they were covered."

SOUTH SARUM VILLAGE INFANT SCHOOL, CLASS 1.
WRITING EXERCISE

My name is Eliny Clay
I am a boy aged 5 years.

My mama is called chayza. She mostly looks
after us but she used to work in the food
factory before. I love her very much.

My Mapa is called Kest. She is a doctor. She
goes to work every day and works very hard.
I love her very much.

My sister is called Soween. She is three. She is two
years younger than me. I love her very much
sometimes.

I am writing this with my new pen. I am in class one.
My sister will also come to this school soon.

In my class there are nine girls and two boys. The
other boy is called Fecge. He is my best friend.
I do not like girls they are too bossy.

Our teacher is Teacher Kluth. I like her very much.

I live in South Sarum Village.

SOUTH SARUM VILLAGE INFANT SCHOOL, CLASS 1.
WRITING EXERCISE

My name is Soween Clay.

I am a girl aged 5 years.

My mama is called chayza. She looks after us but sometimes she used to work in a food factory. I love her very much.

My mapa is called kest. She is a doctor. She goes of to work everyday and works hard. I love her very much.

My Brother is called Elihu. He is Seven. He is two years older than me. I love him very very much.

In my class there is seven girls and two boys.

I am writting this with my new pen.

I am in class one. Elihu is in class two.

Our teacher is teacher kluth. I like her very much.

I live in south sarum Village

SOUTH SARUM VILLAGE JUNIOR SCHOOL – CLASS 3
ENGLISH ESSAY BY ELIHU CLAY AGED 9

What I want to do when I'm older

There is lots of things I would like to do when I'm older. For one I would like to be an Explorer.

The world is very big and there must be lots of places here no one goes very much any more. Till now I have only lived in South Sarum with my family which is a very small place and you keep meeting the same people all the time, most of them girls or women which is boring.

When I get older I would like to meet different people and see lots of different places. My friend Fergo wants to join the Monitors because they are extremely tough and strong and they also learn to fight especially the bad people when they are wicked.

When I am eleven I will leave this school and because I am a Boy I will have a tutor to teach me at home. The Tutor will tell me about all the other things I can do as a Man once I cross the Divide.

I can't wait till I cross over and I'm eighteen and turn into a Man.

But I may be an artist as I am also brilliant at drawing.

SOUTH SARUM VILLAGE JUNIOR SCHOOL – CLASS 2
HISTORY ESSAY BY SOWEEN CLAY AGED 7

I live South of the Divide in South Sarum Village.

Before the Divide happened, it was a part of Salisbury which was a big city with thousands of people. Men lived here as well as Women. Not like today.

Today it has 510 people. 478 women, 28 girls and 4 boys. The Girls will all live here and become Women as soon as they are twelve. They will then all stay here till they grow very old and die.

The Boys when they become 18 have to move over to North of the Divide to live with the Men. That is the rule of the Preacher.

In olden days, Women and Men all used to live together. But they weren't very happy and they used to argue a lot. But when the plague came, millions and millions of people all died until there were only a very few left.

And the Preacher came and in Her Wisdom She created the Divide and told the Men to live to the North and the Women to live to the South, like it is today.

And the Preacher said, So it shall be until the end of Time. And the Preacher still lives to this day though she is extremely old.

And if a Women goes North she has to wear a suit and if a Man comes South he also needs to wear a suit. Women do not go North very much but the Men sometimes come South to teach young Boys on how to be Men.

One day my brother Elihu will have to wear a suit too and I won't see him again which makes me sad. The end.

Sir,

I assume the tone of your leading article (dated 24 Summer 112 PD) was deliberately intended to be controversial for I can conceive of no other reason for having written it. It came over to this reader, along with countless others I imagine, as both facetious and offensive. As a loyal subscriber to your Journal for many years, I never thought I would see the day when you would stoop to penning such pernicious rubbish. To espouse the cause of heterosexuality, certainly closet heterosexuality, flies in the face of the beliefs of all decent people. The notion which logically follows from the implications of your article, namely the reintroduction of Women into our society is surely anathema to the majority of right-thinking Men. Women have no place in a decent respectable community. Since Helen of Troy, history has taught us again and again that their presence is disruptive, counter-productive and frequently downright destructive to the conduct of rational civilisation. Due to an act of nature, some might even claim an act of God, they are now segregated from the rest of us and long may it remain so. Let them primp and preen, scheme and gossip, devise their sexual snares and petty stratagems, well away from the rest of us. Vive la différence indeed, sir!

Yours etc.,

Brigadier J.R. McF. Nordish (Retd.)

North-WestSarum (North).

EDITED EXCERPT OF MINUTES OF MEETING.
SOUTH SARUM VILLAGE COUNCIL, 10 AUTUMN

Present:
Cllr. T. Chilzer (Chair) (Moderate)
Cllr. K. Clay (Orthodox)
Cllr. M. Chalice (Moderate)
Cllr. J. Grosh (Orthodox)
Cllr. F. Harran (Moderate)
Cllr. S. Staint (Orthodox)
Cllr. H. Tarness (Progressive)
Cllr. L. Marling (Orthodox)
Cllr. D. Bunderwell (Orthodox)
Cllr. Doben (Orthodox)
Cllr. L. Kriffitt (Moderate)
Cllr. W. Spanway (Moderate)

Orthodox (6) Moderate (5) Progressive (1)
The meeting as usual was preceded by a brief reading
from The Book of Certitude. Reader: Cllr. Clay (O)
1. Apologies for absence: None

2. Minutes of last meeting dated 25 Autumn were
read and approved.

3. Newly appointed Cllr. M Chalice (M) and
Cllr. H. Tarness (P) were welcomed by the Chair.
Cllr. Chilzer particularly welcomed the Progressive
Party Member, Cllr. Tarness, the first to be elected
in this region. She understood that this newly
formed party was fast gaining a reputation as

advocates for change wherever its members had been elected. She said, amidst laughter, she hoped that, in the case of South Sarum Council, Cllr. Tarness would make a distinction between healthy spring cleaning and total demolition!

4. ~~xxxxdxxxxxxdxdxxxxxxxdxxdxdxdxxxdxdxdxdxxdxd xdxdxdxdxdxd~~

5. ~~xxxxdxxxxxxdxdxxxxxxxdxxdxdxdxxxdxdxdxdxxdxd xdxdxdxdxdxd~~

6. ~~xxxxdxxxxxxdxdxxxxxxxdxxdxdxdxxxdxdxdxdxxdxd xdxdxdxdxdxd~~

7. There being no other business the meeting was concluded

Sir,

Your correspondent, Brigadier Nordish (Letters 2 Autumn) in his somewhat splenetic response to your leading article (24 Summer 112 PD) rather misses the point, surely. The introduction of Women into our society may indeed be disruptive as he claims but surely there is an alternative and one which your brave and clear sighted article implied. For those unfortunate Men harbouring a sexual inclination for Women there is a solution which stops well short of actually re-introducing females back into our society. Let these male deviants, should they choose to turn their backs on our society, move elsewhere to conduct their perversions. Thus avoiding the risk of corrupting by example those innocent, impressionable and fresh faced young men who, weekly, arrive to join our community. Let us think of our young people and not risk their heads being turned by the immoral example of the few?

Incidentally, why does Brigadier Nordish only cite back as recently as Helen of Troy? It goes further than that. All the way to Genesis 3.6, surely.

Yours etc.,

Tamlin Hazzard

WestSarum (North)

DIARY OF ELIHU CLAY, 16TH DAY OF AUTUMN.*

Mapa, today, on my 9th birthday gave me a diary which is bound in leather and is very expensive, she told me. It wasn't really what I wanted, though. I had asked for a football which I could kick around with my best friend Fergo. But instead I got given this diary which Mapa tells me I have to write in every day and record what happens to me. Practically nothing happens to me so there won't be much to write about, really. Fergo's no longer at the school but now has a Tutor. He's usually free most afternoons and we meet up quite often after I've finished school. Fergo's Mapa is something important in the Food Factory and his Mama, with him being a boy, has to stay home to look after him. Boys are special and need a lot of looking after. Not like girls who, Fergo says, are ten a penny. But after the Plague, it's much more difficult to make boys than it is to make girls. Something about Nature compensating or something. I don't really understand it, it's all women's stuff. I'll soon have a Tutor of my own next year. Can't wait! My class is full of girls now Fergo's left. Chit-chat chitter-chatter all day long. They drive me mad! What do they find to talk about all day that is so important?

---

* *Author's note:* all diary entries, both Elihu's and my own, were written originally in longhand (no computers for the likes of us in those days!) To spare the reader, I have transposed these into a more legible typeface, as the traumatic events we underwent during the writing of our diaries, were often refected in the quality of both our respective handwritings, especially that of my dear brother's.
S C-F April 2154

Sir,

I don't know which North Sarum your recent correspondents, Brigadier Nordish and Tamlin Hazzard (Letters 2 & 11 Autumn) are living in but it's certainly not the same one I do. I note from their addresses that they come from the West and North West areas of the town, presumably the privately gated, so-called Elite District. I invite them both to come and spend a day with the rest of us, struggling to and from work, in my case a brief daily commute from south-east to mid central North Sarum. They speak of our "decent, respectable community" and of our "peaceful society" which certainly bears little resemblance to the world that many of us are living in. I travel from my tenth floor apartment to my place of work at the Offices of the Wilts Water Board, a distance of little more than a third of a mile. During my journey each morning and evening there and back, I am forced to run the gauntlet of open gang warfare as hordes of violent and threatening youths confront each other in seemingly endless territorial disputation. Pity the innocent citizen attempting to make his way to work, he takes his life in his hands each day! I have written consistently to the Chief Monitor's Office about the increasingly serious situation over the years but still no action has been taken to stop it. I can only assume our forces of law and order are as powerless to deal with such lawlessness as the rest of us.

As to the reintroduction of Women back into our society, this correspondent, for one, feels it might well prove beneficial. They might serve, at the very least, as a welcome distraction and possibly might even contribute a grain of common sense to moderate the mindless violence we are witnessing all around us every day.

Yours etc.,

Walsice Breen

South EastSarum (North)

LETTER TO *NORTH SARUM JOURNAL*, DATED 13 WINTER

Sir,

Your correspondent, Tamlin Hazzard (Letters 11 Autumn) quotes Genesis 3.6 "And when the Woman saw that the tree was good for food, and that it was pleasant to the eyes, and a tree to be desired to make one wise, she took up the fruit thereof, and did eat ..." He, together with your other correspondents, might do well to read on a little further in Genesis 3 to verses 15 and 16, "and I will put enmity between thee and the Woman, and between thy seed and her seed .... Unto the woman he said, I will greatly multiply thy sorrow and of thy conception; in sorrow thou shalt bring forth children; and thy desire shall be for thy husband and he shall rule over thee."

Certainly, "the enmity of their respective seeds" taken together with references elsewhere to Woman's innate inner and outer uncleanliness, clearly anticipates the Plague itself. With our society now divided as the Bible predicted, that distant prophecy has been fulfilled. It was always originally God's Will that the Divide would eventually come into being. Let us abide by the rulings of the Preacher and leave things as they were intended from the Beginning. There is no turning back now from the true path we have taken.

We are better apart.

Finally, as I have earlier quoted, though there is a clear instruction for a Woman to desire her husband, there is no such equivalent command for a Man to desire a Woman, only that he rule over her. So, as for the abnormal deviants in our society who harbour such unnatural desires, let us rout them out and teach them the folly of their ways by all means at our disposal.

Yours etc.,

Doagul Triffellich, Orthodox Minister

South West Sarum (North)

SOUTH SARUM VILLAGE JUNIOR SCHOOL - CLASS 3
ENGLISH ESSAY BY SOWEEN CLAY AGED 8

What I Want To Do When I'm Older

What I really want to do when I am older is to be a brilliant writer. I would write exciting stories that would be printed in books which people would pay me lots of money so that they can read them. The books would have lots of pictures as well which my brother Elihu would draw. He is a brilliant artist. I would give him some of my money for drawing them.

But since I am a girl and will one day become a Woman, I probably won't be able to do that but instead work in the Food Factory or on a Farm. Or perhaps become a Plumber or a Builder or a Lectrician. I would like one day to be a Mama and have lots of babies with someone and stay at home all day to clear up things. Which I will probably do until I grow fat and old and die. That would also be nice.

The end.

DIARY OF ELIHU CLAY, 20TH DAY OF AUTUMN

(IN MY ELEVENTH YEAR)

This afternoon, Fergo had the brilliant idea of building a model boat. His Mama got sick of him hanging around the house after his Tutor had gone, bored and with nothing to do and she suggested he tries to build something. So his Mapa who's got a small workshop around the back of their house in a shed is going to help us in the evenings when she gets home from work, so that's something to do, anyway. Fergo says his Tutor is just great and full of ideas about what Fergo might do once he's crossed the Divide. There are he says in the North all these different Houses or Guilds as they're called which specialise in different practical things like woodwork or plumbing or electricity for instance as well as metalwork and stone masonry. There's masses to do over there apparently. Not like here with the Women in their black bonnets tiptoeing everywhere, staring at the ground and not really wanting to talk to you. In the North, there's even Fergo says an Arts Guild which I might be interested in joining. We'll see. I might do stone masonry and make a sculptors. I think that might be interesting. I don't know how long I can keep writing this diary. It's getting so boring, trying to remember what I've done all day. But Mapa every evening asks me if I've written in it today and then she says good, good. It's so boring, every single night to have to do it.

SOUTH SARUM VILLAGE JUNIOR SCHOOL - CLASS 4

BIOLOGY ESSAY BY SOWEEN CLAY AGED 8

How Babies Are Made

To make a Baby there must first be two people who love each other very much and decide they want to make a Baby. They must first get married to each other and promise to live together till one of them dies. And then they must decide who will be the Mama and have the Baby and who will be the Mapa to look after them all. Then they must apply to The Village Council for some Seed. And when they get given the Seed they must both go into a room on their own and the one who is going to be Mama lies down with her legs open and the Mapa takes the Seed and very carefully puts it inside the Mama where it mixes with her own Seed and then they both have to sit back and wait and be patient for a long time. And The Preacher says if God is pleased with them both and they are good, then in nine months time they will be given a Baby. Mostly it will be a girl but sometimes it will be a boy. Since the Plague boys are Vulnerable and Nature usually likes to make girls.
The end.

EDITED EXCERPT OF MINUTES OF MEETING
SOUTH SARUM VILLAGE COUNCIL, 20 WINTER

———

Present:
Cllr. T. Chilzer (Chair) (Moderate)
Cllr. K. Clay (Orthodox)
Cllr. M. Chalice (Moderate)
Cllr. J. Grosh (Orthodox)
Cllr. F. Harran (Moderate)
Cllr. H. Tarness (Progressive)
Cllr. L. Marling (Orthodox)
Cllr. D. Bunderwell (Orthodox)
Cllr. Doben (Orthodox)
Cllr. L. Kriffitt (Moderate)

Apologies: Cllr. W. Spanway (Moderate), Cllr. S. Staint (Orthodox)

The meeting as usual was preceded by a brief reading from The Book of Certitude. Reader Cllr. Grosh (O)

1. Excessive noise xxxxxxxxxxxxxxxxxx tolerated.

2. Improper dress xxxxxxxxxxxxxxxxxxxxxxxxxx xxxxxx disciplined.

3. Cllr. Clay (O) raised her concern that, according to Monitors, Days of Reflection were of late being less and less strictly observed, sometimes even ignored completely, by an

increasing number in the community, especially amongst the young. Preacher's Law clearly states that Women are forbidden all speech on these special days but instead should silently reflect and seek forgiveness for past sins through day long prayer and study of The Book of Certitude. Cllr. Harran (M) said she agreed it was worrying. Cllr. Tarness (P) said she felt to continue to observe such Days was both outmoded and unhealthy for Women and she would welcome the relaxation of such draconian traditions. What was past was past, surely and we ought, as a community, to be looking forward rather than backward. It was high time Women did more to restore their self respect and pride. Cllr. Clay argued that self respect was itself a form of vanity, whereas pride, as she was sure the Progressive Councillor was well aware, is the fourth deadly sin. The discussion continued and eventually became sufficiently agitated for the Chair to intervene. Cllr. Grosh (O) then moved that the Council should do all in their power to urge the Monitors to enforce Day of Reflection rules more strictly and if necessary punish habitual offenders. This was seconded by Cllr. Staint (O) and the motion was carried by 10 votes to 1 with one abstention. There being no other business, the meeting was closed.

DIARY OF SOWEEN CLAY, 5TH DAY OF SPRING
(IN MY TENTH YEAR)

Because today I am nine years old, Mapa has given me a diary to write in and to put down what I do every day so I will remember. Also sometimes I can write what I'm going to do tomorrow. She gave one to Elihu when he was nine. It is very special and expensive and is bound in leather. Elihu's is white because he is a boy but with me being a girl mine is black. But mine is much easier to keep clean. Elihu's is already covered in his dirty finger marks after scarcely two years because he often forgets to wash his hands which Mama says is typical of Men. And Elihu said to her, how would you know about men? Mama then hit him on the head. Mapa told me not to lose my diary on pain of death! She said I am forever losing things which is very unfair and untrue. But she still remembers my pencil case which I lost at Junior school when I was only seven years old and because it was a present from her she got very cross and spanked me. I said I didn't lose it, someone must have stolen it, and then she said if you accuse people of stealing without good reason then I'll spank you again. So I shut up. I couldn't sit down properly for ages after. Mapa is really strong. It must be her being a Doctor and lifting people up all the time to examine them. I certainly won't lose this diary. I'm going to write in it **every single day**, I swear! I'm so excited!

DIARY OF ELIHU CLAY, 16TH DAY OF AUTUMN
(IN MY TWELFTH YEAR)

    I am eleven years old today and have finally left school. My last day sitting in that classroom with all those chattering creatures, forever giggling and whispering together in little groups. At last I can concentrate on my studies in peace and quiet. My Tutor who is called Tutor Rudgrin arrives tomorrow. I can't wait to meet him and ask him all sorts of questions about my future, once I cross the Divide. We are still working on the boat! Fergo's Mapa is a real stickler for getting everything just right. We spend hours and hours on every single detail while Fergo and I simply want to get it in the water and see if it floats. But we spend hours cutting every tiny little piece of wood and then even longer waiting while it glues and sets. I rather wish we hadn't asked her to join us in the venture. We could've built a whole armada by now! We're planning to launch it (if we ever do) on our secret pond by the waterfall. Where we all used to swim when we were little. Happy days!

"A BOY BORN SOUTH OF THE DIVIDE will be schooled along with females until he reaches the age of eleven at which point he will be removed from the school and placed in the care of a male Tutor from the North. This tutor will be employed by his parents. The Tutor will conduct classes privately in the boy's home and the parents are required to provide suitable facilities for such tutelage, including a designated, suitable private space for daily use as a classroom. The parents are required to wear shielded visors at all times in the Tutor's presence (apart from those occasions when the Tutor is himself protectively visored). In addition, at least one parent will be required to sit in during their son's lessons in order to ensure the correct curriculum is being followed and that nothing inappropriate occurs. It is intended this contact with male company that the student experiences at this stage of his development will serve to help acclimatise him to future existence in an all-male society. The Tutor in consultation with the parents will endeavour to assess and recommend a choice of potential career apprenticeships suitable for his student when the time comes for him to finally cross the Divide and take his place in Northern adult male society."

DIARY OF SOWEEN CLAY, 16TH DAY OF AUTUMN
(IN MY TENTH YEAR)

The last of the Boys left our class today. Saddest of all it was Elihu, my own brother, being the youngest and only just eleven. I shall have to walk to school on my own now. Boo! We will miss the boys. Mostly. I mean there were times when they drove us all **CRAZY** with their squabbling and fighting and noisiness and as for their teasing! We won't miss that! They were always trying to pinch you or pull your hair. Especially Elihu's so-called best friend, Fergo. I hated him. He picked on me all the time, even though I tried being really nice to him. I asked Elihu why Fergo was like that and he said it was because Fergo secretly liked me and wanted to be my friend. What??? By making my life a misery? I'd hate it if I was his enemy! He left school last year. Good riddance! Elihu's Tutor arrives tomorrow. I hope I will get a look at him before he is shut away in the study. I'd like a Tutor, too. Why can't girls have Tutors? It's so unfair. Boys get **everything** because everyone says they're special. Boo!

EDITED EXCERPT OF MINUTES OF MEETING
SOUTH SARUM VILLAGE COUNCIL, 17 AUTUMN

———————

Present:
Cllr. T. Chilzer (Chair) (Moderate)
Cllr. K. Clay (Orthodox)
Cllr. M. Chalice (Moderate)
Cllr. J. Grosh (Orthodox)
Cllr. F. Harran (Moderate)
Cllr. S. Staint (Orthodox)
Cllr. H. Tarness (Progressive)
Cllr. L. Marling (Orthodox)
Cllr. Doben (Orthodox)
Cllr. W. Spanway (Moderate)

Apologies: Cllr. D. Bunderwell (Orthodox), Cllr. L.
Kriffitt (Moderate)

The meeting as usual was preceded by a brief
reading from The Book of Certitude. Reader: Cllr.
Staint (O)

1. Visors xxxxxxxxxxxxxxxxxxxxxxxxxxxxxxxxxxxxx
xxx demure.

AOB. Daily Reading of The Book of Certitude in
our schools. Cllr. Grosh (O) expressed concern that
she had recently learnt certain Teachers were
disregarding the statutory ruling that all school
days should commence with a reading from The Book
of Certitude. She was concerned that children were

lacking proper guidance with regard to the conduct of their future adult lives. Cllr. Clay (O) agreed, saying there was no excuse as it was clearly laid down in school regulations. She moved that any future lapses result in severe reprimands to those Teachers guilty of this oversight. Cllr. Tarness (P) disagreed saying she had learnt from her own child that there was a growing feeling amongst pupils that the daily readings from the Book, with its constant emphasis on Women's guilt and inferiority, were both dispiriting and demoralising for young girls, blunting their ambition and diminishing their sense of purpose. Cllr. Staint (O) expressed the view that surely it was wrong to encourage ambition in young girls, anyway? In her view, ambition was best left to men. Hadn't the Preacher clearly stated that ambition in Woman was bound to distract her from her main purpose? Cllr. Tarness then asked what did Cllr. Staint consider was Woman's main purpose, anyway? Cllr. Clay said that was also clearly stated in the Book, a Woman's main purpose is the worship and glorification of God and the subjugation of self. Surely she didn't need to remind the Councillor of that? Cllr. Tarness responded that she felt that ambition and the worship of God were not necessarily mutually exclusive. Several Councillors then tried to speak at once and Cllr. Chilzer was forced to call the meeting to order saying she felt members were in danger of straying from the subject and anyhow it was getting late. She appreciated the passion with which both sides expressed their views. She felt this was healthy as the Council Chamber was a proper place for debating such issues. A vote was then taken as to whether, in the members' view, Teachers failing to observe daily morning readings of The Book of Certitude on a regular basis should be reprimanded. The motion was carried by 7 votes to 2 in favour with one abstention. There being no other business the meeting was concluded.

DIARY OF ELIHU CLAY, 17TH DAY OF AUTUMN
(IN MY TWELFTH YEAR)

My new Tutor, Tutor Rudgrin arrived today and he will be teaching me for the next seven years, until it's time for me finally to cross over and join the Men in the North. I hope we both get on! It's a long time to spend in someone's company, otherwise, even if it is with another man. When he arrived, the first thing that struck me was his height. He is very tall and lean and loomed over all of us. Mama and Mapa were both there waiting, to give him the once over. Mapa said we needed to check him over first, just to make PERFECTLY SURE. I noticed, too, Soween lurking in a corner, eager to catch a glimpse of him before she raced off to school. Trust you not to be left out, nosy little sister! Being a Male guest, he arrived of course fully visored but, as is customary and to show common politeness, the Women, after the initial greetings, all promptly visored up. This allowed him, in turn, to show us his face for the first time. It was a kind one, like the rest of him, lean, craggy and naturally solemn. But when he chose to smile he had such great warmth which was instantly attractive. After the briefest of greetings to me and a nod to Soween, he was whisked away to Mapa's study where he spent some time, first with both of my parents and, a bit later, with Mapa on her own. Presumably making doubly sure about him. Once presumably Mapa was satisfied, I was finally allowed in. Her study will be my classroom for the foreseeable future. There are regulations, though, that say in the case of a one-to-one Tutor with an under-age student, it was the law to have at least one parent present at all times. Totally outdated and old fashioned but what else do you expect if you live with Mapa? So in future poor Mama will have to sit with us. So after Mapa left for work, the three of us, Mama, Tutor Rudgrin and I, sat there in awkward silence. I thought to myself, this is never going to work. Tutor Rudgrin tried asking me questions about myself but before I could answer them, Mama interrupted, answering them, saying oh, Elihu did this or Elihu thinks that. Really, she still thinks I'm a CHILD! In the end, I had to ask her politely to shut up and let me answer my own questions! So she sat there behind her visor and never said another word, probably sulking because she never likes it when someone tells her to be quiet. She loves talking. I think I caught a bit of a smile on Tutor Rudgrin's face, but I couldn't be sure. I'm encouraged that this is someone I could get on with but I suspect the real work will begin tomorrow.

DIARY OF SOWEEN CLAY, 17TH DAY OF AUTUMN
(IN MY TENTH YEAR)

Elihu's new Tutor came today. Having left school until he is eighteen and finally crosses, he will be taught by a Man. He is called Tutor Rudgrin and is enormously tall. Like all Tutors, he wears a white protective male suit with the Tutor's black badge showing a book on his chest. Just like our own Teacher, Teacher Olishaw, does, only her badge is white to show up on her black dress. Before he met Elihu, Tutor Rudgrin met Mama and Mapa first. As is the custom, before he arrived, my parents had put on their visors as a sign of respect and modesty (Mapa insists everything in this house must be in observance of the rules of etiquette, laid down by The Preacher. She is very strict and Orthodox!) But it did mean that the Tutor was then free to take off his own visor so we could get a really good look at him! He is quite old, over 35 I should think, but has a kind face and a lovely smile. At least, I thought it was lovely. When I said that to Mapa at supper, she said: Never be fooled by a man's smile, Soween. The Preacher says it can lead to your Downfall. What Downfall? When am I ever going to meet a man? I envy Elihu. He is going to learn about important Men's things, like Architecture and Engineering and Fighting. Which are much more interesting than the things we have to learn, because we are Women and have smaller brains and can only retain Useful Things such as Sewing and Cooking and Cleaning Up. Because most women in South Sarum work in the Food Factory (which doesn't need any brain at all, it seems to me) or on the Farms or basic labouring (where all they need are muscles). Which isn't fair at all! Except when a Woman's extremely clever and brainy like Mapa and then she can become a Doctor or a plumber and serve on the Council.

DIARY OF ELIHU CLAY, 19TH DAY OF AUTUMN
(IN MY TWELFTH YEAR)

Tutor Rudgrin spoke this morning about the
separation of Men and Women and why it was necessary.
We had all grown-up accepting it as a matter of course but
it was important, even before The Plague, to be reminded
exactly why the two sexes should be kept apart. He then
read from The Book of Certitude, Chapter Five. Of course
I'd heard it before, Mapa used to read it to us all on a
nightly basis.

"THE KNOWING OF OUR SEPARATE PLACES.
Men by nature are born to be leaders and should
accept this duty with a diligence and a clear-headed sense of
purpose. Remember, leadership comes with a responsibility to
the weak, namely Women and young Children, who are in need
of Men's protection and guidance. Thus in His Wisdom has
The Preacher created The Divide, South of which Women
and their Children would be safe. For before the Divide,
Women and young children were vulnerable to vile abuse
from predatory Males who heartlessly took advantage of
their weakness, violating or even killing them. So the poor
defenceless creatures lived in constant fear. It is better
therefore that they live apart. The Women for their safety
and security, the Men so they will no longer be tempted. For
Man's most serious weakness is Woman herself who so easily,
in the mere twinkling of her sinful eyes, can reduce a Man,
that most noble and civilised of creatures, created in God's
own image, to an uncontrollable beast. Woman beware Man!
But let Man beware Woman still more!"

I must have read that passage a hundred times and heard it read still more frequently. But seldom with such passion and intensity as Tutor Rudgrin read it this morning. Mama sat in the corner all morning and never said a word. I think she dozed off like she did yesterday. She then made us all some lunch and afterwards we did some English grammar and finished early. Later I went round to Fergo's to carry on building the boat. This mostly consisted of Fergo and I sitting and watching his Mapa taking ages and ages.

DIARY OF SOWEEN CLAY, 2ᴺᴰ DAY OF WINTER
(IN MY TENTH YEAR)

When I woke up this morning my whole body was covered in a red rash which was terribly itchy. I called Mama and she came to my room to look and when she'd seen it she looked very worried. So she went and called Mapa who also looked at it and because Mapa is a doctor she knew what it was. She said I had eczema but it wasn't very serious and she would give me cream to rub on it especially on my arms and legs where it was at its worst and it itchiest. Elihu was already shut away in the study with teacher Rudgrin when I left for school. I tried to listen at the door but they were talking so quietly that I could hear nothing. What were they talking about? Men's things? What on earth could they be? As a result, when I arrived at school I was a bit late and so they had already started and I had to explain to Teacher Olishaw about my eczema. She said, Oh, you poor thing, I expect you'll grow out of it. She is very kind, and I like her very much. In my class is Sassa who is my very best friend in the world. Sassa is nine and the same age as me exactly since our birthday, the fifth day of Spring, is on the very same day. I'm going to marry her as soon as I grow up. In my class too is Silje who is the same age as us and her older sister, Axi. Also Giella, Molwin and Yoteez who are all older than us. This evening Mapa brought home some cream that she rubbed into my arms and legs which made it feel much better. I'm glad my Mapa is a doctor. But she also said that my eczema was sent by God to stop me from becoming vain. Because though I would still remain beautiful in the eyes of God, the eczema will stop me from being beautiful seen through my own eyes. Because thinking of oneself as beautiful

is the very worst form of vanity and I should Beware! I had to go and look at myself in the mirror in the Hall. Women are not allowed mirrors in their bedrooms because of Vanity or in any part of the house except the Hall. There is a mirror in Elihu's bedroom but that is only for him to shave in. He's only eleven and he doesn't shave so why does he need a mirror? I'm the one who needs a mirror! Though I must say, looking at myself red faced, shiny and covered in cream,
I didn't look beautiful. Not at all!

114 PD

EDITED EXCERPT OF MINUTES OF MEETING
SOUTH SARUM VILLAGE COUNCIL, 3 WINTER

———————

Present:
Cllr. T. Chilzer (Chair) (Moderate)
Cllr. K. Clay (Orthodox)
Cllr. M. Chalice (Moderate)
Cllr. J. Grosh (Orthodox)
Cllr. F. Harran (Moderate)
Cllr. S. Staint (Orthodox)
Cllr. H. Tarness (Progressive)
Cllr. L. Marling (Orthodox)
Cllr. Doben (Orthodox)
Cllr. L. Kriffitt (Moderate)
Cllr. W. Spanway (Moderate)
Cllr. C. Nivess (Progressive)

The meeting as usual was preceded by a brief
reading from The Book of Certitude. Reader: Cllr.
Marling (O)

Minutes of last meeting dated 15 Autumn were read
and approved.
The Chair expressed regret at the retirement of
Cllr. D. Bunderwell (O) from the Council due to ill
health. On behalf of the Council, Cllr. Chilzer
wished her a happy and well earned retirement.
This was seconded by Cllr. Clay (O). The meeting
then welcomed newly appointed Cllr. Nivess (P).
Cllr. Clay requested she add her own tribute and
personally thank Cllr. Bunderwell for the years

of hard work and her devotion to the upholding of traditional values. She was a loyal, long serving member of the Orthodox Party and would be sadly missed.

Cllr. Tarness then personally welcomed Cllr. Nivess expressing her delight that the Progressive Party was now being more fairly represented on the Council. Cllr. Nivess then expressed the hope that she could add a valuable contribution to the Council's future proceedings.

1. Central placing of
xxxxxxxxxxxxxxxxxxxxxxxxxxxxxxxx blasphemous.

2. Bright objects
xxxxxxxxxxxxxxxxxxxxxxxxxxxxx more muted hues.

3. Correct footwear xxxxxxxxxxxxxxxxxxxxxxxxxxxx in future.

There being no other business the meeting was concluded.

DIARY OF ELIHU CLAY, 4TH DAY OF WINTER
(IN MY TWELFTH YEAR)

Tutor Rudgrin read some more from the Book of
Certitude this morning. He sometimes arrives looking very
tired as if he'd been up all night. Presumably he has been
studying. Or maybe it's with him making such a long journey
every day through the Divide tunnels and then back again
every evening. It must be exhausting for him, day after day.
I think he enjoys reading from The Book, especially in the
mornings as a way of waking himself up! Mind you, it never
does that to Mama. Whenever he starts reading, she always
falls asleep. It certainly can't be the tone of his voice
that sends her off, as he normally gets very excited like a
preacher, thumping the desk, getting quite dramatic. Maybe
he wanted to be an actor originally, rather than a Tutor. I
must ask him some time. Today he read from The Book of
Certitude Chapter 4.

From her twelfth birthday a Woman will wear black for
the remainder of her life in order that she remind the world
she is in a permanent state of mourning for the deaths she
has caused through her uncleanliness. For a Woman is, by
nature, unclean and has wrought irreparable damage to the
world through this uncleanliness. From the day of her birth,
she is steeped in Sin and is responsible for slowing Man's
progress towards his perfection. A Woman must for ever more
share the guilt of her mother and of her mother's mother for
the harm they have done and must live out her life in shame
and remorse. Whilst Men, when they move among Women, will
wear white as a reminder to the world of their innocence.

Personally, I wasn't quite sure that applied to all Women. It certainly didn't to Mama who, as far as I know, has never caused anyone's death and hasn't done the slightest damage to anything. Generally, in this house, it's the other way round. It's us that do all the damage and Mama's left clearing up after us. But I don't think she's too worried about what the Book says. She seems to sleep through it quite peacefully. Like she usually does in Chapel, apart from when Mapa nudges her awake. After lunch, Tutor Rudgrin said he had a headache and he might go home early and go to bed. I told him if he wasn't feeling well, perhaps he should wait to see Mapa. She was after all a Doctor and might be able to give him something for his headache. At which point Tutor Rudgrin looked even paler and asked me, please, not to say a word about this to Mapa under any circumstances. He left saying he was sure he'd be better in the morning.

SOUTH SARUM VILLAGE JUNIOR SCHOOL - CLASS 4
CLASS REPORT BY SOWEEN CLAY AGED 9

Our Trip To The Village Memorial

This morning our class went with Teacher Olishaw to visit the Men's Memorial in the Village Square. The Memorial is twenty metres high and made of grey granite. It is two and a half metres square. It weighs over 80 tons. The names of all the Men who died of The Plague in South Sarum are carved on it. There are over ten thousand names on it. Our Teacher's great-grandfather's name is on it. His name was Des Olishaw. He was 47 and he used to be a Traffic Warden. (Whatever that was). Teacher Olishaw says The Memorial is there to remind us for ever of all the Men who died in case we ever forget them. In the old days, the children would be brought out here and made to learn whole sides of the Memorial, five hundred names a time. And if they forgot even one single name they were beaten and we should all count ourselves lucky today that we weren't living in those days. I'm glad too! There is another much smaller Memorial in the High Street for all the Women who died too but we didn't have time to go there.

The end.

DIARY OF ELIHU CLAY, 12ᵀᴴ DAY OF WINTER
(IN MY TWELFTH YEAR)

I think Mama is beginning to lose heart, sitting in all day in the study listening in on these lessons of mine. She's finding still more ways to excuse herself, saying she just needs to do something important and won't be a moment. And when she does go, she's away for ages, going shopping or preparing the evening meal, leaving Tutor Rudgrin and me alone for hours by ourselves. As she left the room, Mama always holds her finger up to her visor as if to say, don't tell Mapa, will you? Not that we ever would. We're far happier to be left alone. I think, for one thing, Tutor Rudgrin finds it rather dispiriting, whenever Mama's with us, listening to her snoring whenever he's teaching. I took the opportunity today, once she'd left, to ask him about life on the other side of the Divide. I mean, not general points but more specific ones. I wanted to know more about him. Left alone with just me, he began to talk about himself. He told me he lived with his partner, Orlo, for eight years. Orlo is a composer and jazz musician, a brilliant alto sax player, apparently. He's reckoned one of the best jazz players North of the Divide around at present.

Probably South of the Divide as well, come to that. I'd never seen or heard an alto saxophone, never in my life. Here in the Village that sort of music's totally banned. The only music we have is boring folk stuff for Chapel dances and weddings and so on. Seems to me to be an excuse for people to jump up and down and wave their arms and shout, wheee, occasionally. Rudgrin said yes that was a pity but never mind, once I got North of the Divide, I could hear all the jazz I wanted to.

And I thought, yes, but my sister can't, can she? She'll never get to hear it and I think she would probably have enjoyed it just as much. Soween loves music. She even enjoys jumping up and down and waving her arms about and shouting wheee! I feel a little sorry for her. She couldn't help being born a Woman, after all, could she?

Rudgrin told me that was one of the reasons he'd been so tired in the mornings recently. He'd been up late, listening to Orlo playing in this club. And having the occasional drink. I said to him, alcohol? You've been drinking alcohol? And he said, he did sometimes. But, very, very rarely. And only in tiny amounts. They're allowed alcohol North of the Divide. But here, it's not permitted because Women have a big problem with alcohol and can't absorb it into their systems, not like a Man can. When they drank, Women would often lose all self-control, screaming hysterically and falling down senseless. And sometimes saying, yes when what they really meant was no. Women have very little self-discipline, especially younger ones. I remembered those last few days at school, being in a classroom with all them, chattering, screaming and screeching with laughter. My God, the din! And they'd not had a drop of alcohol either. Probably best to keep jazz and alcohol North of the Divide, for all their sakes. Just imagine Mama out-of-control?

DIARY OF SOWEEN CLAY, 15TH DAY OF WINTER
(IN MY TENTH YEAR)

This morning, Axi arrived at school a little bit late. It was her twelfth birthday and she'd been to a fitting and she was wearing her adult clothes for the very first time. She looked most grown up and we were all very jealous of her in her black bonnet and her long black dress. Giella and Molwin and Yoteez will soon be twelve as well and then they will get to wear dresses. I can't wait to be twelve and to get out of my boring, boring grey check school dress. Sassa and Silje say they feel the same. Sassa and I made a promise that, in two year's time, on our joint twelfth birthday, we're going to invite each other to a huge party! I really do love her so much. I think she knows how I feel about her. She smiles a lot at me which must mean she likes me, surely? Maybe if I don't rush things and scare her off she'll grow to love me too someday soon. Oh please make it SOON!

DIARY OF ELIHU CLAY, 26TH DAY OF WINTER
(IN MY TWELFTH YEAR)

Tutor Rudgrin's headaches are still not getting any better. Every morning he arrives looking more and more pale. I am getting rather worried about him. I've grown quite fond of him over the past few weeks. But this morning, halfway through some complicated equation, he suddenly stopped speaking and I'm certain he had tears in his eyes. He must have been in such pain and I thought, thank goodness Mama wasn't there to see it or Mapa would definitely have got to hear about it. But Mama has given up completely ever sitting in with us now, except on the rare occasions when Mapa's still at home. Then Mama comes into the study and waits till she hears the front door close as Mapa leaves for the surgery. Then Mama tiptoes to the study door and we don't see her again till lunchtime. In the afternoons we're left totally alone. This afternoon after lunch, Rudgrin suggested we take a stroll outside, to help clear his headache. So after he'd visored up, we set off on a walk, avoiding the Village because if someone had seen us and reported back to Mapa, there could have been trouble, us stopping work early. So, instead, we walked in the Woods, which brought back all sorts of happy memories of when Soween and I were both kids, still a proper family in those days and used to spend hours in summer picnicking and playing together. Once we were clear of the Village and into the trees, Rudgrin lifted his visor, saying that if we happened to meet a Woman, he could always pull it down again. But it was a pretty cold day and so we didn't. We talked and talked. Or rather he did. He talked and I listened. It all seemed to pour out of him as if he needed to tell someone, anyone, even me! He said that he and Orlo had been having these terrible rows lately. And that he was afraid it was all over between them. Orlo was becoming more and more restless, starting to find other people. Rudgrin had heard, according to the bass player, Orlo'd been having a relationship with their drummer which Rudgrin said was upsetting enough, but recently he'd started a relationship with their houseboy, the one who comes in to clean and tidy for them. It was bad enough going off every morning to teach, leaving him lying in bed there all day and then coming home and finding nothing had been done, no tidying, no washing up, nothing even cleared away. But then coming home and discovering Orlo lying in bed with that little bastard ... At which point Rudgrin needed to stop and sit down on a tree stump and began to cry. I mean really cry. Worse than my sister at her worst! I stood feeling a bit helpless as I didn't know what to do. After all, he was meant to be my Tutor and I'm only twelve years old. So I stood there looking a bit useless, till he'd finally stopped, said sorry, thank you for listening and it wouldn't happen again, he promised. Then he pulled down his visor and we both went home to do basic algebra.

———————

It's the day of my tenth birthday and I'm feeling a little unhappy today. I don't think Mama loves me as much as she loves Elihu. Since he's being taught at home with his Tutor, he and Mama have had so much time together. Most afternoons after Tutor Rudgrin has left, Elihu tells me he and Mama talk for hours and hours together. They have become very close. I think maybe it's because Mama feels that Elihu is growing up and it will soon be time for him to withdraw from us and be protectively visored in our presence. And so Mama is savouring the moments that they have left together as mother and son. But he doesn't have to put on his suit until he is fifteen, for goodness sake! He's still only eleven. They've got masses more time together, they really have. It's just not fair on me being left out. Sometimes, in the evenings, they both start giggling together and it's really, really annoying. When we were young we all used to all of us go for picnics in the woods. Even Mapa came with us occasionally when she wasn't working. One of our favourite places was the Secret Pool by the waterfall. It wasn't really secret but very few people went there apart from us. If they wanted to swim they preferred to go to the lake which is much bigger and has long sandy beaches. Our secret pool is shaded by lots of trees so it gets less sun and is hard to find if you didn't know where to look. It is quite small but very deep. No one knows how deep it is. I know it's impossible to swim to the bottom. On one side is this little waterfall which comes pouring down from the cliff above. It is very beautiful and most of the time we had it all to ourselves and would swim and play there all through the summer days. One reason many people don't go there is there are rumours that, in the middle at the deepest point, there lives a Merman. A terrible monster who will catch anyone who dares to swim too deep dragging them down to the very bottom and devouring them. In all the days we used to swim there we never once saw any monster. Mapa anyway said it was ignorant nonsense. I said to her once that wasn't it strange that the monsters in the stories, even the unreal ones, were usually Men. And Mapa said, that's probably because most of the monsters in real life are also Men.

DIARY OF ELIHU CLAY, 10TH DAY OF SPRING
(IN MY TWELFTH YEAR)

———————

    In the middle of my geometry lesson this morning, Rudgrin sank down into one of his depressions again. They seem to come from nowhere and just sort of grab hold of him, like he's been struck down by an invisible fist. I'm getting used to his moods now, though. They happen fairly regularly and we have to just wait till they've passed and then we just carry on again with the lesson from where we left off, as if nothing had happened. But I do worry about him, sometimes. It's really great to have a Tutor especially one who's so good and kind and a good friend, most of the time. But not when you have one who's totally MAD, as well! I tried to cheer him up the other day by telling him he wasn't useless and total rubbish at all, not like he was saying. I personally thought he was brilliant. When he used to read to me from The Book of Certitude in those first early days, I found him so inspiring. I wanted him to know that. And he said I didn't believe all that crap, did I? And I must have looked so shocked, with him coming out with that and in Mapa's study, too! I thought all the religious pictures and texts would drop off the wall! And then he said he was sorry and he didn't mean to say that, not at all. And I wasn't for God's sake to tell Mapa and he didn't mean it, not really, not a single word of it.

EDITED EXCERPT OF MINUTES OF MEETING
SOUTH SARUM VILLAGE COUNCIL, 2 SUMMER

———————

Present:
Cllr. T. Chilzer (Chair) (Moderate)
Cllr. K. Clay (Orthodox)
Cllr. M. Chalice (Moderate)
Cllr. J. Grosh (Orthodox)
Cllr. F. Harran (Moderate)
Cllr. H. Tarness (Progressive)
Cllr. L. Marling (Orthodox)
Cllr. Doben (Orthodox)
Cllr. L. Kriffitt (Moderate)
Cllr. W. Spanway (Moderate)
Cllr. C. Nivess (Progressive)

Apologies: Cllr. S. Staint (O)

The meeting as usual was preceded by a brief reading
from The Book of Certitude read by Cllr. Clay (O)

Minutes of last meeting dated 15 Spring were read
and approved.

1. The warmer weather xxxxxxxxxxxxxxxxxxxxxxxxx
correct dress.

2. The state of the roadway xxxxxxxxxxxxxx repaired.

3. Under any other business, Cllr. Tarness (P) raised
the question as to whether the regular readings from

The Book of Certitude preceding Council Meetings were
now outmoded as they tended to delay more pressing
business and surely the duty of the Council was to
facilitate public matters rather than delaying them
by readings, however entertaining, from Orthodox
Party Councillors. Cllr. Clay (O) responded angrily
saying the readings had always been part of tradition
ever since Village Councils were first formed,
following the Divide. There was absolutely no question
of the readings being discontinued, indeed, in her
view, they were often far too brief. They served to
remind members of all Parties of their solemn duties
and responsibilities as Councillors. Moreover she
found Cllr. Tarness's frivolous and flippant attitude
verging on the distasteful. Cllr. Tarness in response
regretted if she'd upset the Councillor but she had
noticed over the weeks a number of the members
struggling to stay awake during the readings and
surely this was equally disrespectful for members
to doze through the Prophet's wise words. She then
proposed that in future, readings from The Book of
Certitude before Council meetings be discontinued.
An animated debate then ensued until Cllr. Chilzer
called for a vote to be taken. The voting was 5 in
favour and 5 against. The Chair withheld her casting
vote, proposing instead that those members in favour
of continuing the readings could do so at a separate
brief meeting in the antechamber, prior to joining the
main meeting. Cllr. Clay wished it to be minuted that
she felt this was a disgraceful compromise and that
every Woman present who supported the motion should
be thoroughly ashamed of herself. Cllr. Clay then left
the chamber.

DIARY OF SOWEEN CLAY, 3RD DAY OF SUMMER
(IN MY ELEVENTH YEAR)

I'm sure nobody loves me and I don't want to live here any more. I think when I'm a little bit older, I'll run away from home with Sassa and we'll both find another village nearby where we can live together and get married. And we can decide then who could be Mapa and who could be Mama. And then the one that is Mapa can find work somewhere, in a shop, or on a farm, or in a factory. While the other one stays home in our cottage to have the babies. I think that's a really good plan and as soon as we are alone together I'll talk about it with Sassa.

DIARY OF ELIHU CLAY, 5TH DAY OF SUMMER
(IN MY TWELFTH YEAR)

———————

Tutor Rudgrin said in the middle of our lesson quite suddenly out of the blue that Men could be such total bastards sometimes! He shouted it out so loudly I'm sure Mama heard it in the kitchen where she was preparing our lunch. Then he said, sorry, he didn't mean me. He was talking in general. And I asked if he meant his partner, Orlo? And he said, yes, his ex-partner. He and their houseboy had both taken up residence together in their apartment and kicked Rudgrin out. He was having to sleep at a friend's flat on his sofa. Just so long as his friend's partner lets him. Which was the reason he wasn't getting much sleep as it was quite a small sofa. Poor Rudgrin. I tried to cheer him up by suggesting we both went for another walk this afternoon. So after lunch, I took him to our Secret Pool with the waterfall, the one we used to swim in years ago. And I told him about the fun we used to have. And he brightened up immediately. And then he took off all his clothes and jumped straight into the pool. Naked! Without any clothes on at all! He's completely MAD! He splashed about laughing for some time, calling me to join him. So eventually I took my clothes off as well and jumped in, too. And we both messed around, splashing each other. What if anyone had happened to be passing? Then we climbed out and ran around until we were fairly dry and got dressed again. And Rudgrin said it was the best fun he'd had for years and he was feeling much better, thank you. And we must do it again soon. Only next time we'd better bring some towels!

DIARY OF SOWEEN CLAY, 6TH DAY OF SUMMER
(IN MY ELEVENTH YEAR)

Elihu told me, after swearing me to secrecy, that while he was out walking with Tutor Rudgrin yesterday, they both went swimming in the Secret Pool by the waterfall. With no clothes on at all! It isn't fair that they're allowed to do that. Just because they're Men! What did they think they were doing? It was really, really dangerous. What would have happened if a Woman had happened to walk past without her visor and she stopped by the pool and was so completely shocked that she'd breathed on them? And they'd both got infected? That would have been terrible! When we were young we used to go down there and swim together and have picnics. Now we don't have those any more. At least I don't. Now it's just Elihu that has them with his Tutor. That is just so not RIGHT! He is twelve years old now. What's happening to him? His Tutor must be completely crazy! At school, I told Sassa about them both swimming together but I told her to promise on her honour not to tell anyone else. I can trust her. We have lots of secrets together. We are secretly going to plan our wedding soon, only I think Sassa wants to be a Mama, too, that's the problem. And I really, really want to be a Mama, I really do. I've decided that. And I want to have two babies. Sassa told me that Axi was forming a gang with Giella and Molwin and Yoteez called The Falcons. She has also asked Sassa and Axi's sister, Silje to join but not me! I will be the only one left out. Life is just awful!

DIARY OF ELIHU CLAY, 12TH DAY OF SUMMER
(IN MY TWELFTH YEAR)

We went swimming again today. It's become quite a regular habit recently. We've started to swim every afternoon, apart from the days when it's overcast. As it's in the shade of the trees, our Secret Pool never really gets that warm, unless it's a really bright day. Rudgrin has been telling me more and more about himself over the days. I'm sure he's not supposed to but I sense he has few people he can talk to apart from me. So I try to listen as a friend and to sound sympathetic, even when some of the things he talks about, I really don't understand, not at all. It's odd to think that, in little over a year, he's moved from being just my Tutor to being my friend as well. I never thought I'd make a friend who'd be quite as old as him but I seem to have done. I told him about my drawings, too. He seemed particularly interested in that and asked if he could see some of my sketches. I promised to show him some. Apart from Soween I haven't shown them to anyone. Well, only Mama but then she thinks anything I do is wonderful, so she doesn't count! I certainly haven't shown them to Mapa who I'm sure would not approve. I think she'd think of drawing as wasteful and non-productive. I think she's ambitions for me to become a doctor like her when I go North, but I'm not sure I want to do that. I'd like to become a proper artist and spend my life drawing things and people. But I don't really know, once I've crossed the Divide, whether there will be any work there for an artist. Maybe North of the Divide is just filled with brilliant artists! I'll be interested to see what Rudgrin thinks of my sketches. If he tells me I'm rubbish, I'll probably give up drawing and be a doctor after all. I trust him.

SALISBURY VILLAGE JUNIOR SCHOOL - CLASS 5
HISTORY ESSAY BY SOWEEN CLAY AGED 10.

Why the Divide is important

Before the Divide, Men and Women all lived together in towns and cities and villages and were mostly very unhappy, especially the Women, because the Men used to threaten them or hit them because they were not as strong as the Men. And sometimes the women would just be walking down a street and the men would jump out and hold them down and take them by sheer brute force. This was called rape. Most men did this to women whether they liked it or not. Which made a lot of women very nervous and angry and there were terrible arguments often between the Men and Women as to who was to blame. But as the Plague spread, more and more people died, especially the men who were more Vulnerable. And instead of being friends they became greater enemies than ever and the men became afraid of the women and started shooting them. Until The Chosen One ordered the Divide and told the Men to live on one side of it and ordered the Women to live on the other because otherwise everyone in the whole world would have died. But He said because of The Plague it showed that in the end it was really the Women who were to blame. But after that there was peace because men are much happier living with other men and fighting each

other and getting drunk and only really need
women for sex and to clean up after them.
And the Women, though they quite enjoyed sex
sometimes, they certainly didn't enjoy always
cleaning up after Men and so were quite happy
as well. Which is why the world today is a
much better place than it was. The Chosen One
wrote that God had really intended it this way
but in the beginning everything got muddled up.
And that Women and Men are really separate
species and it makes no more sense for a Man
to live with a Woman than it does for him
to live with the giraffe or her with a jellyfish.
It was never meant to be because Men and
Women are a danger to each other.
The end.

EDITED EXCERPT OF MINUTES OF MEETING
SOUTH SARUM VILLAGE COUNCIL, 24 SUMMER

Present:
Cllr. T. Chilzer (Chair) (Moderate)
Cllr. K. Clay (Orthodox)
Cllr. M. Chalice (Moderate)
Cllr. J. Grosh (Orthodox)
Cllr. F. Harran (Moderate)
Cllr. H. Tarness (Progressive)
Cllr. L. Marling (Orthodox)
Cllr. Doben (Orthodox)
Cllr. L. Kriffitt (Moderate)
Cllr. W. Spanway (Moderate)
Cllr. C. Nivess (Progressive)
Cllr. G. Whipple (Progressive)

The Orthodox Party members, Cllrs. Grosh, Clay,
Doben and Marling, having concluded their private
reading in the antechamber, joined the main meeting
as usual.

The Chair, Cllr. Chilzer (M) expressed regret at
the retirement of Cllr. Staint (O) due to ill-
health, thanking her for her loyal service to the
Council. She then welcomed Cllr. Whipple (P) saying
she felt sure that the newly appointed Councillor
would further enliven future debates. Young faces
were always welcome. Cllr. Whipple said she hoped
she could make a valuable contribution to future
proceedings. She felt honoured to join and, despite
her youth, assured the Council that what she lacked

in years she would attempt to make up in enthusiasm!

1. A suggestion xxxxxxxxxxxxxxxxxxxx defeated.

2. Concern was expressed xxxxxxxxxxxxxxxxxxxxxx
needless.

3. Several members complained xxxxxxxx spoken to
severely.

There being no other business the meeting was
concluded.

DIARY OF ELIHU CLAY, 25ᵀᴴ DAY OF SUMMER
(IN MY THIRTEENTH YEAR)

Our boat is finally finished! Together with my best friend, Fergo and his Mapa we took it out to the Lake rather than the secret pond because there was more wind. It looked quite wonderful, I must admit, and we drew quite a crowd of admirers. Fergo's Mapa spent a great deal of time adjusting each sail and then tweaking the rudder, etc. before wetting her finger and holding it up to establish wind direction and throwing a handful of dry grass into the air to determine its speed. Then finally she launched it with a gentle shove, pushing it clear of the shore. The wind in the middle of the lake was clearly stronger than it had been on the edge where we were standing and the boat gathered speed and, for all of twenty seconds, it really looked spectacular and what we'd always dreamt it would be. And everybody cheered. But then the thing suddenly blew over onto its side, its sails became sodden, the hull filled with water and the whole thing sank without trace. Everyone booed and we went home. That's the last boat I'll ever build.

116 PD

DIARY OF SOWEEN CLAY, 30TH DAY OF SUMMER
(IN MY TWELFTH YEAR)

My heart has been broken today. Sassa told me after school that she was going to marry Axi when she grew up and not me after all. I came home and cried for ages and ages. I feel my life has come to an end and I can't bear to live any longer. I don't even have anyone now that I can run away with and marry. I can't even write in my diary. But I had to write this in case this is my last day on earth. My eczema has now spread to my face, so what's the point? I'm now ugly as well and can't bear to look at myself any more even supposing I had a mirror.

DIARY OF ELIHU CLAY, 20TH DAY OF AUTUMN
(IN MY FOURTEENTH YEAR)

Rudgrin, today, stopped in the middle of geometry to talk some more about his private problems. I thought a Tutor was supposed to guide me and help me to face my own problems, but he seems to have more problems than I do. So we need to sort his problems out first. I see in this diary I'd written that I wanted to know more about my Tutor. I'm not sure that I need to know this much! We sat by the Secret Pool. It was too cold to swim, and we were throwing stones into the middle trying to wake up the Merman. And Rudgrin said, he thought one of the reasons that none of his relationships worked out was he realised he'd never fully committed to any of them. He told me that the friend, the one he'd been staying with had last night asked him to leave. The friend and his partner had had a terrible argument, shouting and screaming, till the neighbours threatened to summon the Monitors. And when I asked him what the cause of the argument was, Rudgrin said, he thought it was probably because of him. They'd got fed up with him sleeping on their sofa. And I said it sounded as if there were a lot of unhappy people North of the Divide. And Rudgrin agreed that there were. Men could sometimes get very angry and violent with each other and it can get quite dangerous, sometimes. Which is why it was important that I shouldn't cross there until I was at least eighteen which in his opinion was still a bit too young. But I wasn't to worry because he was there to prepare me for when I did cross. He explained that a Tutor was more than just a teacher, he was also intended to be a Father figure as well. It was important for a Boy to have a Father. I asked him where he was going to sleep tonight if he'd been thrown out again. He said I wasn't to worry, he'd find somewhere. Never fear. He was here to take care of me, he promised. All the same, it's very worrying. I hope he has somebody over there to take care of him.

DIARY OF SOWEEN CLAY, 21ST DAY OF AUTUMN
(IN MY TWELFTH YEAR)

A big important day for me today! Sassa told me that Axi wants to talk to me! Axi who never talks to me at all! The great Axi, leader of The Falcons. The gang I wanted to join more than any other. I don't belong to any gang, at present. They told me at first I was too young to join and that they didn't take Kids (though they took Sassa and Silje) but now I'm older they still hadn't asked me. Not being in a gang is very lonely. You never have any real friends, not really. Well, I have Sassa of course, but even she — well most of the time I think honestly her heart is with Axi and The Falcons and not with me. But today all that's changed! Now Axi wants to see ME, perhaps to ask me to join The Falcons? What a tremendous thing that would be in my life! For though my one time friend, Sassa, is Axi's partner now and everybody knows they will eventually marry, settle down and apply for children, Mama Sassa and Mapa Axi, nevertheless Axi has always been very unfriendly towards me. Like she thinks I'm so incredibly stupid! I don't know why she feels like that about me. I always try, whenever I'm with her, to be interesting but when you're with someone who you know thinks you're boring, you try so hard that you end up looking and sounding really, really boring! Axi does that to me all the time. I asked Sassa why she thought Axi was like that towards me and she said she thought maybe Axi was a little bit jealous of our friendship, Sassa's and mine. Which amazes me.

116 PD.

DIARY OF ELIHU CLAY, 22ND DAY OF AUTUMN

(IN MY FOURTEENTH YEAR)

I think Rudgrin senses that he's probably confided in me a bit too much. When I asked him today about how things were North of the Divide he avoids the question and says, fine, they're fine, and I wasn't to worry about him. But I do worry. I think he feels guilty that he's talked about himself so much in the past few weeks and he really ought to be concentrating on my education and upbringing. So I have no idea where he's sleeping or whether he's sorted out his own life or not. He doesn't seem to be any happier, though. When he thought I wasn't looking I caught him staring out of the window with tears in his eyes. It's been raining for the past few days so we've not been able to go for a walk or even to swim in the secret pool. We've been stuck in Mapa's study, working hard. So there's no way of cheering him up at present.

DIARY OF SOWEEN CLAY, 23RD DAY OF AUTUMN
(IN MY TWELFTH YEAR)

———————

Today I met with Axi and Sassa in the Square. We stood behind the Men's Memorial in secret and it was quite exciting. Till I found out what Axi wanted! It was to do with Elihu (of course!) She told me she'd heard that Elihu and Rudgrin went for walks together in the Woods and occasionally stopped for a swim in the Secret Pool by the waterfall and bathe **naked** together! I don't know how she'd found that out, unless Sassa told her! And Axi said I was to find out the next time they were planning to go on one of their little walks together, so we could spy on them. She knew a great hiding place and if I agreed to help them then she'd let me become a member of The Falcons. I don't know why they want to see my brother naked. It wasn't **that** exciting! I've seen him naked masses of times ever since he was a tiny baby and it was never very much! And then Axi said, What about seeing his Tutor naked as well? I bet you haven't seen that before, have you? Wouldn't that be exciting? And I nearly said, what do you think I am, some kind of **pervert** or something? Seeing a **MAN** naked? Who wants to see that? Yuurrk! That's perverted! But I didn't say it because though I don't really want to see either of them naked (why should I?) I really want to be a member of The Falcons more than anything. Then I can be with my dearest friend, Sassa **every single day**! Even though I can't marry her, I can still be her friend. Apart from the times when she's shut away with Axi (which is nearly **all** the time). So here I am at last, a member of The Falcons! Thank you, Elihu. I feel a bit bad, though. Like I've just sold a part of him. A very private part of him, too. (Tee-hee!) I feel very excited! (But a little bit nervous, too!) My eczema is still there and is still spreading, I think. I've started itching behind my ears now!

DIARY OF ELIHU CLAY, 24TH DAY OF AUTUMN

(IN MY FOURTEENTH YEAR)

———————

First thing this morning, before she went to school Soween was behaving very oddly, even by her standards. She asked me in rather a sly way, if, because it was such a beautiful day, whether Rudgrin and I would be going for another of our swims together. And I said, probably, why? And she said, all innocent, oh, no, reason, I just wondered. And I said, you haven't told anyone, have you? She'd better not have done! Note: Never tell your sister anything important that you want kept a secret!

When he arrived, Rudgrin seems much happier and back to more like he used to be. He told me he'd moved into this single room apartment, just him. He much preferred living on his own, he was perfectly happy now and it had all turned out for the best. I didn't say anything to him but I thought that sounded a bit sad, if he was going to have to live in one room on his own for the rest of his life. I hope I'll find another Man to live with, someday. Though I can't imagine it. But then I haven't met many other Men, apart from Rudgrin and, though I like him as a friend, I don't think I'd ever want to live with him all the time. I think we'd probably drive each other crazy, in the end. We went swimming in the Secret Pool this afternoon, which I think cheered Rudgrin up a little.

DIARY OF SOWEEN CLAY, 25TH DAY OF AUTUMN
(IN MY TWELFTH YEAR)

After morning school was over, at lunchtime The Falcons met in the Square by the Memorial. At least some of us did. There were actually only four of us, Axi, Sassa, Giella and me. Axi said she hadn't asked everyone or there'd be too many. At the edge of the woods, Axi stopped and said from this point I should be blindfolded because we were going to a secret place and, as a new member, I was not to be trusted because I hadn't yet taken the sacred oath. I think she secretly hates me and wants to make my life miserable. So I was blindfolded and we walked on, me stumbling with Sassa and Giella holding my hands. Soon, I could hear the waterfall up ahead of us. I knew exactly where we were, of course. I'd been there millions of times! But Axi told me to be quiet and they led me very close to the falling water till I could feel the spray on my face and I thought for a moment they were going to push me over the edge but then we seemed to step through the water like it was a curtain. Then at last my blindfold was removed and we were in a small cave behind the waterfall. All the years we'd been swimming here and I'd never known about it. Axi said it was a secret which only her family know about, going back years, long before the Divide and now, apart from her parents, we're the only people who knew about it. As I was the newest member of The Falcons, first of all you have to be initiated. I was made to kneel down on the wet stone floor and swear an oath and then forced to drink some of Axi's wine to seal my vow. Which was **foul**. We then waited for Tutor Rudgrin and Elihu to arrive. I hoped I'd got it right. Looking out of the cave through the curtain of water, we had a good view of the pool. But looking in from the other side the cave was hidden, making us invisible. It was a brilliant hiding place. Axi isn't very nice but she is clever. As we waited, I began to get anxious that maybe they wouldn't come. And then I worried what they were doing was something private between them and maybe I was betraying them. And just then, my brother and Rudgrin appeared through the trees, laughing and talking. They both stripped off their clothes and jumped straight into the pool, laughing and splashing each other, unaware of their uninvited audience behind the waterfall. As we watched to my *disgust* I saw Axi staring at Rudgrin and lifting her long black skirt and starting to play with herself – down there. Worse still, Sassa, sitting by her, then lifted her school dress and started to do the same. Both at first separately and then eventually doing it to **each other**! All the time staring at Rudgrin and giggling. Whilst Giella sat very still, in the opposite corner, seeming to be unaware of them. She was staring as well, not at Rudgrin, but at Elihu with a strange look of sort of wonder on her face. Like she was seeing some heavenly vision or something. Strange. But Giella is always a bit strange. Remote somehow. Perhaps not having a brother, she'd never seen naked Men before. As I write this, just before I go to sleep, I feel today was a day which started excitingly but ended with a feeling that I have finally lost Sassa for ever, even as a friend. In a few months it will be our joint twelfth birthday, the day when we will finally be fitted with our grown-up dresses, the day we promised each other our big joint party. But that will never be, not now.

DIARY OF ELIHU CLAY, 5TH DAY OF WINTER
(IN MY FOURTEENTH YEAR)

When Rudgrin arrived this morning he had a black eye and a nasty cut on his forehead. Mama immediately ran and put a dressing on his wound. She's great like that. The smallest cut and she's there with the ointment. We asked what had happened to him. Rudgrin explained that it was his own fault really and that last night he went across the road from his new apartment to a café opposite but on his way back he didn't look where he was going and stupidly walked through the middle of a gang fight. It was usually alright, they generally leave you alone, providing you don't bother them. It was entirely his fault, he just hadn't looked where he was going. Mama looked rather worried and Rudgrin said, it was only a gang fight, you must have gangs over here too, mustn't you? Girls must have gangs, surely? And I said, not that I know of. I'm sure Soween doesn't belong to one, anyway. But Mama still looked uncertain. As if she knew something. Perhaps Soween does belong to a gang, whoever would've thought it? I asked Rudgrin whether he'd ever belonged to a gang and he said once he did when he was younger, before he was with Orlo. But that now he was single again, maybe he should join one. It was safer. North of the Divide, a single Man was better off belonging to a gang. Safety in numbers. I asked if that meant he had to take part in fights, if he joined one and he said, occasionally he might have to but only when they were fighting for territory. That's when Men fight. To stop others taking over your territory. It's all to do with territory. But Men always had been territorial, since time began. I suppose when I cross the Divide, I'll probably need to join a gang. I hope I don't have to fight. I've never been good at that. Whenever I wrestled Fergo he always beat me. But then Fergo loves to fight. He says he can't wait to fight someone properly, because at present, there's only girls and they're never any fun to fight. There's only me and he says I'm no better at fighting than most of the girls. He'll be very happy once he's North of the Divide.

Next year will be my fourteenth birthday and, in a few months, my sister will be fitted with her first grown-up dress. It's strange to think of us all getting older. In a year or two, whenever she's with me, she'll have to visor up, so I'll never see her face any more. Somehow, it'll be like saying goodbye to her.

"ON HER TWELFTH BIRTHDAY, a girl will first have a blood sample taken at an approved Medical Centre before being fitted with appropriate adult clothing. This will consist of officially approved items as supplied by a designated local outfitter. For full details of officially approved items see Note 5 below

A WOMAN WILL CONFORM to this official dress code at all times throughout her lifetime without deviation.

ONCE SHE HAS BEEN FITTED with her clothes a Woman, when in public, should contrive to walk demurely, drawing as little attention to herself as possible, never staring at others but keeping her eyes cast down in humility.

ITEMS WORN will only be purchased through an approved local outfitter.

FAILURE TO COMPLY with these regulations will be punishable by law."

DIARY OF SOWEEN CLAY, 5TH DAY OF SPRING
(IN MY THIRTEENTH YEAR)

Sassa and I didn't go straight to school this morning. Instead, we both went first to the Medical Centre in the High Street where, because we were both twelve years old, we had to give some blood just to confirm we were infectious. All Women have to do this on their twelfth birthday. It was very quick and didn't hurt a bit. We both then went to the Outfitters in the High Street where we were fitted with our first grown-up dresses. We have now reached the age when we are considered mature enough to be possible Carriers and therefore a danger to Men. We had been measured a few days earlier and now here we were, sitting side-by-side outside the fitting room, waiting to be called in. I was the first. As I stood there, half undressed whilst the assistant fussed and fumbled with the fastenings, I felt very self-conscious, aware of the awful rash covering my body and face. My eczema came and went, some days were better than others. Today was a bad one, probably because of my nerves! First, I tried on the underwear which, as Axi had warned us the year before, was scratchy, every inch of it, from the tight black vest, flattening your chest, to the black baggy bloomers. All of which did little to help my skin condition. Over this, the black dress with its floor length full skirt and front fastening, stiff bodice with long sleeves tapering at the wrists. Then the gloves to be worn outside the house and the flat lace up black shoes. Finally the black brimmed bonnet fastening under the chin and from which, by reaching up into its brim, you were able to pull down the built-in protective visor to cover your face. Which I would now need to do, of course, whenever I was with Elihu. Later, Sassa and I left the shop together both of us walking back through the High Street, feeling slightly self-conscious. And, it has to be said also feeling somewhat restricted and uncomfortable, especially for me with the new underwear rubbing against my skin. I mentioned this to Sassa. She said, I wasn't to worry as no one bothered with official underwear, not after the first day. I asked her what most people wore. I was sure my own family were perfectly correct and proper, certainly Mapa. And Sassa laughed and said, you wear something that makes you feel good, something sexy and pretty. Or even nothing at all! God, I have lived such a sheltered life! My parents tell me nothing! And Sassa said, that when you thought about it, if we're going to have to spend the rest of our lives in black clothes, all of us identical black blobs, you need to wear something to make you feel special, don't you? I will so miss Sassa. I will really miss her so much. Now we are twelve, we start at the Senior School, soon. When we will no longer have Teacher Olishaw. I will miss her TERRIBLY, too. We all will. Even Axi will, I think, secretly. Our new Teacher in Senior School is called Teacher Jollie. I hope she is! But I've heard she's a real dragon!

END OF PART I

Part II
ATTRACTION

EDITED EXCERPT OF MINUTES OF MEETING
SOUTH SARUM VILLAGE COUNCIL, 19 SPRING

Present:
Cllr. T. Chilzer (Chair) (Moderate)
Cllr. K. Clay (Orthodox)
Cllr. M. Chalice (Moderate)
Cllr. J. Grosh (Orthodox)
Cllr. F. Harran (Moderate)
Cllr. H. Tarness (Progressive)
Cllr. L. Marling (Orthodox)
Cllr. Doben (Orthodox)
Cllr. L. Kriffitt (Moderate)
Cllr. W. Spanway (Moderate)
Cllr. C. Nivess (Progressive)
Cllr. G. Whipple (Progressive)

The Orthodox Party members, Cllrs. Grosh, Clay,
Doben and Marling having concluded their private
reading in the antechamber, joined the main meeting
as usual.

1. Sadly the xxxxxxxxxxxxxxxxxxxxxxxxxxxxx great
regret.

2. Men's Memorial xxxxxxxxxxxxxxxxxxxxxxxxxxxxx
respect.

3. Inappropriate use of xxxxxxxxxxxxxxxxxxxxxxx
discouraged.

4. Mirrors. Cllr. Whipple (P) apologised for bringing up such a trivial subject before the Council but felt it was important. She was conscious of being, by some years, the youngest member of the Council, this might not be so pressing for others present. But ever since she was a small child she wondered why, under Preacher's Law, mirrors were not permitted in Women's bedrooms but only, in most houses, the hall or a public room. And then just a single mirror per household. All the time she had been growing up, with all a normal young Woman's insecurities and wavering self-confidence, she had felt a need to check her appearance on an almost regular basis throughout the day. Most of her friends of her age felt the same. She believed it was only natural, a normal part of growing up. At this point, Cllr. Clay (O) interrupted to enquire how regularly did she consider regularly? Cllr. Whipple said, at least once an hour. Cllr. Clay replied that someone needing to look at themselves on an hourly basis could hardly be described as natural but rather as grossly narcissistic. Did the Councillor consider herself vain? Cllr. Whipple replied, no more than most people. Cllr. Clay said, in her opinion, the Councillor must reside in a cesspit. Cllr. Tarness (P) objected saying this was highly offensive, demanding Cllr. Clay withdraw her remark. Cllr. Clay then added that if Cllr. Whipple was an example of the new bright Progressive Party then we were all of us, to use an historic phrase, going to hell in a hand cart. Cllr. Whipple said all she was proposing was that regulations regarding mirrors within private homes should be

relaxed but, in the face of such aggression, she would withdraw the motion. Most people, anyway, had mirrors everywhere in their houses including their bedrooms so it made little difference. It was just such absurd and outmoded rules that brought the law into ludicrous disrepute. Cllr. Whipple then left the meeting in tears. She was applauded by other members of the Progressive party. Cllr. Chilzer said, if nobody wished to add anything further to the discussion, perhaps they should move on.

DIARY OF ELIHU CLAY, 20TH DAY OF SPRING.
(IN MY FOURTEENTH YEAR)

Today, I decided to show Rudgrin my drawings for the very first time. He's been asking me for ages if he could look at them and I eventually decided to pluck up courage and show some to him. I think I was frightened he'd say they were no good and then I would never have had the heart to carry on because I do value his opinion, even though he has his up and down days. He's very wise about most things and has good judgement, I think. I showed him the ones of birds and animals, occasionally of flowers. He studied them for a long time, without saying anything. After a long pause, he told me he thought they were very good and that I showed promise. Though I was still quite young he'd like to encourage me to carry on and that he felt I might develop into something quite special as an artist. He actually liked them! Then he asked me if I'd ever thought of drawing people rather than just birds and animals and flowers. He thought people would be more of a challenge for me. Perhaps I should ask someone to pose. I said I'd try and find someone. But I can't possibly think who to ask.

DIARY OF SOWEEN CLAY, 10TH DAY OF SUMMER
(IN MY THIRTEENTH YEAR)

Sassa said she wanted to talk to me today after school. For a moment, it was like the sun had come out, but when we met it went back behind the clouds. She told me that she and Axi, last night, had got engaged and in a year or so, as soon as they'd both left school, they planned to get married. And because I was her best friend, she wanted me to be the first to know! And I pretended to be ever so casual saying, really! That's great! How lovely for you both! Congratulations! Wonderful! But inside I felt like someone who knew they're dying but all the same hopes it isn't true, and then finally hearing from the doctor that it was. I suppose in my heart I knew it would happen. It was just too good to be true, Sassa and me. Besides, if Sassa is really set on being a Mama, it's just as well, I suppose. Because if we had married I'd probably have wanted to be a Mama too and you can't really have a family with two Mamas, can you? It wouldn't be fair on the children. I talked to my Mama about it later. Telling her how miserable I was. She was very sympathetic. She said she knew all about hearts being broken, hers must have been broken dozens of times when she was my age because young girls can be very fickle and fussy when it comes to pairing. But once I did meet the Woman of my dreams, I'd know it at once. (I thought I had already found the Woman of my dreams already, but I didn't interrupt her!) Mama said when she came along, it was often the very person you least expected. Perhaps even someone who at first you didn't care for very much. But in the end turns out to be just perfect for you, being interested in the same things, loving all the things you love. But, most important, they'd love me for myself. For what

I was, myself. That was exactly how it had been with her and Mapa. She couldn't stand her at first. So stiff and stuffy, Mapa seemed to have no sense of humour at all. She never laughed. Never. Not once. Mama had made a vow early on she'd never live with someone who didn't make her laugh. Someone she could laugh with, now and then. And she was sure Mapa found her empty and frivolous, too, with not a serious thought in her silly little head. But the more they got to know each other, the more Mama saw in Mapa. She came to admire her strength, her honesty, and above all her sense of what was right. Which in the end, counted for more than all the laughs in the world. What you need most from a partner is strength and loyalty. After all, you could always giggle with your girl friends, couldn't you? Or, I wanted to say, with your children, especially Elihu. They're terrible those two, she and Elihu, always whispering and giggling. It drives me crazy sometimes. I don't know how Mapa puts up with it either, night after night. Once, as we were leaving the table after supper, Mapa said to me quietly that I should try to ignore them. That at this time, they both needed it, mother and son. For they both knew in their hearts that the day was soon coming when they would be separated for ever.

Out of the blue this evening, Elihu asked me if I'd pose for him. Me? At first I said, no, you don't want a picture of me! But he said please and promised to give me this wonderful drawing of a vixen he'd done which I specially liked, for my bedroom wall. So I said yes, alright. So now I'm going to be an artist's model! He really is a wonderful artist. We still haven't written our book together. I don't think we ever will now. Teacher Jollie is just horrible. She said today she was going to knock all the girlish nonsense out of us and bang us into shape! Help!

When Rudgrin arrived this morning, he was covered with yet more bruises. He'd hurt his arm and his hand and was limping slightly and the side of his face was badly discoloured. Mama squawked in amazement as soon as she saw him and rushed to fetch the first aid box again, insisting on dabbing him with all sorts of lotions and creams to ease the bruising. Rudgrin seemed a bit embarrassed by all the attention and kept telling us he was fine and that this time it was entirely his own fault. He'd been talking to someone, a neighbour outside his apartment, hadn't been looking where he was going, missed his footing and fell down the stairs. Mama said he was lucky nothing was broken and suggested Mapa should check him over just in case. But Rudgrin seemed horrified at the thought of this idea. Maybe he's afraid of doctors. I hope he'll be all right. He sat there for the rest of the day and wincing every time he moved. Rudgrin really has an awful lot of bad luck, one way or another. To take his mind off things, I told him my sister had agreed to pose for me. Which managed to get a bit of a smile out of him.

DIARY OF SOWEEN CLAY, 24TH DAY OF SUMMER
(IN MY THIRTEENTH YEAR)

Mapa summoned me to her study today first thing to tell me she'd had the results of my blood test and (surprise) I had, like every other Woman in the Village, been confirmed positive and infectious. I asked her why she had needed to send the blood sample away to be analysed, north of the Divide and she explained that safe screening was a delicate and complicated process and needed to be done by the Hospital on the north side by experts. It required equipment far beyond the limited facilities in her own surgery.

After we'd had supper, Elihu and I went to my room to start on my portrait. We told Mama and Mapa that he was very kindly going to help me with some schoolwork which I was having difficulty with. Which was sort of true because he does help me occasionally especially with mathematics which I'm just useless at. My room is tiny, compared to Elihu's and I asked him why we couldn't go to his room instead. He said, no, he needed to capture me in my natural surroundings which made me sound like a squirrel or a badger. So we both sat in my room. In the early days, we used to share this huge room together. But, later on, when Mapa decided it was time we both of us slept separately, this big room was divided up, with a huge area given over for Elihu because he's a Boy and needs Much More Space while I was given what was left because I'm a Girl and don't need Very Much Space at all. At least that's what Mapa said. Which I thought was totally **unfair**. Mama told me, never mind, once Elihu moves on and crosses the Divide, I could have the whole big room back, all to myself. But it won't be the same, once he's gone, will it? I don't want him to go, not ever!

So we both sat in my broom cupboard, me and Elihu, while he shifted me about, first facing this way and then facing that, then sideways on. And finally he settled for me sitting in my dress and bonnet with my back to him and looking back over my shoulder and smiling. I begged him not to draw my eczema as I didn't want a picture of me covered in sores and blotches and he promised he wouldn't.

Which I know is Vanity and will send me straight to Hell. But I don't care. I can't help it if I'm not beautiful, can I? He spent ages frowning and squinting at me and I hoped I didn't have to sit still for too long as my neck was beginning to ache and I felt less and less like smiling. He promised he'd be as quick as he could but in the end he spent ages and ages scratching and scraping with his pencil on his sketchpad and then rubbing things out and scratching away again until I was in sheer agony!. But just as I was about to scream, he left just like that. Without showing me anything of what he'd drawn. I don't think I'm going to enjoy modelling very much.

DIARY OF ELIHU CLAY, 16TH DAY OF AUTUMN
(IN MY FIFTEENTH YEAR)

—————

My birthday! For the past few days, every evening, I've been working on my picture of Soween but I'm not sure I'll ever be a portrait painter. I'm finding it terribly difficult to express through what I draw, my feelings for her. With animals, it's much simpler, it's either joy at their beauty or simply awe at their sense of freedom. With Soween, although she's always denying she is beautiful, she has an inner beauty which is very hard to capture, the laughter behind her eyes, ready to jump out at you when you least expect it. Which people don't often notice unless they know her very well, like I do. I'd like to show what I see in her through my picture. The secret side of her. When we were all in school together, surprisingly, Fergo really rated her. He said she used to make him laugh just by the way she said things. I think that's why he teased her as much as he did, just to get her attention. I tried explaining that to her once, but she just said she found him vile and horrible. Because Rudgrin every day asks me how the portrait is getting on, I was forced to let him see something. Yesterday I showed him my progress so far. And he was very encouraging but said he felt I was not serving my subject at all well by insisting she keep her bonnet on. He said a Woman's hair was, after all, one of her most dominant features. And that the black frame of her bonnet gave Soween such a bland impression of severity, cancelling out the natural softness of her beauty. I said I was already taking a terrific risk by drawing her in the first place. The Book of Certitude clearly forbade Images of Self for a Woman and that portraits certainly came under that heading, surely?

Which is why photographs south of the Divide are forbidden. Apart from, under special licence, landscapes, animals or inanimate objects — besides Mapa is highly Orthodox. Didn't he realise, mine was the only room in the house with a mirror! Surely he didn't expect me to draw compromising pictures of my own sister and risk having her brought up before the Morality Committee? Is that what he wanted me to do? At which point he got very angry and agitated, angrier than I've ever seen him and ended up shouting, for Christ's sake, he wasn't asking her to strip naked, he was only suggesting she took her bloody hat off!

And we heard Mama clearing her throat in the kitchen and realised we'd been talking bit loudly. Tonight, I'll probably try and persuade her to take off her bonnet. Casually, of course. I'll tell her it's in the cause of Art.

DIARY OF SOWEEN CLAY, 10ᵀᴴ DAY OF WINTER
(IN MY THIRTEENTH YEAR)

The most dreadful thing happened tonight. Elihu and I were still working on my portrait which I have to admit has taken ages, far longer than either of us imagined it would. But it's really beginning to take shape. He showed me his earlier efforts when I sat stiffly looking like some burnt currant bun which had been left in the oven too long. But his Tutor was right, once I took off my bonnet it made sense and my face somehow looked a far better shape. I resisted at first as I knew inside that what we were doing was probably awfully wrong but it just didn't feel wrong, not at all and if I could help Elihu with his art in any way I was happy to take the risk. So once I got rid of the bonnet, the picture began to take shape and at least gave me a bit more personality. Which I suppose the bonnet is designed not to do but to take all that away from us. Whenever we're all out together, we Women must look to a stranger almost identical. Presenting a series of what Sassa would call identical black blobs. I am as indistinguishable from my own parents, presumably, as they were from their parents. And my daughters, if I'm blessed with any, will look identical to me. Deep inside, I feel despite that, we all still manage in some way to cling on to bits of our little secret selves. The part of me that says, I'm ME! So we dispensed with the bonnet and, in a day or so, Elihu persuaded me (though, looking back, I must admit I didn't take that much persuading!) to loosen the top of my dress as well, just enough to expose one of my shoulders, my left one where the eczema had yet to take over. And I was sitting there in my customary pose, gazing at him over one bare shoulder with my hair flowing free, smiling, when the door opened and without warning Mapa walked in. She took one look at me and then at Elihu's picture which she promptly tore from the sketchpad and ripped in half, ordering Elihu to his room and me to make myself decent at once. So much for the cause of Art! Before she left, Mapa said grimly, she would deal with me in the morning. I'm sure she'll blame me entirely for everything because I'm a *girl*. Whereas Elihu, I know, will get away with nothing more than a telling off. Life just isn't *fair*!

95

I told Rudgrin what had happened last night. How Mapa had burst in on us and how angry she'd been. Not only had she destroyed the portrait but she later also made me hand over all my earlier sketches of Soween and destroyed those as well. Rudgrin got quite angry at this but I pointed out that really, I got off fairly lightly whereas poor Soween was condemned to a month of nightly penance, just bread and water for supper, followed by a session in Mapa's study where she or Mama read to her from "The Book of Certitude". I must say, despite all that, Soween stays reasonably cheerful, and appears to bear me no grudge, despite the fact that I talked her into doing it in the first place. I think she must have considerable strength of character and self-control. If I'd been her, I would have punched me into next week! I expected Rudgrin, once he'd heard what had happened, to have another of his outbursts but instead he went very quiet. It was again far too cold to go for a walk so instead we had to work on here all day.

DIARY OF SOWEEN CLAY, 11TH DAY OF SUMMER
(IN MY FOURTEENTH YEAR)

I'm planning to stop going to meetings of The Falcons in future, although technically I'm still a member. But I don't think I can face watching Axi and Sassa gazing into each other's eyes. It makes me feel slightly sick. Do they have to make it so public? Anyway, Axi never makes me feel that welcome to meetings. She always finds some new initiation ceremony for me to do, because I'm the newest member (yes I'm still that, apparently!) I find it strange no one else in the group ever has to undergo initiation rites like me. At the last meeting, I was made to stand in a tiny cupboard, holding a pencil between my teeth, for two hours in the dark. If that is Axi's way of trying to get rid of me then she's succeeded. I'm going to no more meetings just so they can humiliate me. She still demands that I attend meetings of The Falcons, too and that I had sworn an oath, a sacred oath. (Though I can't **ever** remembering swearing any oath!). But she said, if I didn't attend, I would be put into Solitude. I asked what Solitude was and Axi said darkly that I really didn't want to know! And then Sassa sniggered. (I really so **loathe** her now!)

———————

"A MAN DISPLAYING SEXUAL DESIRE for a Woman or a Woman expressing desire for a Man, whether publicly or privately, will henceforth be classified as sexually abnormal.

ALL CITIZENS who suspect such tendencies exist either within themselves or those close to them, are legally bound to report such suspicions to the relevant authority.

PERSISTENT OFFENDERS if found guilty of such abnormal inclinations will be subject to imprisonment or, in extreme cases, sexual modification or physical neutralisation to dissuade them from corrupting others.

IN ADDITION, the possession of sexually provocative images of either sex, either partially clothed or nude, shall be deemed an offence and will be looked on severely, especially in cases of the circulation of such images to an under-aged person."

DIARY OF ELIHU CLAY, 11TH DAY OF SUMMER

(IN MY FIFTEENTH YEAR)

When he arrived today, as soon as we were alone,
Rudgrin showed me this picture. It was really quite shocking.
It was of a Woman, completely naked and standing, for some
weird reason, in a large sea shell, surrounded by other people
also wearing very few clothes. Seeing how shocked I must
have looked, he explained it was a famous classic picture,
painted hundreds of years ago, in the fifteenth century,
in more enlightened times by a painter with an incredibly
complicated name but also known as Botticelli, of the
goddess of Beauty, Venus emerging from the waves. He asked
me if I liked it. I had to admit it was very well painted.
Even though there was something in me telling me I shouldn't
really be looking at it, and Mapa's voice whispering in my
ear, whispering: SINFUL! SINFUL! Rudgrin said that he
wanted to show me that the female body was something to be
celebrated by art, a thing of beauty, not torn up by ignorant
people who don't understand. He said he was sorry, he knew
she was my Mapa but she was wrong to do what she did
and should know better. After all, she was a Woman herself,
wasn't she? Underneath she had an identical body to the one
in that picture, doesn't she? I somehow doubted it. I mean,
I really love and respect my Mapa, but I hope I'll never
have to see her naked, let alone standing in a giant seashell.
Having looked at it for a while I've hidden it away carefully
in the pages of my geometry book.

DIARY OF SOWEEN CLAY, 12TH DAY OF SUMMER
(IN MY FOURTEENTH YEAR)

———

Last night, I missed an important meeting of The Falcons. I really didn't mean to. I just had so much school work to do and I'd hurried home and it was only halfway through the evening I suddenly remembered about the meeting. And I thought, oh well, too late now. I'd probably be in worse trouble if I'd turned up late. But this morning when I arrived at school, I found out what Solitude meant. No one in the entire class would even acknowledge my existence. No one spoke to me or even looked at me. Not even Giella. It was like I was invisible. And it went on like that for the entire day. It was just so awful. Axi told me when I arrived that the class had put me into Solitude and from now on no one would speak to me and I was to speak to no one except the Teacher. I was only to look at the floor and not try to catch anyone's eye, except the Teacher's. At break time, I was completely ignored, left standing in the corner of the playground. When I got home, Mama could see I was upset. She asked me what the problem was. I told her I had a slight tummy ache. I went to bed early and cried myself to sleep.

DIARY OF ELIHU CLAY, 13ᵀᴴ DAY OF SUMMER

(IN MY FIFTEENTH YEAR)

After our swim together, this afternoon, as we both sat drying off in the sun, Rudgrin began to talk about himself more personally. And though I was dying to interrupt and ask questions, I sensed I needed to sit and listen quietly or he'd stop and close up again. He said that one of the reasons he'd had trouble with his relationships in the past with his various partners was, after a time, he gradually stopped feeling it was "normal", to be that way with another man. What was more he was very certain, in fact he knew for certain, there were others North of the Divide who felt the same as he did. He was by no means alone. There were plenty of others. Only most of them were too afraid to reveal their feelings for fear of prosecution. There were strict Preacher's rules, just as there were South of The Divide. Heterosexual sex, sex between a Man and a Woman was unthinkable. Even just admitting to having such feelings, the consequences didn't bear thinking about.

I asked him, did he mean to say he'd had these feelings himself? Wanting sex with a <u>Woman</u>? And his voice suddenly got very quiet and he whispered, yes, all the time. I must have looked so shocked that he said, sorry. It was just something in him. Something he couldn't help. I listened to this with a growing sense of horror. My Tutor, my friend was a self-confessed deviant. It went against everything I'd ever been taught, that I instinctively believed. How could he? I admit I came closer, at that moment, to reporting him to Mapa than I've ever been. I think only the friendship between us prevented me. Instead I put my hand over his by way of reassurance, pretending that I sympathised and understood. Indeed, in a way I did sympathise. After all, that was the way he was born, poor man, and there was nothing he could do about it, was there? As we walked home, I insisted on holding his hand, hoping that my presence by his side would help to keep his thoughts free of Women. Though I somehow doubted it.

DIARY OF SOWEEN CLAY, 13TH DAY OF SUMMER
(IN MY FOURTEENTH YEAR)

Today at school it was exactly the same as yesterday with everyone ignoring me again! Halfway through the day, I tried to sneak a sly look at Giella but she managed to avoid my eyes. How long are they going to keep this up? I think I'll die of loneliness if someone doesn't talk to me soon. When I got home at the end of the day it was obvious I'd been crying and Mama looked at me anxiously but again I told her, it was nothing. Although it's everything, really.

DIARY OF ELIHU CLAY, 14TH DAY OF SUMMER
(IN MY FIFTEENTH YEAR)

Rudgrin brought more pictures today. He opened his satchel and fumbled beneath the lining for a moment where he had them concealed. More reproductions of paintings featuring naked or semi-naked women. He seems to have an inexhaustible supply of them! He's obviously deeply into pornography. He tried to explain them away saying that they were all classic images from an enlightened time when they were perfectly acceptable, even admired. None of the Women had any clothes on. I asked him, in this so called enlightened time did none of the Women ever wear clothes? In some of the pictures, where there were Men, they were wearing clothes, lots of clothes. I told him to take the pictures away because they were upsetting me. But he persisted, showing me this newspaper article from The North Sarum Journal.* At which point we had another of our arguments, only this time I got quite angry with him, refusing to read it and accusing him of trying to corrupt me. I was fourteen years old and couldn't cope with this, I really couldn't.

I didn't really mean to get so angry with him but I honestly believe he is, he's starting to corrupt me. I dreamt last night of that Woman in the seashell.

In my dream that Woman was advancing on me, holding out her arms, her breasts pushing forward at me, almost as if she were threatening me with them. I awoke shaking, in a terrible sweat, feeling very aroused. I do think he's beginning to corrupt me and I'm getting rather frightened. I'm torn between reporting him or worse still of forfeiting (as Mapa would say) my Immortal Soul. I don't quite know what to do.

I told him to take the pictures away and never to bring any more of them!

* *Author's note:* Elihu refers in his diary entry 14 Summer 118 PD that Rudgrin, along with the pictures, also gave him an old newspaper article. I have no idea if Elihu actually read it or not but no trace of it was found amongst his belongings so I can only assume it was lost or destroyed. It is my guess a leading article in *The North Sarum Journal* (dated 24 Summer 112 PD) might well be the one referred to.

A DIVIDE TOO MANY?

We are made aware almost daily of the Divide just to the South of us. It separates us all, us here in the North from the Women only a few yards away on the South side. But for yards you may as well read, miles. As years pass, the distance between us grows greater and greater. Ever since that wretched disease decimated our species, threatening at one stage to wipe us out entirely, the sexes have been forced to live separate lives, a situation in itself which potentially threatened the future of the human race. Fortunately, Science had advanced sufficiently to ensure this did not happen. Women were still able to conceive children, albeit from Men whom they'd never met and certainly never had a chance of loving or with whom they could ever properly share the child. But, despite that, for generations now, we have survived and indeed, if statistics are true, the population is gradually on the increase again. But as long as the danger continues, any genuine congress between the sexes remains impossible. What future do heterosexual relationships have while one partner still remains lethally toxic to the other? We can but wait and see. The agnostics and atheists amongst us praying for good old Science to come up trumps again or, for the followers of The Preacher (and there must still be a few of those left, surely?) for the arrival of the long prophesied Immune One. In the meantime, the Divide not only remains but grows deeper with each passing year. The truth is that, here in the North, Men have learnt over the years to cope perfectly well without Women and I have no doubt, Women in the South have adapted in much the same way. We are, each of us, gradually growing self-contained and independent from the other. So be it, I hear you say, *vive la difference*. In most areas we're coping perfectly well. After all when it comes down to it, who needs Men/Women anyway? After all, what *difference* is there these days? A bit more muscle on the North side perhaps (but they can always compensate for that, can't they? They've got gyms in the South too, haven't they?) and babies being exclusively produced in the South (but, God forbid, who in his right mind ever wanted voluntarily to stand watching *that* happening!) But when it all boils down, the *difference* really isn't any big *difference* at all. And yet . . . And yet . . . Something is missing for some of us. A certain something that no amount of Man on Man grunting or Woman on Woman groaning can ever quite replace. Don't get me wrong, I've been in Man on Man relationships most of my adult life and the majority have been sheer heaven (with a few exceptions, no names mentioned!) But what of those Men in our society who secretly long for the intimate touch of a Woman? Those we currently classify as "abnormal" or (more hatefully still) as "straight"? The ones we vilify or shun socially or even seek out on street corners to beat the hell out of? What of these poor souls? I'm certain, though of course I have no direct knowledge of this, that South of the Divide there are Women who feel the same way about Men, who are equally encouraged through social pressure to suppress such "unnatural urges". Something must surely be done to help these people. We must stop referring to them as criminals or threaten them in extreme instances, God forbid, with castration and seriously consider how to integrate them back into our society. It can not be beyond the wit of Science, surely, to come up with a solution for that?

DIARY OF SOWEEN CLAY, 15TH DAY OF SUMMER
(IN MY FOURTEENTH YEAR)

———————

A third day of misery. Again the terrible isolation. Just for missing a stupid meeting! I sensed teacher Jollie is also getting concerned for me and she made special attempts to single me out and talk to me which was kind of her but in a way made me feel even more alone and isolated. Solitude is really the most terrible punishment. People can be so CRUEL. And I can't tell anyone. Not Mapa, nor Mama or Elihu who is rarely around these days, anyway. Either he's shut in with his Tutor or off on one of those walks of his with his sketchpad.

Rudgrin didn't turn up this morning. At first I thought following our quarrel, I may have badly hurt his feelings. But then I thought again he may have just been delayed. He says that often in the Tunnel when you're crossing the Divide especially from North to South, the officials can sometimes get very fussy and hold you up for hours, checking for illicit materials they suspect you're trying to smuggle in. But when he hadn't arrived by lunchtime, Mama and I began to get a little worried. But of course we had no way of contacting him since we didn't have a direct link to North of the Divide. That was closed down ages ago to prevent Improper Exchanges. So, in the afternoon I went for a walk on my own. I had a nice quiet swim and then came home again. I hope he's all right and hasn't had another fall. I think, sometimes his falls are maybe due to alcohol though I'd hate to say that to his face.

DIARY OF SOWEEN CLAY, 16ᵀᴴ DAY OF SUMMER
(IN MY FOURTEENTH YEAR)

This evening, after another long day of silent torment at school when I got home, before supper, Mapa summoned me to her study which she rarely does, except to punish me or to tell me off for something. And as I went in, I thought to myself, I don't think I can bear it if Mapa's going to punish me after what's been happening to me again today! But Mapa sat behind her desk and smiled at me and gently told me to sit down. Which was a good start. When she intends to punish you, she makes you stand. (Later on, through bitter experience, you can't sit down!) Mapa said she'd heard from Mama that I was having some trouble at school. I just sat there staring at my feet. Blushing and for some reason just feeling so terribly ashamed! Mapa's voice was so gentle and soft. Then, all of a sudden I started to cry. When I had stopped, she handed me a tissue and said, girls could be very cruel sometimes, even more so than boys, in their own way. I wasn't the first person to be bullied and she feared sadly, I wouldn't be the last. She told me when Mama was my age, she suffered in much the same way. It's something that went on, generation after generation. It might be that things seemed unbearable at present but it was sure to pass. Bullies were generally stupid creatures with small brains and a limited attention span. And if I could just hold out, show them how little they were hurting me, how they were failing to get to me, then sooner or later they'd grow bored and move on in search of some other poor victim. But for the time being, I needed to be brave. She knew I could be. After all, I was her daughter and she was very proud of me. And then she pulled me to her and hugged me. Mapa actually hugged me! And, oh.

God, I was suddenly two metres tall. Tonight I truly loved my Mapa, really, really for the very first time! Mama's right! She's so strong!

DIARY OF ELIHU CLAY, 17TH DAY OF SUMMER
(IN MY FIFTEENTH YEAR)

Another day without a Tutor. I'm getting very worried. It's never the same swimming on your own. There's no one to splash! Mapa said at supper last night that, if Rudgrin didn't turn up soon, she was going to make some enquiries.

Although I've got out of the habit of late, tonight before I go to sleep, I will say a prayer for Rudgrin. I think I need to pray for me, as well! I keep opening my geometry book and taking sly looks at that Woman in the seashell. I think she's put me under some sort of spell.

DIARY OF SOWEEN CLAY, 17TH DAY OF SUMMER

(IN MY FOURTEENTH YEAR)

After Mapa's talk to me last night, I slept much better and went off to school this morning full of new resolution. But when I got there, miracles! Things were back to normal and people greeted me and said good morning as if nothing had happened. When I sat at my desk, I saw a note informing me that this evening there was a meeting of The Falcons at Axi's farm. There was no way I was going to miss that one! Axi's parents had a farm and The Falcons usually met in their barn. The seven of us, Axi, Sassa, Giella, Molwin, Yoteez, Silje and I, all went straight from school and arrived together. It was soon apparent, though, as soon as the meeting started that my trials were far from over. Axi hadn't yet got that bored! She started by sarcastically welcoming me back to the group saying how delighted she was that I had deigned to join them. Since it had been so long, my membership had now lapsed and I was going to have to re-apply for membership. I was then made to kneel down and go through the whole nonsense again with Sassa sniggering throughout. Drinking yet more wine, not just Axi's this time but from all of them. Disgusting! I thought I was going to be sick! When I finally choked and couldn't swallow any more, Axi poured the rest of it over my head. When the meeting broke up, as we were leaving the barn, Giella ran her hand secretly up my back and gave me a quick smile, as if to say, it's going to be all right. Thank you, Giella! My new friend! My only friend, come to that. As soon as I was home, I avoided Mama and cleaned up as best I could in the bathroom. Washing my stinking bonnet to start with. Mama knew something was wrong, though, and kept giving me these sorrowful looks of hers. I wish she wouldn't. they're no help at all. I woke up in the night with a terrible stomach ache. God. I think they must have poisoned me! Pee poisoning! Help!

CLERK: EDITED EXCERPT OF MINUTES OF MEETING

SOUTH SARUM VILLAGE COUNCIL, 19 SUMMER

———————

Present:
Cllr. T. Chilzer (Chair) (Moderate)
Cllr. K. Clay (Orthodox)
Cllr. M. Chalice (Moderate)
Cllr. F. Harran (Moderate)
Cllr. H. Tarness (Progressive)
Cllr. L. Marling (Orthodox)
Cllr. Doben (Orthodox)
Cllr. L. Kriffitt (Progressive)
Cllr. C. Nivess (Progressive)
Cllr. G. Whipple (Progressive)

Apologies: Cllr. J. Grosh (Orthodox), Cllr. W. Spanway (Moderate)

The Orthodox Party members, Cllrs Clay, Doben and Marling, having concluded their private reading in the antechamber, joined the main meeting as usual.

Before the commencement, Cllr. Chilzer, Chair, informed Councillors that earlier today, Cllr. L. Kriffitt had spoken to her telling her she wished to resign from the Moderate Party and would be joining the Progressive Party. Cllr. Chilzer said whilst she regretted the loss of Cllr. Kriffitt from the ranks of her fellow Moderates, she wished her every success with her new Party. Members, she added, must always act according to their own

political consciences, of course. Councillor Clay
commented, however bad that conscience might be.

1. Maintaining the xxxxxxxxxxxxxxxxxxxxxxxxxxxx
be arranged.

2. Improper dress codes
xxxxxxxxxxxxxxxxxxxxxxxxxxxxxxx penalties.

3. Mirrors. Relaxation of current legislation.
Cllr. Clay (O) asked why this subject had again
been included in the minutes. To her recollection,
the item had already been discussed and dismissed
over a year ago. If members of the Progressive
Party were once again attempting to introduce
modifications to mirror legislation, then she
wished to inform councillors that the Orthodox
Party would still strongly oppose any further
attempt to do so. Cllr. Tarness then reminded the
meeting that the item had indeed been included
at the meeting of 21 Spring last year and it had
not then been voted upon and so they were at
liberty to reintroduce it for reconsideration
by Councillors. Cllr. Clay accused her of
deliberately reintroducing this again, taking
advantage of the absence of Cllr. Grosh (O) thus
allowing the Progressive Party a numerical
advantage. Cllr. Tarness responded that she had
had no foreknowledge of Cllr. Grosh's absence,
how could she? And that it was somewhat ironic
that the Councillor should be accusing her of
unfair tactics after the way last time she had
shamelessly bullied her colleague, Cllr. Whipple

and had been doing so at every opportunity since.
Cllr. Clay was, in her opinion, a cowardly bully
and a bigot. The Chair then interceded and asked
Cllr. Tarness to lower her voice and moderate
her language or face disciplinary procedures.
And that this constant bickering between her
and Cllr. Clay had to stop. As Chair, she would
no longer tolerate it. She felt she was speaking
for members of all parties in saying she was
becoming heartily sick of it, meeting after
meeting. A vote was then taken on the motion. Did
the Council agree to the relaxation of current
legislation regarding mirrors in private homes
and allow them in future to be used throughout
the home, including bedrooms? A vote was taken
and the motion was passed by 5 votes to 3 with 2
abstentions. There being no other business the
meeting was concluded.

DIARY OF ELIHU CLAY, 20TH DAY OF SUMMER
(IN MY FIFTEENTH YEAR)

Rudgrin returned again today. He was using a walking stick and was limping quite badly and in obvious discomfort. I asked him if he walked all the way from the north side in that state and he said, apart from the moving walkway in the tunnel, yes he had. When I asked what happened to him this time, he refused to answer, saying it was too complicated to go into. I thought, either he doesn't want to tell me, or he's running out of excuses. I wish he'd just be honest with me. He's my friend and if he's in trouble he ought to feel able to tell me. But I suspect there's some dark secret about himself that he doesn't want to reveal to me. So, this afternoon when we finished lessons and we'd had lunch, although it was a lovely day I assumed he wouldn't want to go for our usual walk and certainly wouldn't want to swim. He agreed to walk with me but in the end I had another swim whilst he sat and watched me, smiling to himself. No doubt thinking of naked women, if I know him.

DIARY OF SOWEEN CLAY, 21ST DAY OF SUMMER

(IN MY FOURTEENTH YEAR)

Some kind of miracle happened today. After school, as I was on my way home, Giella came running after me, calling out my name and asking if she could walk home with me, saying she urgently needed to talk to me. And the strange, distant Giella tagged along beside me all the way home and I thought considering I'd hardly exchanged three words with her the whole time we'd been growing up together, it was a bit peculiar. Halfway home, she suddenly burst out saying she did so want to be my friend and would I mind? She was sorry about what happened in the barn at the last meeting. She was forced to join in with the others. She'd never personally have made me drink her urine. And I said, ever so casually, well once you've tasted one lot, it tended to taste much the same, really. Which made her laugh and then she hugged me. What did she want?

When we reached our front door, I looked at her properly for the first time and it occurred to me that she was probably terribly shy. The reason she never spoke much, never talked about herself at all, appeared to be so mysterious, was she was actually very shy. Looking at her, she was pretty rather than beautiful. Not beautiful like Sassa and, though I hate to say it, not handsome like Axi. Now, here she is running after me. No one has EVER run after me before. What is she up to, I wonder? I suspect some dark Falconish plot by Axi! Help! What are they planning for me next?

DIARY OF ELIHU CLAY, 16TH DAY OF AUTUMN
(IN MY SIXTEENTH YEAR)

It's my fifteenth birthday today. Mama baked me a cake and had knitted me some enormous swimming trunks that start at my chest and come down to my knees. She said if I must insist on swimming, I could at least be decent. I thanked her very much but secretly I certainly never intended ever wearing them! If they filled with water, they'd probably drag me under and drown me!

Mapa gave me a framed embroidered sampler with the text: "If Love Is The Answer, Why Should We Question?" Soween gave me a set of charcoal pencils and when Rudgrin arrived he was carrying a large rolled up picture which I dreaded would turn out to be an enlarged diagram of female genitalia. But turned out, after all to be an ancient historic map of Salisbury when it was still a large city, before the Divide. Which was really rather interesting.

In the afternoon, Fergo arrived, resplendent in his new white suit and visor, walking with just a bit of a swagger. He gave me what he described as a joke present, the tiniest boat imaginable, made it out of a half walnut shell which he said I could float in my bath. We both agreed we must meet soon and catch up.

DIARY OF SOWEEN CLAY, 16TH DAY OF AUTUMN
(IN MY FOURTEENTH YEAR)

Well, I did it! I saw Giella at school this morning and told her she could be my friend. I'd kept her waiting for a few days as I didn't want to look too eager but I felt very grand saying it. She got very excited and hugged me (again, that's twice!) crying out, thank you, thank you! I'm still extremely suspicious of her! I'm certain someone somewhere is up to something! I'm sure of it! I looked towards Axi but she was, as ever, ogling Sassa in a dopey lovesick manner. And Sassa was doing the same back! Yeeurrk! It's quite sickening, it's really is! But now, I don't need either of them. I have a new friend of my own. Although I don't fancy ogling Giella, but she keeps smiling at me whenever she gets the chance. I must say, she has lovely even teeth, lucky thing. Life is very strange and confusing just at present.

DIARY OF ELIHU CLAY, 5TH DAY OF WINTER

(IN MY SIXTEENTH YEAR)

A disastrous day. At breakfast, I noticed Mapa looking extremely grim faced saying she wouldn't be going to work, not until she'd had a word with Rudgrin. I felt a little sick wondering what she'd found out or indeed what Rudgrin could have done, since we saw him yesterday. As soon as he arrived, she took him into her study and closed the door. From the kitchen we heard them talking animatedly, certainly from Mapa's side. Eventually Rudgrin came out looking rather white, as if he'd just had a terrible shock. Mapa followed him out and announced that he was no longer to be my tutor and that he would not be coming to the house again, ever. And that she'd shortly be finding a new Tutor for me, one more suited to my requirements. And with that, she swept out for work. Leaving us all, Mama, Soween and I looking a bit stunned. Rudgrin still seemed very shocked and refused to say what had happened. Other than it was entirely Mapa's decision as she felt apparently he was no longer suitable. And that it had been a pleasure while it lasted and he was very sad to be leaving but that was that. I was especially devastated. This whole thing had happened without any warning at all. I had no idea Mapa was dissatisfied with him, she'd never shown the slightest sign of it. A huge gap had suddenly opened in my life which I was certain no new Tutor was ever going to fill. I realised how close I'd grown to Rudgrin over the past years, how good a friend he'd become, deviances and all. I was so going to miss him! I think, at that point we all started crying, Mama, Rudgrin and me. I think even Soween started too, probably coming out in sympathy, although it really didn't affect her, not at all. Protocol forbade Rudgrin, as a Vulnerable Male, even to shake hands with either of the Women, and it was left for us Men to retreat into the privacy of the study for the last time where we could embrace each other and say a proper goodbye. He still seemed very upset, muttering under his breath, "The bastard. That little bastard ... He outed me! I know he did. It was him, I know it was him!" He said Mapa had obviously heard rumours probably through the Council — concerning things that happened recently on the other side of the Divide. But when I asked him, he refused to say what those things were apart from the fact that she clearly had doubts about his Moral Stability, saying she wasn't prepared to expose her son to further danger. He'd had a letter this morning telling him he was to be charged under section ten of the Deviancy Act, which if he was found guilty automatically means the revocation of his Tutorial credentials. So, then he wouldn't be able to work anywhere. He then wrote his address on a piece of paper which he pressed into my hand, saying if in future I ever needed a friend at any time, I knew where to find him. Finally he embraced me once again and hurried out of the house and out of my life, as far as I know, for ever. Later on, I went for a walk but chose to walk through the Village today. The prospect of visiting the Woods, let alone the Secret Pool, with so many memories of Rudgrin, I really couldn't have faced just now.

DIARY OF SOWEEN CLAY, 5TH DAY OF WINTER
(IN MY FOURTEENTH YEAR)

———————

Mapa has dismissed Tutor Rudgrin and a new one will be coming to teach Elihu in a day or so. What can have happened, I wonder? Poor Elihu! He and his Tutor seemed to get on so well, more like close friends. Mama seemed particularly upset at the thought of him not coming back again. I wish somebody would sack my Teacher. Jollie, she isn't!

DIARY OF ELIHU CLAY, 7TH DAY OF WINTER

(IN MY SIXTEENTH YEAR)

———————

Mapa called me in this morning before she left for work. She told me she had arranged a new Tutor for me, Tutor Morden. It had been very short notice to find a replacement and he wouldn't be arriving for two weeks. Until then, I should spend my time revising and studying. Tutor Morden will only be here to teach me in the mornings. He has another pupil in the afternoons. But he comes highly recommended by another member of the Council, her colleague, Cllr Grosh, and she felt confident he'd more than make up for any lack of schooling over the past few months. Tutor Morden had a reputation for being firm but fair.

Which all sounded a bit ominous! I feel I'm really going to miss Rudgrin a lot. If they debar him as a Tutor, I hope he finds other work instead, North of the Divide. And he won't have any more of his "accidents". I'm still wondering what he meant by being "outed" and who on earth the "little bastard" could be? I did a lot of walking today trying to sort out my head. I must confess that now he's gone, I keep opening my textbook to take another look at the Woman in the seashell. I wish now that he'd left some of the other pictures with me, too. Oh, God, I think I might be turning into a pervert! Oh, Rudgrin, my friend, what have you done to me?

118 PD

CUTTING FROM *THE NORTH SARUM JOURNAL*

25 WINTER, P5

EX-TUTOR JAILED ON SEX CHARGES

Former Tutor Rudgrin Obolos (26) appeared before North Sarum Magistrates Court on 12 Winter charged with sex offences including possession of heterosexual pornographic material. On 7 Autumn last year, Mr Obolos whilst in an intoxicated state reputedly approached Undercover Monitor, Officer F Hackwith in Rudy's Bar, Sefton Street and suggested they go off somewhere to 'try and pull a couple of girls'. When the Officer declined, Obolos then produced several pornographic images of young Women, in partial or totally nude states, inviting the Officer to 'feast his eyes on those'. At which point Officer Hackwith arrested and subsequently cautioned Obolos under Section 10e of the Sexual Offences Act. Presiding Magistrate Jethrin Page, sentencing Obolos, described this as one of the worst examples of sexual deviancy that he had come across for several years. The Magistrate said it was doubly shocking to learn that Obolos, until only recently, had been a Tutor responsible for the moral upbringing of impressionable young men. Since this was his first offence and in view of his comparative youth, the court was in this instance going to deal leniently with him. Obolos was warned if he persisted in offending, he would be dealt with far more severely. Were he to come before them in future, he faced the maximum penalty of chemical castration. Obolos was then sentenced to 3 months imprisonment pending psychiatric counselling.

Giella asked if she could walk home again with me after school today. She's taken to following me around like a puppy. Anyway, this afternoon, I brought her home. I introduced Mama to my new friend, Giella. They seemed to get on really well. Probably partly because Giella insisted on walking about everywhere and crying out about what a beautiful house it was! Which obviously delighted Mama. What is this girl up to? She's too good to be true! She wanted to see all over the house, at least what there is of it. So we walked from room to room, including Elihu's room, with Giella, as we entered each new space exclaiming, "wonderful" or "marvellous" like we were living in a palace. We finally finished up in my tiny bedroom where we sat practically nose to nose and talked together for ages. She wanted to know everything about me and we talked about little else for hours on end but ME, ME, ME! She seemed genuinely interested, like no one had ever been, not even Sassa in the old days, when we seemed to talk mostly about her! At first, I wasn't really comfortable talking about myself. Mama always taught me it was rude to talk endlessly about yourself as it was generally extremely boring for other people. With Giella, though, I found myself telling her everything. My childhood, my friendship with Sassa, (of course!). Even my deepest private feelings of loneliness, now that I was about to lose Elihu. And eventually with both my parents now well into their forties, my very worst fear of growing old, all alone. Giella was a great listener, not interrupting or trying to switch the conversation to herself, like most people try to do. Nodding and saying, she understood, she really did, though she'd never had a brother, nor even a sister. And she looked so lost and wistful as she said it, that I felt a sudden warmth for her. Then she suddenly asked me what it must be like to have a brother, she couldn't imagine. So then I told her all about Elihu. What it was like growing up with him. I told her of the fun we'd both had when we were young and how much I'd come to rely on him being there for me. And of the great love I still had for him still and how I missed him. How terrified I was when the time finally came to lose him. How I already felt him drifting gradually further away from me. Now he'd lost Tutor Rudgrin, how he'd lately taken to going for walks all alone in the Woods with his sketchpad. Giella said she remembered the afternoon in the hidden cave, seeing them both swimming. We ended up talking for so long that finally Mapa returned home from work and I introduced her to Giella. I thought I detected a certain coolness from Mapa towards my new friend. Why should that be? Giella grows more and more fascinating. I'm still unable to discover much about her though she now knows all there is to know about me. I feel our friendship can only grow.

DIARY OF ELIHU CLAY, 20TH DAY OF SPRING
(IN MY SIXTEENTH YEAR)

My new tutor, Tutor Morden arrived today. He is very different to Rudgrin, I must say, being rather short and stout and, once he'd removed his visor, bald headed, round faced, with a small grey beard and moustache. He has a rather high voice and speaks in short sharp sentences, always appearing to be in a bit of a hurry. He'd evidently been briefed by Mapa that we should concentrate to begin with on The Book of Certitude because we spent the morning reading aloud from it together, each of us taking turns to read to the other. Mama, poor thing, was back sitting silently in the corner, presumably dozing behind her visor. Tutor Morden doesn't seem to smile much. I think laughter between us will be a rarity. Unlike with Rudgrin when, apart from his days of depression, laughter was the rule rather than the exception. I was quite relieved when Tutor Morden and I reached the end of the morning and had to stop. He stayed for lunch though, before going off to his afternoon pupil. He appears to enjoy his food. He had seconds of everything, which delighted Mama, of course. She always warms to people with healthy appetites, does Mama. Venus in her seashell still haunts my dreams and is becoming a recurrent nocturnal visitor. Each night she comes to me, she draws closer and closer, till I can almost taste the salt on her skin and smell the seaweed in her hair. When I wake up, I often find I've soiled my pyjama bottoms and have to rinse them and hang them out of the window to dry, in case Mama finds out. I wish I could talk to someone. Another man. Maybe I should talk to Fergo? Anyone but Tutor Morden.

" **A** WOMAN MUST ACCEPT the body she was born with and as God had originally intended her to inhabit. All enhancements, modifications, additions or concealments are considered expressions of Vanity and will be punished severely and in persistent cases by public flogging.

A WOMAN SHOULD NEVER attempt to modify or enhance her body in any manner, either by decoration such as jewellery (rings, earrings, necklaces, bracelets, bangles, etc.) or bodily decoration, including tattoos, piercings, etc. Nor should she engage in the use of make up, either to her face or any other part of her body. The removal of bodily hair, apart from in cases of excessive overabundance, is also strongly forbidden.

THE CONCEALMENT of physical blemishes (spots, growths, warts, rashes or other natural disfigurements) by creams or by applications intended for the purposes of concealment is also prohibited.

MODIFICATIONS TO THE BODILY SHAPE either in the form of specially designed cosmetic procedures or in the adoption of figure-enhancing clothing or underclothing is also forbidden. (See regulation clothing page 326)

A WOMAN SHOULD AT ALL TIMES be content to remain as God intended her. A Woman left to her own devices is easily led into the paths of personal vanity. (See also section Mirrors and Self Worship, paragraph 9, Appendix 15)."

DIARY OF SOWEEN CLAY, 15TH DAY OF SUMMER
(IN MY FIFTEENTH YEAR)

In the past few days, Giella and I have spent a great deal more time in each other's company, walking together in the Woods, even passing our Secret Pool by the waterfall. Giella began to talk about herself a little. She's certainly exhausted all there is to know about me! Her family are very interesting, though. Her Mama, Desollia, is a sculptor and a designer and her Mapa, Hork, is a joiner as well as being a Councillor like my own Mapa. Though they're both on different sides, my own Mapa being strictly Orthodox whereas hers belongs to the recently formed Progressive Party. Both her parents are strongly Progressive, full of new and exciting ideas. I hope I'm not in danger of being led astray! Needless to say, Mapa disapproves of Progressives and told me, if I ever came across any, I was to have nothing to do with them! Maybe that's why she frowned when I introduced her to Giella the other day when she came round. Today, Giella took me home to her house for the first time. Her parents were still at work and she took me to their bedroom and showed me her Mama's secret cupboard where she hid her great-great-grandmother's dresses and other beautiful treasures like jewels and face paint and shoes to make you taller. But best of all were some books called Magazines, filled with pictures of extremely thin beautiful women wearing these flimsy clothes and showing — well you could see nearly **everything** they had! I asked her, did her great-great-grandmother really dress like **that**? And Giella said, of course, nearly everyone did in those days. I must have looked very shocked, in the pictures they were wearing practically nothing at all! And Giella laughed, seeing I was blushing and hugged me, again, laughing and saying I was so sweet! And she told me her Mama, Desollia, some evenings, dressed up and painted her eyes and lips and wore perfume and jewellery to please her Mapa and then they'd both go off to the bedroom for hours. Giella'd said she heard them laughing and giggling all night on occasions. And I told her, they'd better not let the Monitors catch them, or they'd be in all sorts of trouble! And Giella shrugged and said, Monitors? Who cares about Monitors. In this house, we're Free Spirits. And she explained that The Free Spirits were a secret group within the Progressives, like-minded Women who totally reject The Preacher's teachings as being old-fashioned and wrong. Worse and worse! Then she took me into her own bedroom which was huge, compared with mine, and full of light with rugs and everywhere painted in these bright colours. She showed me, hidden behind a picture, the secret shelf which her Mapa'd built for her, with her collection of battered old books, most of them banned since the Divide. Our house doesn't even have as much as an illegal saucepan! And when I look back at my own pathetic attempt at rebellion! Eight years old and painting my bedroom walls and ceiling an ever so gentle (not even a bright) pink! And Mama crying out asking me if I'd gone completely mad? And then Mapa marching in with a tin of white paint, telling me to redecorate it all immediately or face the consequences! When I told her this, Giella smiled and said that if you can't be a tiny bit girly in your own bedroom, where else can you? Please, God, bring some colour into my life before I die. Colours like Giella has in her life. Maybe that's why she's come to me? To bring colour to my life? I think I may be falling in love.

DIARY OF ELIHU CLAY, 12TH DAY OF AUTUMN
(IN MY SIXTEENTH YEAR)

This afternoon, after the usual gruelling morning session with Tutor Morden, I went back to the Secret Pool. I realised that in a few days time it would be my sixteenth birthday. And, in two days time, the Monitors would come and fit me with my first adult Protective Suit and visor which I will then have to wear for the rest of my time this side of the Divide, whilst among the Women. This was one of my few remaining days to walk in the Woods to get direct sunlight on my face and to feel unrestricted and free. One last chance for a swim. In future I'll be confined, when I'm outdoors, in a Protective Suit. I shall miss swimming more than anything. Though the past few times I've swum, I've had the strange feeling I'm being watched. I can't be sure. Though I've never actually seen anyone, I have a sense that someone is there and watching. Maybe I should start wearing the vast swimming costume, the one Mama made me! Too late now. For my last swim today I certainly went in naked! All things will change for me in a couple of days, anyway. It's a significant time in your life, your sixteenth birthday, reaching the age The Preacher decreed when I'm Vulnerable. Then my family will have to visor up in my presence. In future either I will, or they'll have to. It's always difficult, holding a conversation between Men and Women when one side can no longer see the other's face. Which I suppose was The Preacher's intention all along, to make intimate conversation more difficult between us and to mark the distance that exists between us. I'm sure, by the time I leave here in two years time, I will no longer feel part of this Village. As my friend Fergo put it, even after his one faceless year in his suit, he senses people increasingly ignore and exclude him. Day by day, he says, he's becoming more and more of a stranger, even to his own family. How strange.

DIARY OF SOWEEN CLAY, 13TH DAY OF AUTUMN
(IN MY FIFTEENTH YEAR)

—————

Today is three days before Elihu's sixteenth birthday and the Monitors came to fit him with his Protective Suit. It's plain white with the male hood instead of the female bonnet, and white face visor instead of our black ones, in many ways identical to the Monitors but without their Insignia. The Monitors hardly spoke at all, but then they rarely do. Even at my age, I still find them a bit frightening. Probably the result of all Mapa's threats whilst we were growing up warning us that if we didn't behave, the Monitors would come and get us! Now, they were standing in our tiny living room, heads bowed slightly because of the low ceiling. Once they'd fitted it, Elihu stood for a moment, extended both his arms, as if to say, Well? How do I look? Mama and I, in turn, made various noises of approval. But I felt, in a way, he'd become as anonymous as the Monitors. He was no longer Elihu. He could have been anyone. Every visible, familiar scrap of him had been taken away from us. I was really going to miss him, as I knew Mama would even more so. Poor Elihu, poor Mama. His suit would put an end to all their giggly games together. Quite a relief for Mapa and me, I can tell you, both of them carrying on like a couple of kids. In two days time his Apprenticeship would start and in two years, when he was eighteen he'd be gone forever across the Divide. I'm not looking forward to it, not at all. Protective visors are suffocating, especially in the hot weather. I do believe, though, Elihu actually enjoyed putting on his suit, looking on it as a symbol of his approaching Manhood. A few months ago, we all of us went to his friend Fergo's own Apprenticeship ceremony at the Chapel and he'd later come swaggering round here showing off in his suit. (Horrible boy! I still haven't forgiven him.) And I noticed then, while he was here, Elihu looking at him with envy. Boys! They're a mystery! Mind you, we're just as bad, us Girls, in our own way!

No Tutor today. Instead, my official talk from Mapa prior to my Apprenticeship Ceremony in the Chapel tomorrow. I was really dreading our talk but in the end it turned out all right. Mapa didn't get all fiercely Orthodox with me (well, not that much!) She told me that tomorrow was a significant day for me and I must look on it as a farewell, a farewell to my family, a farewell to all of my female friends. From tomorrow, I must start preparing myself for my final entry into the world of Men, where I would take my rightful place to live among like-minded fellow human beings for the remainder of my life. I must look back on the years I'd spent in the Village as a preparatory period. Over the next few years, all the Women whom I'd spent time with here, Mama, Soween, herself, all my childhood female friends, I'd find would gradually become an increasingly distant memory, an irrelevance. Women would be, indeed ought to be, no longer a significant part of my life. The next two years, until I was eighteen, would be a time when I'd need to harden my heart and shut all of them out of my life forever, in order for me to face the final crossing without nostalgia or regret. I should look forward rather than back, put childhood behind me! I need to think of myself as one of the birds I was so fond of drawing, leaving its nest for the first time. For them too, it must be a traumatic experience, testing their untried wings in uncertain maiden flight and requiring courage! I found that last bit quite moving, partly because I knew such flowery metaphors were not part of Mapa's usual vocabulary and she'd obviously gone to a lot of trouble thinking up something that she thought I'd find relevant. I wanted to tell her, in my experience, for every single baby bird which manages to fly first time, there's at least two that crashed helplessly to the ground and promptly got eaten by predators! But I didn't think it was the right time to tell Mapa that. Nor to tell her about my recurring dreams. They're getting increasingly vivid. Last night I dreamt Venus actually climbed into bed with me and gently stroked my hair. And I licked the salty skin around her shoulders and she breathed in my ear and it was as if I was holding up a seashell listening to the sea, like Mama had shown us to do when we were both little. I really look forward to going to sleep these days!

DIARY OF SOWEEN CLAY, 15TH OF AUTUMN

(IN MY FIFTEENTH YEAR)

This evening, after school, Mama came to my room and talked to me about the significance of tomorrow and what it would mean to Elihu. This was traditionally the role a Mama plays with her daughter on the eve of her brother's Apprenticeship. She said it was not only going to change his life, it was going to change all of ours, too. Though she didn't need to remind me of that. I knew! I **knew**! My whole life was going to change, too! And we both sat there on my small bed, her holding both my hands and both of us being very brave and trying not to cry. Then she picked up my copy of The Book of Certitude which I kept by my bed (by law!) and she read to me the section from Chapter One. (Though I knew all this by **heart**, it's practically the first thing you're taught at Infant School!)

FOR IN TRUTH for Woman to place her trust in Man is as foolish as for her to try to cross a river using stepping stones made of straw. In the end, she will most certainly drown. For Man will always betray Woman, however noble his intentions, however honourable his initial declarations of love and fidelity. It is truly inherent in Man's nature to destroy all the things in Woman which he first loved. Like a wolf you adopt as a cub and try to domesticate, a Man will eventually turn and harm you. He is bound to cheat and betray the one he claims to love. Likewise with Woman. No matter how much she convinces herself she loves a Man, she will finally betray him.

At this point Mama, noticing I was mouthing the words along with her, closed the book. And said it was best for us to start saying our goodbyes to Elihu now and his to us whilst there was still trust between us. Before he turned on us. As a Man, he was bound to eventually. He was not really to blame. It was in his nature

Though, even as she said this, she began crying again and I felt all the love she had for Elihu, bubbling up inside her. These were words which I knew, like me, she'd been made to learn as a child. But now, as a Mama, having to say goodbye to her son, they no longer seemed to make sense to her. They certainly made none to me! This was dear, sweet Elihu she was talking about. Turn on us? Never!

———————

"UPON REACHING his sixteenth birthday, a Boy residing South of the Divide will then be termed an Apprentice and will there reside for a further two years before travelling North of the Divide on his eighteenth birthday, when it is deemed he will have matured into a state of Full Manhood.

FOLLOWING HIS FORMAL Apprentice Ceremony which will be held in a local chapel (for details of this, see Section 7, Note 12) the Apprentice will thereafter be suited and in a full state of protection during the remaining three years he resides South of the Divide.

WHENEVER ABSENT FROM HIS HOME, he will wear his protective suit and visor at all times. When at home amongst his family, he is also obligated to remain protected, except on certain occasions when his family may alternatively choose to protect themselves. (For precise details of this see Section 9, Note 14, Family Procedural Practices)

UNDER NO CIRCUMSTANCES are a family and a Boy, during his period of Apprenticeship, to engage socially or otherwise make contact without one or both sides being fully protected."

DIARY OF SOWEEN CLAY, 16TH DAY OF AUTUMN
(IN MY FIFTEENTH YEAR)

It's Elihu's sixteenth birthday and we all went to the Chapel to say a sort of goodbye to our darling Elihu. Physically at least. All the family were there, me, Mama, Mapa plus a handful of family friends and Orthodox Councillors. At the start, none of us were visored with Elihu bare headed. Monitors were in attendance, of course, and after the first hymn (Oh, Lord put steel within our feeble hearts) they accompanied Elihu and the Priest into the vestry. The rest of us sung another hymn (Woman, thou art born of sin!). Then the Priest returned and she read the official Coming Of Age text. And how significant this was in the life of a Boy as he stepped into Manhood. And, I thought again, he'll soon be lost to us for ever. Once they go North, Men rarely return, except to teach other Boys to become Men. Then Elihu, impressive in his white suit, returned flanked by the two Monitors and stood before the altar. He turned to face us and declared a dramatic Farewell! He then pulled down his visor which was the signal for us women also to shout out our own farewell and then to cover our own faces. Mapa told me this was a symbolic act to denote the Separation. After another hymn, (God bless this Man he may resist base Woman's wicked wiles) we all returned home. Later that evening, Mama, Elihu and I held our own private separation and hugged and hugged each other till our ribs started to crack, for the very last time. And then we all crept away to our own beds. In the very early days when we were both tiny we'd both even shared a room together. Poor Elihu! What loneliness. For one thing, our mealtimes had to change. It's physically impossible to eat a meal whilst wearing a visor! Mapa decided that in future, to save Mama work, we would all continue to eat at the same time but in different rooms. We Women would continue to eat in the kitchen as normal, whilst Elihu would be banished to the sitting room in solitary state. No more family dinners together, then. One of the few times in the day we actually manage to talk to each other for any length of time. Mapa decreed that, instead, after we'd eaten our separate meals, we'd meet up in the sitting room for our usual nightly conversation. In keeping with common tradition, we would alternate our so-called 'visor days', Elihu wearing his one evening, us the next. Tonight we tried this out, allowing Elihu to go visor-free whilst we three sat faceless round him. It was the most awkward and embarrassing evening, ending up with Mapa and Elihu making stilted conversation whilst Mama and I sat crying with frustration behind our visors! I'm sure we'll get used to it eventually (she said bravely!)

EDITED EXCERPT OF MINUTES OF MEETING

SOUTH SARUM VILLAGE COUNCIL, 17 AUTUMN

Present:

Cllr. T. Chilzer (Chair) (Moderate)

Cllr. K. Clay (Orthodox)

Cllr. M. Chalice (Moderate)

Cllr. J. Grosh (Orthodox)

Cllr. F. Harran (Moderate)

Cllr. H. Tarness (Progressive)

Cllr. L. Marling (Orthodox)

Cllr. Doben (Moderate)

Cllr. L. Kriffitt (Progressive)

Cllr. C. Nivess (Progressive)

Cllr. G. Whipple (Progressive)

The Orthodox Party members, Cllrs Clay, Grosh and
Marling, having concluded their private reading in
the antechamber, joined the main meeting as usual.

Before the commencement, Cllr. Chilzer, Chair,
told Councillors that Cllr. Doben had written to
inform her she had resigned from the Orthodox
Party and was joining The Moderate Party. She said
this was as a result of irreconcilable differences
between herself and other Orthodox Party members.
She declined to elaborate further. As a fellow
Moderate, Cllr. Chilzer formally welcomed Cllr.
Doben to the Party. Progressive and Moderate Party
members then applauded Cllr. Doben. Cllr. Grosh (O)

commented that this was inappropriate.

1. Graffiti was xxxxxxxxxxxxxxxxxxxxxxxxxxxxxxxxx
xxxxxx punished.
2. Unnecessary use of xxxxxxxxxxxxxxxxxxx be
discouraged.
3. For the fifth time in xxxxxxxxxxxxxxxxxxxxx
severely.

4. Proposal for A Day of Colour. Cllr. Tarness (P)
informed the meeting that The Progressive Party
was proposing a Day of Colour to be held in the
Village sometime next Spring. This would encourage
all members of the community to dress publicly
for one day in the brightest possible colours
they could find. The only colour that would not
be permitted would be black! This would have the
effect, she suggested, of raising the morale of
the entire community, bringing both symbolically
and literally a little colour back into their
monochrome lives. This was vigorously opposed by
first Cllr. Clay (O) followed by Cllr. Grosh (O). The
former claiming that this was simply a stratagem
by the Progressive Party to open the floodgates
to a sea of debauchery. Cllr. Whipple (P) commented
that she couldn't see how wearing a modest brightly
coloured dress for a single day constituted a moral
decline and she felt the Councillor's arguments
were predictable and antiquated. Cllr. Marling (O)
said that once a Woman was permitted a brightly
coloured dress, it was only a matter of time before
she started showing her naked flesh and next be
painting her face. Those members with a knowledge

of recent history knew where that would lead. She, for one, had no desire to live in a bordello. The argument continued for some time until the Chair finally brought the meeting to order and called for a vote for those in favour of holding A Day of Colour next Spring. The proposal was defeated by 7 votes to 5. There being no other business the meeting was concluded.

DIARY OF ELIHU CLAY, 18TH DAY OF AUTUMN
(IN MY SEVENTEENTH YEAR)

This afternoon, following my morning session with Tutor Morden and after he'd devoured both his lunches, I took a deep breath, pulled down my visor and stepping out of the front door, I set off on my first solo expedition through the Village. Fergo was absolutely right. It's a disturbing experience. Once you're visored, even though there are very few Men in the Village apart from Monitors and people must have had some idea who I was, most of them pretended not to recognise me and some even averted their gaze or looked deliberately at the ground as if I wasn't there at all. I felt virtually invisible. I passed Women I recognised and knew well and I'd greet them but very few replied. If they did, it was always awkward and a bit sheepish as if they weren't comfortable in my presence. Separation was already starting and, if Fergo's anything to go by, I'm in for pretty lonely time over the next three years. I had to eat my dinner all alone in the living room this evening. I could hear the others talking in the kitchen. Afterwards, they came to join me and, sensing I was a bit depressed, they courteously kept their visors lowered allowing me to raise my own. Not much of a choice as I then spent the evening talking with three faceless people, trying to guess what they were thinking. I think I would have preferred it the other way round. We'll be doing that tomorrow. I expect I'll get used to it in time. Perhaps I'll go round soon and see Fergo. We don't really have that much in common, not these days, but at least he's a Man. Someone to talk to or rather to talk at. Even he's better than nothing.

DIARY OF SOWEEN CLAY, 1ST DAY OF SPRING
(IN MY FIFTEENTH YEAR)

———————

One day I'm going to marry Giella. I've decided. I will be her Mama and have all our children and she will be my Mapa and take care of us, me and the girls, however many we're allowed to have. They'll probably be girls, if Nature has her way. Since my visit to Giella's house yesterday, my head's been filled with colours. I even dreamt of colours last night! They say you don't dream in colour but I did. Bright colours, swirling around me, like they're dancing. And I have this feeling of hunger as if I wanted to eat them. I wake up feeling slightly sick though oddly I'm still hungry. I told Giella about this later. And she laughed and said I was obviously suffering from colour deprivation. Later, when no one was looking, she passed me a book which she'd been hiding, whispering in my ear that I might enjoy it. It was one of those from her secret banned collection. Immediately, I hid it under my dress where it burnt a hole in my vest for the rest of the day, till I got home and hid it in my room, well away from Mama. Imagine her face, if she ever found it? And as for Mapa! She'd probably have me burnt as a witch! Giella said to me later while we were walking home together, what was the harm in reading something which might bring a little colour inside me as well? Maybe she'd let me come and stand in her bedroom, now and again, so as I could get my regular colour fix. After all, this black and white life we were forced to live was suffocating, wasn't it? We were Women! We were naturally creatures of colour and light, weren't we! All of us! But it's drilled into us from birth that choosing bright paint for our homes or choosing clothes with colours to express our moods and our personalities is sinful and unnatural. But it surely wasn't half as unnatural as making us all dress forever in black or paint our homes a dull monochrome? Women were deliberately subjugated and suppressed, forced to live in fear of their lives if they dared to speak out of turn. We should be free to dress as we pleased and say what we like and to hell with The Monitors and the whole stupid Council! She said she couldn't wait till she was older. She'd wear bright clothes and paint her face and have jewels all over her body! I'd never seen Giella get so excited. When she gets like that she becomes so different. At school she's quiet, hardly ever speaks. Now, she's fierce and passionate and she becomes so completely beautiful! She then shouted out terribly loudly that she sometimes felt like marching into the Village Square with a tin of red paint and setting about that dreary grey Men's Memorial!

In fact she spoke so loudly people were turning round to stare at us. God! I'm beginning to understand what it's like to associate with the daughter of Free Spirits! Elihu has grown very distant of late. I think he's lonely, poor thing. If only I could cuddle him to show I still love him. I think he misses Tutor Rudgrin. He certainly seems less fond of this new one. I asked Mapa why Rudgrin had been told to leave. She replied rather coldly that it was because Tutor Rudgrin was not a person she wished to have under the same roof as her teenage daughter. Oh dear! Rudgrin was dismissed because of me! How terrible. But rather exciting at the same time! I thought he hardly knew I existed!

FROM *THE BOOK OF CERTITUDE*
APPENDIX 5: "DAYS OF REFLECTION"

"**T**HERE WILL BE FOUR DAYS EACH YEAR to be designated as Days of Reflection in Spring, Summer, Autumn and Winter.

THESE WILL BE OBSERVED by all Women, regardless of age.

THE DAYS will be conducted from dawn till dusk in complete silence, without any form of vocal communication.

THE MAJORITY OF THE DAY should be set aside for the study of and re-acquaintance with *The Book of Certitude*.

THESE OCCASIONS ARE INTENDED to serve as a reminder to all Women of the historical wrongs they have inflicted upon Men and to remind them, whilst they continue to remain Infected, in the eyes of God, they remain Unforgiven and in an ongoing state of sin.

ALL WOMEN SHOULD STRIVE, on these days especially, towards greater humility, repentance and self-abasement."

DIARY OF ELIHU CLAY, 20ᵀᴴ DAY OF SPRING
(IN MY SEVENTEENTH YEAR)

———————

Today, for all the Women of the Village, this is the Day of Spring Reflection. There are four of these days over the year. They're always a bit odd if you're a Boy, I find. An eerie silence settles over the place, as the Women, who make up over ninety five percent of the inhabitants, are all supposed to stop talking for twenty-four hours. At least, they do in most houses, including ours. But I've heard that in the less orthodox ones, they just talk in whispers all day, as the Monitors prowl round outside trying to catch anyone breaking the Vow. Mapa, typically, insists that our family follows the law to the absolute letter and she, Mama and poor Soween sit all day silently crouching over their respective copies of The Book of Certitude lest they forget, in Mapa's words, The Sins of Their Sex. Being excused from all this, it seemed the perfect day to get together with Fergo. We met up in the Square and then walked around for a bit chatting and generally catching up, with just the sound of our footsteps and the birdsong. I told him about my change of Tutor, of Rudgrin's departure and of his replacement by the solemn, ever hungry Tutor Morden. Fergo's Tutor sounds a lot more fun. His parents, in an attempt to encourage their son's ambitions to become a Monitor, engaged a suitable Tutor. Fergo said he was great and did a lot of physical stuff, Martial Arts and stuff. I must say Fergo does seem amazingly fit. I wish my parents had found me a Tutor who specialised in the Arts. But then perhaps they did try at first and look how that turned out! Poor Rudgrin. Fergo told me he'd heard that Rudgrin was the talk of everywhere North side. Suspended, then dismissed. Now he's even in jail for a bit. He's quite famous, apparently.

Poor Rudgrin.

DIARY OF SOWEEN CLAY, 20TH DAY OF SPRING
(IN MY SIXTEENTH YEAR)

The Day of Spring Reflection and so far as this house is concerned, , a day of complete silence as enforced by my Orthodox Mapa. Years ago, I once committed the deadly sin of talking aloud during Reflection and she made me spend the next Reflection with a wooden spoon wedged in my mouth all day. Agony! More rebellious talk from Giella yesterday! She told me that in the days before The Divide there was something called the World Wide Internet which was a system of separate screens which everyone used to have and so they were able to talk to each other and have access to practically all the knowledge there was in the World. But it was switched off and destroyed after the Divide. Because those in power, in their so-called wisdom, decided that knowledge was a dangerous thing and should be restricted to a very few. And that the World was better off without it. That those in power said it led Men into depravity and gave them Unsavoury Ideas and put Women in danger of Abuse. But of course it also meant that no one any longer had access to information of any sort and that's just criminal. People need to know about the World, don't they? They need to be able to look beyond their own narrow circle, surely? Knowledge is power. Ignorance is weakness, she said and didn't I agree? And, though I pretended to agree, secretly I wasn't sure I needed to have information about the whole Wide World with all its problems. My own little world gives me enough problems, thank you very much! Like I never even knew, in my innocence that Tutor Rudgrin posed any sort of threat to me! I'd all the time been in real danger! And I risked undergoing, according to Mapa, A Fate Worse than Death. Thank goodness for Giella! I must say that when she talks about things, immoral as some of them often are, she becomes so animated and lively. There's a passion in her, probably she's got from her parents, that's attractive and exciting. Her face becomes so alive and her voice almost trembles. And her eyes! I never really noticed their colour before. Brilliant and bright, not quite blue, in some lights much sharper than blue. Sapphire! There I go about colour again! I think I'm growing fonder and fonder of her. Please God, I don't want my heart broken again! I'm torn between shutting my ears to her because, in my head, I know what she's saying is wicked and wrong, but in my heart . . . I'm getting myself into a state again as usual! I've started reading the book she lent me yesterday. It's called Jane Eyre. It's really, really good! I feel Jane's a lot like me, poor thing.

DIARY OF ELIHU CLAY, 10TH DAY OF SUMMER

(IN MY SEVENTEENTH YEAR)

These glorious summer days drag on and on. Once Tutor Morden has departed for the day, it gets so stifling and stuffy in the house I'm forced to go outside. I've taken up sketching again and, rather than brave the Village where I feel so conspicuous and unwelcome, I've taken to walking for hours in the Woods drawing anything and everything that catches my fancy including, lately, tiny insects. What started me with these was I became fascinated by this greenish brown multi-legged creature as it attempted time and again to climb over this obstacle in its path. This small twig must have been, so far as the creature was concerned, roughly the equivalent of a vast tree trunk and yet it scrambled and climbed and fell back and started again only to fall back again. And again. Such determination and persistence. Walk round it, I shouted, why don't you walk round the thing? Do you think somewhere, God's looking down, shouting similar things to us which we can't hear? Or simply don't choose to hear? As we're struggling with an apparently insuperable obstacle? Once I'm deep enough into the Woods it's such a relief to raise my visor. I never meet anyone and it gets unbearably stuffy in this heat, at times I can scarcely breathe. Today, I stopped by the Secret Pool to rest. I find the sound of the waterfall incredibly relaxing. After a minute or two, I really couldn't resist it any longer and I stripped off my suit and dived in. What the hell, there was no one about and the temptation was just too great. It felt glorious! Afterwards I lay on the grass till the sun had dried me sufficiently to put my suit on again. Just like old times, really! I did sense again, though, that I was being watched. It's happened before, nothing I can quite define, just a vague sense of someone nearby. Probably my imagination. Or a feeling of guilt because technically I was doing something illegal, risking my health, possibly my life. It only took a chance meeting with a solitary unvisored Woman out for a stroll to put my whole life in danger. Still, the swim was worth it.

DIARY OF SOWEEN CLAY, 11TH DAY OF SUMMER
(IN MY SIXTEENTH YEAR)

Well, I thought it was too good to last! There was another meeting of The Falcons last night in Axi's barn and I went along there believing, in my blissful innocence, that having undergone my second Initiation Ceremony I would be left in peace. No such luck. This evening I was to be "baptised" or putting it crudely have my head held underwater in the filthy horse trough in the yard. Axi is very strong and she held me under several times, for longer and longer until I really thought I was truly going to drown. Sassa found this simply hilarious and giggled and giggled. She really must hate me so much. But worst of all was Giella. She just stood there watching and said and did nothing at all. Why didn't she try to stop Axi? My so-called friend might have said something! I can't make her out at all. She's two people. When I'm alone with her, she's sweet and kind and yet at these Meetings she's distant and indifferent. Almost as if she doesn't care for me one way or another. I read some more Jane Eyre this evening. She and I really have a great deal in common! I'm still enjoying it, though I have to keep stopping because there are words in it that I don't know. I need to look in my school dictionary. But sometimes they're not even in that. Teacher Olishaw told us once that there were certain words that we wouldn't find in our dictionaries, words that are banned and considered Unsuitable for Women and are on what is known as The Inflammatory List. I must ask Giella if she knows what these words are. That's if she ever speaks to me again.

FROM *THE BOOK OF CERTITUDE*
APPENDIX 9: "RESTRICTIONS ON ARTS
AND LITERATURE"

———————

66 **A** SIDE FROM THE RESTRICTIONS on visual art on both sides of the Divide (see section 4, Chapter 5), there are also restrictions on other areas of the so-called 'Arts' field. The Preacher has ruled that, with very few exceptions, large areas of this much overrated area of human activity are both a distraction and without relevance in a civilised God-fearing society. The Arts can all too often lead us from the light of the True Path into dangerous dark side alleys. Too often the Artists begins to imagine themselves as creators, rivals to God Himself in the erroneous belief that they too are capable of true originality, crediting themselves with everything and the True Creator with nothing.

THE ARTS can frequently lead the perpetrator into a state of self-delusion, immoral pride and a disproportionate self gratification. Moreover by portraying their own alternative, often distorted visions of God's true universe, they are also liable to lead others astray.

THERE CAN ONLY BE one Truth and that is God's Truth.

BOOKS
These are strictly proscribed apart from certain (but by no means all) religious texts, most works of fiction and other material considered light-hearted, frivolous or irrelevant to the conduct of seemly and proper everyday life. (See Appendix X for a list of permitted titles).

All textbooks and volumes of a strictly informative and educational nature (apart from certain graphic books dealing with human biology) are permitted.

MUSIC

It is forbidden to play, either publicly or privately, any form of recorded music. Music players are illegal and will, when discovered, be confiscated and the owner liable to severe punishment.

The only music permitted is of an acoustically produced nature, designed for religious ceremonies or services. Limited exceptions will be made, subject to licence, for single events which involve non-tactile dancing of a virtuous nature.

It is considered that music, at best, can raise the soul closer to God but, at worst, it can debase the body and distract the mind.

PERFORMANCE ARTS

THEATRE

All performances of live theatre are strictly prohibited.

FILM AND TELEVISION

Following the demolition of all transmitters and the disbanding of all TV networks these categories are no longer relevant.

OPERA AND BALLET

All performances of Opera or Ballet are strictly prohibited

FINE ART AND PHOTOGRAPHY

Still life portayals of landscape, animals, wildlife and inanimate objects, subject to restrictions outlined in section g, clauses 5 to 13 (colour & content), are occasionally permitted.

Representation of the human form is strictly forbidden. Photography, moving or still, is prohibited."

DIARY OF ELIHU CLAY, 13ᵀᴴ DAY OF SUMMER
(IN MY SEVENTEENTH YEAR)

———————

Another afternoon walk today but a very significant one. I met someone! After my usual circuit of the Woods I ended up, as I usually do, by the Secret Pool and considered this time I might have a go at trying to sketch the waterfall which I thought would be impossible, attempting to capture its ceaseless ever-varying motion and would probably be beyond me completely. But worth a try, if I could catch even a slight feeling of it, I'd be happy. So I sat for a while and I tried but it really would have taken a far better artist than me and the urge to dive in and cool down overcame me and I stripped off and plunged in. I swam up close to the fall where it was really turbulent and tossed you this way and that, threatening to push you under and hold you there. Then, teasing, releasing you again and allowing you to bob up to the surface. Probably risky but what's life without a bit of danger? Exhausted, I paddled gently to the bank and crawling ashore, turned to lie back. And then I caught sight of her. Sitting across the other side, in her black dress, visor raised, leaning against a tree trunk, smiling. Startled, I yelled out, Sorry!

And then I rather coyly grabbed my sketch pad in an attempt to cover myself up. This seemed to amuse her still further and she laughed. And then we sat, separated by the Pool, far enough apart that she posed no immediate threat, me naked, her fully clothed, in a sort of impasse. Still wet from my swim till I dried out, I couldn't possibly get dressed again. The noise of the waterfall made conversation impossible and the prospect of bellowing small talk to and fro across the pool didn't appeal to either of us. So I casually pretended to continue my sketch of the waterfall, keeping the pad discreetly positioned, which made any further proper drawing virtually impossible. Nonetheless, I tried to give the impression it was quite normal for an artist to sit naked and sketch with his drawing pad propped against his private areas. Meantime, she sat across the other side, continuing to smile, never taking her eyes off me. Why didn't she move away? Irritating girl! So we both sat like that for about half an hour until she called out suddenly, asking if she could have a look at my picture. My first instinct was to shout back, certainly not, go away, you stupid girl! But there was something about her smile which persuaded me. So awkwardly I made my way around the edge of the Pool, holding the sketchpad in front of me, half slithering, half walking on my knees and left my drawing for her to collect. I then crawled back to my suit, presenting her with my hindquarters which caused even greater hilarity than my front view had done. As she collected the sketchpad, I struggled into the safety of my suit. She stood there studying the contents, slowly turning the pages and nodding to herself. Finally, she put it down, saying she thought they were excellent and she loved them. And then, with a brief thank you, she walked away, and I thought, as I returned to collect the pad, she'd gone, but at the last moment she turned back to ask whether I was going to be there tomorrow? And I said, not wanting to look too eager, that perhaps, I might be. And she said, then perhaps she might see me tomorrow. And I thought, yes perhaps you might. But if so, I'll be wearing that swimming costume Mama knitted for me!

DIARY OF SOWEEN CLAY, 13TH DAY OF SUMMER
(IN MY SIXTEENTH YEAR)

———————

I really had the strangest dream again last night. It was to do with colour but it was more than that really. When I woke up I was hot and feverish and sweating and needed to wash myself in my basin from head to toe. In the dream, I went round to Giella's house and into her parents' bedroom where I opened their secret cupboard, the one she'd shown me, and I started trying on all those revealing, bright coloured dresses of her Mama's that I'd seen hanging at the back. And I strutted up and down in them, shimmying and shaking, like some shameless abandoned woman with absolutely no morals whatsoever. And after admiring myself in her full-length glass, I sat down in front of the table mirror and started painting my face all sorts of vivid colours, like I'd seen in their magazines. And at that point—horrors!—suddenly there was Mapa in the doorway, staring at me in such contempt, I began to cry. And when I did, I saw in the mirror all the paint and the powder on my face had started to run like a watercolour until I looked simply dreadful, as if my face was melting like wax and I heard myself in my dream shouting, "Giella! Help me! Somebody help me! Help me!" And then, thank goodness, I woke up.

DIARY OF ELIHU CLAY, 14TH DAY OF SUMMER
(IN MY SEVENTEENTH YEAR)

As she promised, she was there again today when I arrived, sitting in the same place across the other side of the Pool. As soon as I arrived I lifted my visor and we sat for a time, rather shyly I thought, both on our separate banks, smiling and wondering what to shout across to each other. We weren't technically doing anything wrong, well, not really. But I think we both felt a bit guilty. Our first meeting had been accidental, at least so far as I was concerned it had been, but, this time the whole thing had been prearranged like some furtive tryst and yet so far all we'd done is to exchange a smile. She seemed happy sitting there looking across at me, though I probably wasn't as much at ease as she was, so I hid behind my sketchpad again, pretending to draw but really just doodling. She called across and asked me if I had ever tried drawing people. And I told her how I'd started to try to draw my sister, Soween, until our Mapa had put a stop to it. And she sounded surprised at the mention of Soween, saying she was a friend of hers. She told me she was Giella Tarness and didn't I remember her from Junior School? And I pretended I did but, really, I didn't, she'd only been about eight when I left and she'd changed so much and grown quite tall and back then I recalled she was quite small and slightly chubby. I said I was sorry I hadn't recognised her she'd changed quite a bit since those days. And she laughed and said she hoped she had! And she said it was a shame that I couldn't have carried on drawing Soween as, from what she'd seen, she thought I'd probably be quite good at doing people. And I doodled a bit more, pretending to draw and she sat there, staring. And we seemed to have run out of conversation which was what I always found with girls. (Apart from Soween of course.) Girls always seemed to me, whenever I talked to them, which wasn't very often, they always appeared to be saying one thing and at the same time thinking about something completely different. As if they were secretly thinking the opposite of what they were saying. And suddenly she said that she'd just had an idea and how would it be if she posed for me? Sitting on the other side of the pool, of course, as she was now? Would I consider that? She'd really love to have her picture drawn, she really would. And I said, not wanting to disappoint her, well I'd have a try. She was a bit far away but I'd have a go. It was getting a bit late to start today but we could try tomorrow, if she liked. But now, if she would excuse me, I was going to have my swim. And she said fine. But she continued to sit there making not a single effort to move or even turn away. But, I'd come prepared this time. She wasn't catching me out again! And I nonchalantly took off my suit. But this time, ha-ha, underneath, I was wearing my woollen bathing trunks, the ones Mama'd knitted for me. But even as I was about to jump in, I knew I'd made a big mistake. As I feared, it looked worse than if I'd had nothing on at all. They were huge and drooped practically to my knees. And the moment she caught sight of them, they caused her great hilarity. I thought she'd never stop laughing. She nearly fell in the pool herself. Serve her right if she had! I tried to keep my dignity and jumped in but as soon as I submerged, I could feel the wool in the trunks begin to absorb water until they became heavier than lead. As I moved about, they gradually slipped down my legs until they finally slid off my ankles and dropped into the Pool's bottomless depths. For all I know, for the mythical Merman to keep. He's welcome to them. Needless to say, when I climbed out, I was naked, YET AGAIN!

120 PD.

DIARY OF SOWEEN CLAY, 16TH DAY OF SUMMER
(IN MY SIXTEENTH YEAR)

Here we go again! Another meeting in the barn yesterday evening and, guess what, another humiliation! This time, the worst yet. At the start, Axi turned to me and said that it clearly stated in the Falcon's rules – (what rules, no one ever said there were any rules?) it clearly stated, if I'd ever bothered to read them properly that there should be amongst its members a minimum standard of beauty which I'd fallen well below with my ugly unpleasant fat little face, covered in disgusting skin rashes. And I wanted to shout back, never mind, God finds me beautiful, anyway! But I didn't because I thought that would just make her angry. And she said that the Beauty Sub-committee (her and Sassa, obviously) had decided I was to undergo immediate compulsory beauty treatment to bring me up to standard. This would start with a face pack. Before I could even ask what a face pack was they'd seized hold of me and the next thing I knew, I'd been marched out into the meadow and was threatened with having my face ground into a pat of cow dung. When I resisted I was made to dip my fingers in the stuff and smear it all over my face till I was coated in it. We then returned to the barn. Axi told me to wait outside till they'd finished the meeting, as they didn't want me in there stinking the place out. So I stood outside in the yard, with flies swarming all round me, whilst the rest of them carried on with their meeting till finally the stuff had dried and my face was stiff. I walked home all alone (thanks again, Giella!) right through the Village with everyone staring at me. Thankfully, I was practically unrecognisable. When I got home, Mama led me straightaway to the sink and rinsed my face, sighing and tut-tutting, and then gently patting it dry like she knew exactly what was happening as she'd been through it, too, all those years ago. This morning, during the night, my skin had reacted and come out in great red blotches, worse than anything I'd had previously. Mama (more tutting) smeared some ointment on to the worst areas, around my mouth and eyes. Before I left for school I had a quick look at myself in Elihu's mirror. I looked terrible. My whole face looked like it was on fire! When I walked into the classroom, there they all were, Axi, Sassa and the others waiting for me, laughing and calling out, great improvement, Soween! Ha-ha-ha! I smiled back at them as I knew Mapa would've wanted me to, but inside I really wanted to kick someone! Most of all I wanted to punch Sassa's stupid little sniggering face! Though I know for sure, if I'd tried that, Axi would almost certainly punch me first.

DIARY OF ELIHU CLAY, 17TH DAY OF SUMMER
(IN MY SEVENTEENTH YEAR)

Over the past couple of days we've both of us settled into our respective routines, the artist and his model. Giella, right at the start, did as I suggested and took off her bonnet and let her hair flow free ... She really has the most glorious glossy hair, almost golden, it's a crime to keep it covered up. The problem remains with the physical distance between us. She suggested, if she moved a little bit nearer, did I think that would help? And I said, yes, well maybe just a tiny bit, maybe halfway round the pool and she did and though it still wasn't ideal, it was better. Yesterday I'd also suggested she did the same as Soween and loosen the top of her dress and expose her shoulders. She has the most beautiful clear skin, unlike Soween's, poor thing. Today, as we worked, I told her about Rudgrin and about the picture of Venus in the seashell and how it had affected me, which appeared to interest her a lot, especially when I told her how I'd had this recurring dream about it. She seemed particularly interested in that and kept asking me how the picture made me feel. In fact she went on and on about it. Asking questions which were far too personal to answer! Now that she was closer to me, I was able to fill in the finer details of her face which is quite haunting, especially her eyes. She has this attractive habit of occasionally running her tongue backwards and forwards over her top and bottom lips as if she was all the time trying to keep them moist. She has the most delicate pink tongue. And I couldn't swear to it but, since yesterday, I'm almost certain her eyelashes have got darker than they were yesterday. Maybe it's our increasing closeness, I can't be sure. Today especially, it's been almost unbearably hot and I've had trouble concentrating. I think I might even have a mild case of heat stroke. Eventually, the dizziness really got to me and I had to jump into the pool to cool down. Poor Giella, in her long heavy black dress, looked slightly envious as if she wished she could do the same. I think, in the end I'm generally quite pleased with the portrait. I hope she'll be as well. I think I've caught the essence of her, anyway. Mind you, hers is a face that continually changes, moment to moment. The more you look at it, the more beautiful it becomes.

120 PD

DIARY OF SOWEEN CLAY, 20TH DAY OF SUMMER
(IN MY SIXTEENTH YEAR)

Giella didn't come to school today. Teacher Jollie said she didn't know why as she'd had no note from her parents to explain her absence. And I worried about her all morning and through the lunch hour and into the afternoon session, till school ended. I was afraid she might be ill. After school I went straight round to her house. But when I got there, no one seemed to be home. Finding the front door unlocked, I crept into the hallway, tiptoeing across the shiny wood floor. Her parents were both in the living room, lying on separate sofas, apparently fast asleep. The room was filled with a smoky haze, there was a curious, unusual smell in the air and weird unearthly noises coming from their music player, like I'd never heard before. Probably banned music on an illegal music player, knowing them! Her Mama opened her eyes and smiled at me and sleepily asked me what I wanted. I told her Giella had not been at school all day and I was worried she might be ill. Her Mama seemed perfectly calm about it. (If I'd been missing, my Mama would've have been screaming in circles!) Instead Desollia told me Giella wasn't there but I really wasn't to worry and she'd let me know the minute she came home. Her Mapa, meanwhile, slept through all this! They're certainly extremely weird parents. Free Spirits indeed! I went home, still very anxious. Where could she possibly be? I looked so worried, Mama said she hoped I wasn't sickening for something. Then, about an hour later, there was a knock on the door and when I opened it, there she was, Giella, bright eyed and fresh as ever. And I ran and hugged her, almost crying with relief. She laughed and asked me what was the matter? When I asked her where on earth she'd been, she said mysteriously, she'd just been out walking, that was all, and when I wanted to know where, she said even more mysteriously, oh, you know, here, there and everywhere. And, before I could ask anything else, she kissed me on the forehead and left, just like that, leaving me like a limp dish rag! I think I really must love her, because the pain I felt when I thought I'd lost her was so painful, so sharp, it can't be anything else, can it? I've made a vow that tomorrow, straight after school, providing she turns up, I'm going to suggest to her in a few years we get married. I will be her Mama and she my Mapa. Or the other way round if that's the way she wants. I really don't care. I couldn't bear to lose her again, I really couldn't, not even for a few hours. I feel so confused. Why does love always do this to me? Why does it have to hurt so much? Does it do that to everyone? It can't do surely? My skin's nearly back to normal anyway, that's one good thing. Still reading Jane Eyre. It gets better and better, more and more exciting, though Mr Rochester is really scary! I would like to write like Charlotte when I become a proper writer.

DIARY OF ELIHU CLAY, 20TH DAY OF SUMMER
(IN MY SEVENTEENTH YEAR)

I swear her lips were different today, more sharply defined and a richer, deeper red than they were before. Now she's had to move still closer to me (although still at a safe distance) I'm beginning to be able to smell her as well, a musky bittersweet fragrance, far stronger even than Mama's scented soap which Mapa made her throw away, telling her it was like living with a whore of Babylon.

I got the impression that the heat was beginning to affect Giella as well. She was beginning to take shorter, more rapid breaths like some exhausted animal. She loosened her dress still further, pulling it down lower and exposing some of her chest. I asked her, if the heat was affecting her, would she like me to stop and take a rest. But she urged me to continue though her face was so flushed I was afraid she might faint. So finally I insisted we stop as I too was tiring in the heat and needed a swim to cool off. I stripped off my suit and jumped straight into the Pool. A second or two later, something landed beside me with a mighty splash and sank for a second beneath the surface. When it bobbed up again a moment later, it was Giella, hair flattened straight, water streaming from her face now inches from mine. Before I could stop her she'd raised both her hands and was pulling my face close to hers, fingernails digging into my neck, she pressed her lips on mine, forcing my mouth open and thrusting inside it with her tongue. We both sank beneath the water, our mouths still locked together. Still she clung to me, refusing to let go. She was deceptively strong for a girl. Just when I was sure we were both about to drown, she released me and we both bobbed up again to the surface, floundering and breathless, treading water, gulping in air. Only then did the awful realisation of what we'd just done gradually dawn on us. Giella took hold of me once more, this time more gently and, putting her lips close to my ear, she whispered, I'm sorry. I'm so sorry. And I said, as a reflex really, sorry, as well. But, I knew the truth was neither of us at that moment was in the least sorry. As we left the Pool together, she led me — God knows where she led me, I'd no idea — down some hidden path, along a ledge behind the waterfall and into a concealed cave, cool and safe. And we lay close together on the floor, our minds floating free of any trace of 'sorry' and we let go of our bodies to explore each other in the most magical moment of my life. I knew I might have been, I surely must have been, Infected by this glorious creature but what a way to die! Giella was not to blame. It was all my doing. If necessary I'll tell the world that.

END OF PART II

Part III
RISE AND FALL

"AND SO IT SHALL BE for many years, Men remaining to the North and Women staying to the South of the Divide.

AND THEY SHALL REMAIN SEPARATE for many decades until such time as a Chosen One will arise from amongst the Men. And the Chosen One will be found to be Immune and thus safe once more to enter unprotected into the company of Women.

AND AT SUCH A TIME will it also become safe for all Men to join with Women and for all Women to unite with Men again. For it will then be shown that both have accepted their responsibilities and their duties to each other.

FOR BY THE SENDING of the Chosen One, God will declare Himself content that Men have finally learnt to master self restraint and that Women will at last have returned to a blessed state of humility.

BUT THIS WILL NOT BE for several generations. In the meantime there will come others declaring themselves a Chosen One and to be Immune who will prove false and are not to be trusted."

DIARY OF SOWEEN CLAY, 25TH DAY OF SUMMER
(IN MY SIXTEENTH YEAR)

Giella is deliberately avoiding me. That's the only thing I can think of. After school she rushes away before I can say a word to her. On the day after her mysterious disappearance, the day she didn't come to school at all, I had planned to suggest to her we got married, as soon as we were allowed to, and to become life partners, having children together and so on. But I suspect she must have guessed that was what I was about to ask her which is why she's avoiding me. That's all I can suppose. I must have shown my feelings to her so much that I've frightened her off. She doesn't want the commitment at this stage. Why do I always need to rush into things? Maybe she's meeting someone else? While she's been walking here, there and everywhere, as she puts it? Or maybe meeting up with Axi and Sassa and the rest of them and they're all sitting round and laughing about me? I am, I'm a laughing stock, I'm so pathetic. I feel more alone than ever. The problem is that I have no one to turn to, except Mama and she'll only tut-tut and say, it's just age and she was the same at my age and I would grow out of it, etcetera, etcetera, etcetera! Which simply means, shut up, you're identical to everyone else, kid, and dead ordinary. But I already know I'm ordinary. I know that. I need to feel special. I need someone to tell me I'm special. Like Elihu used to do. But where's Elihu now? He's become so distant. It's like he's no longer part of our lives. Oh, Elihu, where are you when I need you? There's another meeting of The Falcons tomorrow. I don't think I'm brave enough to face another one. Not if they're going to do horrible things to me, again. But the alternative is not to go and then endure days and days of Solitude which is even more worse. I'm very near to wanting to kill myself, really. But then I see Mapa's face so disapproving and Mama going tut-tut -tut!! I realise I haven't even got the courage to do that!

Since Giella and I first touched and made love in the cave, this is the fifth morning I've woken up without displaying a single sign of The Plague, which either means it's still lying dormant in my body or, dare we even hope, I'm not infected and we have somehow escaped the consequences of physical contact. Over the past few days, we've not even dared mention the subject, for fear a mere reference would bring it upon us. Every time we meet, Giella looks at me anxiously and, when I shake my head, we simply carry on as normal. Giella said one time she believed that I might be very special and I could possibly be the Chosen one that was prophesied in the Book of Certitude. But neither of us believes that nonsense and besides I think she's only saying that because she loves me. Anyway, nothing's happened so far. I've shown no symptoms though by rights I should have done days ago. In my heart I know what we've been doing has felt so right, so perfect. Giella said that, even if I was infected, if she found she'd been responsible for my death then she was ready to die as well. She'd have nothing to live for then, anyway. She said it so passionately that I was left in no doubt she meant it! "Let them put me into one of their awful collars or whatever they used to do, I don't care!" Which surprised me. "Ten day collars? They can't still use those, surely, they're barbaric?" But apparently they did. Though no one's used them for years — long before we were born. But Giella's Mapa said apparently they still have them. And, knowing our Council, I'm sure the Orthodox party would be only too happy to use them. My own Mapa among them,

if she thought someone had dared to harm her precious son!
We were taught early on in History class about the Ten Day
Collars, probably intended as a dire warning to the girls.
If a Woman was found guilty of Primary Infection, that is
knowingly and wilfully infecting a Male, the Woman was put
into a device called The Ten Day Collar, spring-loaded, made
of steel, which was locked round her neck. On the front of
the collar were ten lights which, as the days progressed,
went out one by one, counting off her days till finally, at
daybreak on the tenth day, the last light was extinguished
and the collar would snap tight, choking her to death. In
most cases, long before this happened, she'd already done
away with herself. I can't bear to think of that happening to
my darling Giella. These secret meetings in the cave can't go
on indefinitely without someone finding out. This is too small
a community for a secret like ours to be kept for long. Our
lovemaking gets better and better. Giella is so adventurous
and continually anxious to try new things! I marvel at her
inventiveness. It gives me such happiness seeing the pleasure
I bring her and I'm sure she feels the same. I've grown
so fond of her body, I never grow tired of looking at it. I
finished the portrait of her a couple of days ago and she
seemed pleased with it. Yesterday was her sixteenth birthday
so I gave it to her as a present. She says she's framed it
and it now hangs by her bed. It seems strange to have a
picture of yourself in your bedroom, a little vain. I'm sure
Mapa would say that. She said she'd hung it there to remind
her of me. It was a picture of her but her seen through my
eyes. It would always remind her of our first meeting. I've
started drawing her naked body. It gives me such pleasure
tracing every line and curve of her. She seems happy to lie
there, posing for hours at a time whilst we talk and make
plans for the future, wild plans like marrying in secret and

running away where no one will ever find us. If such a place exists in this world, which I doubt. Unless we plan to run away and hide in our own dreams. The moment she gets bored lying there, she reaches out for me and I happily lay aside my sketchpad and, dear God, it starts all over again. These days together are just perfect! I want them to go on for ever!

DIARY OF SOWEEN CLAY, 26TH DAY OF SUMMER
(IN MY SIXTEENTH YEAR)

In the end I decided to brave it and went to The Falcons meeting after all. When we assembled, I braced myself for the worst but for a few moments I really thought Mapa's prediction had come true and, following the so-called beauty treatment, they'd actually run out of ideas for things to do to me. There were just the four of us. Axi, Sassa and Giella and me. The other three sent apologies for absence. (I bet nothing ever happens to them!) The meeting started badly though when I wasn't allowed to sit down but had to stand throughout whilst the three of them sat on the straw bales and started leafing through one of the magazines that had belonged to Giella's great grandmother. And they chattered on about this and that, like how long or short should the hemline on a skirt be? (Do we even have a choice?!) And all sorts of useful tips regarding make up (how useful is that?). And then they got on to the subject of body hair and whether it was preferable for a woman to remove it completely or keep it. And then there was a useless debate about which removal method was best. And what did everyone think? And I thought to myself, well this is really, really stupid, what's the point of this? No one's ever going to see it, are they? They can't even see the hair on our heads, most of them, because it's stuck under a bonnet for God's sake! But they kept on discussing it, wondering how women in the old days used to do it, whether they shaved themselves like men did, or what. And Sassa said she'd read somewhere that they used to cover their entire bodies in wax. And Axi said, what? Candle wax? And Sassa said she supposed so and then they just must have set fire to it. And Giella said, OW! That must have been so painful! And Axi said in a nasty voice, Yes, mustn't it. Very painful. I wonder if it works? We ought to try it. And then my heart sank as she said, Soween, dear, perhaps you can help us out with this? At our next meeting, you wouldn't object if we removed all your body hair, would you? Just in the interests of research? And before I could utter a single word, she said, no objections? No. Let's put it to the vote then. Since Soween has no objections, we'll try it at the next meeting. All those in favour? And she and Sassa both stuck up their hands immediately and they looked to Giella to do the same. But Giella sat with her hands in her lap, not looking at them but at me. And after a long silence, Axi got up, marched to the door, muttering grumpily, Meeting closed, then! And she stormed out with Sassa scampering after her, leaving Giella and me alone. And she came over to me and took my hand and whispered, I won't let them harm you ever again, Soween, I promise. And it all flooded out of me and I cried my eyes out! And I didn't care what Mapa would have said, I didn't care. And Giella, my precious darling Giella, put her arm around me and then she walked me home.

DIARY OF ELIHU CLAY, 27TH DAY OF SUMMER
(IN MY SEVENTEENTH YEAR)

We've started to live dangerously! We are now meeting at night as well. We simply can't get enough of each other. Tonight, as soon as the rest of the house was asleep, I crept out of the front door as far as the edge of the Woods where we met up and then made love under the trees. Softer than the cave floor, and doubtless observed by dozens of pairs of curious nocturnal eyes, though none of them human, we hoped! Afterwards, we lay and talked softly in the darkness. Giella said she was getting concerned for Soween lately. She looked on Giella as her best friend and Giella feared my sister might have fallen in love with her a little. Giella said she was very fond of Soween, too, she was the sweetest, most kind hearted person she knew and at present she was being badly bullied by her classmates. I said I'd heard as much from Mama but as a Man there was not much I could do about it. Giella told me that yesterday, she'd had to step in and protect her and if Soween misinterpreted her concern, she would undoubtedly cause her to grow even fonder of Giella. And that when she finally found out the truth, it would break her heart, completely. She suggested we should tell Soween about us now, to spare her even greater pain. I was reluctant to agree to this. No one is fonder of Soween than I am, but knowing her with secrets! It would be a matter of minutes before the whole world knew about us!

I fully expected, when I arrived at school today, to find Axi had put Giella in Solitude after her defiance at last night's meeting. But I guess whatever revenge she's planning for Giella is for later. Knowing Axi, I'm sure she won't have forgotten. Anyway, the day started well enough. Giella smiling at me a lot and me smiling back and I felt such warmth coming from her I knew it was only a matter of time till one or other of us proposed. I wasn't going to be the one to rush into it, though. I won't panic her again! Let her come to me, this time! Later on after supper, I lay on my bed, fully clothed, and started to plan how best to approach her that would be subtle but wouldn't take too long either. Easy, girl, easy! And I must have fallen asleep because the next thing I remember is waking up and it was well past midnight. I thought at first it had been Elihu going to bed that had woken me. The makeshift wall dividing our bedrooms is embarrassingly thin some times! But then I heard a board creak outside in the passageway. I got off my bed, moved to the door and listened. No sound. Pulling down my visor as a precaution, I sneaked out. Seeing his bedroom door was still slightly ajar, I gently eased it open to see if he was already asleep. But his room was empty. What I'd heard was not him going to bed at all, but him leaving. He wasn't in the living room or the kitchen or even Mapa's study — I looked in there just to make sure. He must have left the house entirely and was now roaming about outside in the darkness somewhere. I felt extremely worried. Had my brother already developed into a full blown man? Was he out there in the night leaping out at unsuspecting people, forcing them to the ground? And then doing unmentionable things to them? Hadn't The Prophet written that this was what happened to Men, once they became active? A solitary Male, all alone on the loose, out-of-control, indulging his worst excesses on innocent female victims? Oh God, was this actually happening to Elihu? Had my brother gone prematurely feral? I crept back to my room and lay awake, listening out for his return, praying he hadn't harmed anyone. Forgive him, God, please forgive him. He can't control it, it's just in his nature.

I must have fallen asleep again because the next time I awoke it was daylight and I heard people getting up. I slept all last night in my clothes. How disgusting!

DIARY OF ELIHU CLAY, 28TH DAY OF SUMMER
(IN MY SEVENTEENTH YEAR)

We made love again in the Woods but tonight I swore someone was watching us and it wasn't just little nocturnal animals, either. Giella sensed it, too. The result was we both got a bit tense and nervous so the lovemaking wasn't quite as good as usual and we both went home a little earlier. Giella said she'd told her parents. They were delighted and, horrors, actually want to hold a wedding party for us at their house. I asked her suspiciously what sort of party? And she said just the four of us, us and them. Her parents, Hork and Desollia, had both set their hearts on us having a proper wedding, apparently and Giella couldn't bear to disappoint them. After all, they'd given her such a wonderful childhood and she owed them so much. I said, please don't invite my family, that's all. And she hugged me with tears in her eyes and said, thank you, I knew you'd understand. And told me I was the most wonderful of men! Quite conventional underneath, these so-called Free Spirits, I find!

DIARY OF SOWEEN CLAY, 28TH DAY OF SUMMER
(IN MY SIXTEENTH YEAR)

If I didn't get much sleep the previous night, last night I got none at all! As I did before, I sat on my bed fully dressed with my light switched off, till I heard Elihu going to bed next door. A few minutes later, I heard Mapa and Mama, along the passage, doing the same. A few bumps and clumps, distant voices and then silence. I stayed sitting up, determined this time not to fall asleep although I was really tired. I waited till I heard Elihu's door softly opening and closing. Then, once again, the creak of the floorboard in the hallway as he crept along the passage. I counted slowly to ten and then followed him through the house and out of the front door. There was a slight moon so it wasn't completely dark. Anyway, his white suit stood out clearly and he was easy to follow. Whereas I, all in black, had the advantage. There are some benefits to being a woman! Rather than making his way to the Village, which I expected, he turned off towards the Woods and disappeared amongst the trees and I thought for a moment I'd lost him. Then I heard the sound of a woman's voice, half a moan, half a stifled cry and I saw him again. He had stopped and was now standing, apparently fighting with a black clad figure. I couldn't make out her face as she had her back to me. Elihu had pulled back his hood and his own face was clearly visible. He was gripping his victim's head with both hands, bending over her, using his mouth and teeth to attack her face and neck with a savagery I'd never seen before. Meanwhile, for her part, she clawed ineffectually at both his hands with her own, as if trying to prise herself free from his steely grip, constantly groaning pitifully as she did so, uttering little stifled whimpers of distress. For one terrifying moment, it appeared he might succeed in tearing out the poor creature's throat, as she writhed and twisted helplessly, powerless to escape from his merciless masculinity. Then, just as suddenly as it had begun, it was all over. Both broke apart, facing each other, panting and breathless. Then Elihu, seizing both her wrists, dragged her still deeper into the trees where they disappeared from my sight. I debated at first whether to follow, fearing the worst for her, to save the poor Woman from a Fate Worse than Death ... But what could I do, even supposing I caught up with them? Beat off Elihu with my bare hands? Finally, I decided to return home, fully intending that, once there, I would raise the alarm. But once back home in the quiet of the house, I had cause to reconsider. Were I to rouse the household now with Elihu still missing, Mapa would probably have summoned the entire Village and it would end in a manhunt for my dear brother, putting his life in danger. But if I did nothing, what of his poor victim out there at his mercy in the Woods? Still undecided, I fell asleep on my bed. The second night running, I have slept in all my clothes. At this rate, they will have to cut them from me!

DIARY OF ELIHU CLAY, 29TH DAY OF SUMMER
(IN MY SEVENTEENTH YEAR)

I'm certain Soween is beginning to suspect something. Maybe it was her watching us out there amongst the trees last night? Or perhaps one of us has let something slip accidentally? The plain fact is, little sister is behaving rather strangely. During our after-dinner family conversation, since it was their night to do so, the women sat visored whilst I was open faced. And Soween brought the conversation round, under the pretext of writing some history essay, which I didn't believe for a minute and started asking Mapa about the Plague. And this, as Soween knew full well, was one of Mapa's favourite topics and once she got going there was no stopping her. In the end, Mama was forced to flee the room whilst Mapa revelled in the full grisly details. How the man would die an agonising death once he became infected. And as I sat there gradually feeling iller and iller, though I couldn't see her face, I was sure Soween was smirking behind her visor. To think I felt sorry for her the other night at being bullied at school. Tonight I wanted to put her over my knee and smack her smug little bottom. Because of her, we've had to give up our nocturnal meetings, Giella and I. How am I going to get through a whole night without her? My dreams are full of her now. Poor old Venus has had to take second place.

DIARY OF SOWEEN CLAY, 29TH DAY OF SUMMER
(IN MY SIXTEENTH YEAR)

I tried to find out today if there was anyone missing from the Village or had been found somewhere savaged to death or horribly gnawed. But no one was missing, apparently. His victim had evidently contrived to escape—or worse still, he'd chosen his victim carefully, and she was someone who would not be missed and he'd killed and buried her! For the sake of the entire Village, it was up to me, from now on, to keep a close watch on my brother. This evening, after supper, it was our turn to be visored so we had a clear view of Elihu's face while he couldn't see ours. I decided to give him clear warning as to the probable consequences of his behaviour, without alerting either Mama or Mapa. Under the pretext of having to write a history essay, I asked Mapa if she could tell me something about The Plague. She said it was extremely virulent and that once a Man was infected, he invariably died. From the first signs of primary symptoms, he faced an increasingly agonising ten day death sentence where his major organs failed one by one as the virus took hold. Mapa was in full flow (as I knew she would be!) and Mama excused herself and retreated to the kitchen. I saw Elihu turning increasingly green and I thought he was bound to leave as well but instead he sat there swaying slightly as Mapa got properly into her stride. Of course, she said, in most cases, the Man was infected usually as a result of accident or sheer ignorance. Few Women, however vengeful or vindictive, would ever wish it on another human, not even a Man. And then, suddenly and quite unexpectedly, Elihu spoke for the first time since we'd started this conversation. He asked what would happen to a Woman if she infected the Man knowingly? And Mapa replied, in that case, she'd be locked in a ten day collar and serve her right. Long before it had killed her, in most cases, the wretched creature had invariably done away with herself. I'd heard about these terrible Collars at primary school, of course, Teacher Olishaw, describing them and sparing no detail. It was probably well intended and meant as a Terrible Warning to us girls. I know several of us had nightmares for weeks afterwards, waking up choking and gasping for air. At the very thought of them, I too began feeling short of breath and asked Mapa whether the Collars were still around. And she said she imagined they were and that the legislation was certainly to her knowledge still in place though, thank God, there had never been a need to use one in recent years and hopefully there never would be again. Elihu looked as if he was going to be sick at any minute. It was good to have reminded him that every time he attacked a Woman, he was risking the Plague. But I don't know why he was so interested in these Collars. Weirder and weirder, my brother.

DIARY OF ELIHU CLAY, 30TH DAY OF SUMMER
(IN MY SEVENTEENTH YEAR)

I told Giella about the conversation we had last night after dinner, when Soween started asking Mapa about the Plague under the very unconvincing excuse that she had to write an essay about it. Nonetheless it didn't stop Mapa from launching in describing every gory detail. Since she was visored I couldn't see her face, but I sensed Soween was staring at me the entire time trying to tell my reaction. What was she up to? In the cave today Giella and I talked about little else but her. How much does she know and how much is she really guessing at? It has to be resolved one way or the other. As once again we both felt a bit edgy, for the first time we didn't really feel like making love. Well not properly. Instead we both lay together, clinging to each other like Babes in the Cave. Sisters! Don't you want to murder them sometimes? As we lay there, Giella told me her parents had come up with some master plan but she couldn't tell me the details because she had been sworn to secrecy. I have a feeling, knowing what I do of her parents, that this master plan might well land us in greater trouble than we are already. How on earth did this simple Orthodox boy end up with a blazing, unorthodox Progressive?

DIARY OF SOWEEN CLAY, 30TH DAY OF SUMMER
(IN MY SIXTEENTH YEAR)

Elihu still insists on going for regular walks, his so called 'nature walks', complete with sketchpad. I've begun to grow suspicious that this might not be all he was up to on his walks! Maybe he's out laying snares, digging traps for unsuspecting Woman walkers to fall into and lie there helpless? Then later on, at night time, he can return to ravage them? This evening, during supper I slipped away from the kitchen making an excuse to Mapa and Mama and, whilst Elihu was still eating in solitary state in the living room, I crept into his bedroom to examine his sketchpad to see for myself. Perhaps he'd even been drawing designs for his traps. At first, turning the pages there were his usual beautiful drawings of birds and animals and then, halfway through, I turned the page and there was an incomplete sketch of a section of a Woman's body, a back view from the top of her shoulders to midway down her legs which included her back and both her buttocks, drawn carefully and in great detail. On the following pages I discovered other drawings, presumably of the same Woman, this time of her arms, her legs, her feet and even of her breasts. Both of them. Everything apart from her face. How could he have possibly obtained these pictures? It was almost as if someone had posed for him, but that was surely impossible. I can only presume he'd hidden and spied on her, perhaps whilst she was innocently swimming, unaware, poor thing. I carefully replaced the sketchpad and returned to the table. More worried than ever. I had to tell someone about this, somebody!

DIARY OF ELIHU CLAY, 31ST DAY OF SUMMER
(IN MY SEVENTEENTH YEAR)

———————

Soween's been in my room, I know she has. Snooping. I'm sure she's been through my sketchpad, I'm almost certain because she left sticky little finger marks on the corner of one page. If you want to be a successful spy, dear sister, then learn to wash your grubby little hands first! If she's seen any of those drawings of Giella, they don't leave much to the imagination. Thankfully there are none of her face, none where she's recognisable. I really must tackle Soween before she blurts it all out to Mapa. If she's guessed about Giella and me, I'm sure she doesn't mean us harm, she can't do? Unless she's blind with jealousy and hates me for taking her beloved away from her? It can't be that, surely? Heaven knows what's going on inside that weird head of hers, though. Who can ever tell? She's nearly a Woman, for God's sake!

DIARY OF SOWEEN CLAY, 31ST DAY OF SUMMER
(IN MY SIXTEENTH YEAR)

———————

This morning, I decided it had to be Giella I would tell. Giella would know what to do. I considered telling Mapa but a single word about this to her and I knew it could be disastrous! So, after school, I walked home with Giella and told her everything. Of my suspicions about Elihu and of his sinister habit of creeping out late at night and prowling the Woods, in search of victims. Of my fears that he'd become feral. And lastly the discovery of the terrible sick drawings he'd made in his sketchpad of some poor unwitting Woman. Giella listened quietly and when I'd finished, looked at me with great seriousness and firmly held my shoulders, saying to me fiercely that I was not to tell a living soul, I was to swear. I was to leave it to her to deal with and to put it out of my mind. I must say her sudden urgency seemed a bit frightening and I promised solemnly not to tell another living soul. Though what on earth she, Giella, could possibly do about it, I can't imagine I finished Jane Eyre tonight. I do! I want to write like Charlotte, I really do. I'll live with Giella and write wonderful novels that I'll dedicate to her and we can both, when we're married, sit up in bed and read to each other. She's promised to bring me another one tomorrow. This one's by Charlotte's sister and Giella says it's even more exciting!

DIARY OF ELIHU CLAY, 1ST DAY OF AUTUMN
(IN MY SEVENTEENTH YEAR)

Today, Giella told me Soween had talked to her about me. And how my sweet misguided sister had got completely the wrong idea. I think she pictures me as some mad baying creature, prowling the countryside at each full moon, tearing out the throats of my victims with my teeth! Such is the nonsense Girls are taught at school these days about Men. Mind you, our education isn't much better, teaching us that Women are lurking on every corner, plotting to beguile and ensnare us and ultimately to infect us and then leaving us in the gutter to die slow painful deaths. A few days with Giella has taught me better. Never in a million years is she that cunning, deceitful, scheming female creature described in the Book of Certitude. There isn't a dishonest bone in her body, I'm certain of it. If she deceived me for a second, I'd know at once. She's an open book to me. I know her better than I know myself.

DIARY OF SOWEEN CLAY, 2ND DAY OF AUTUMN
(IN MY SIXTEENTH YEAR)

Last night, fast asleep in bed, I woke up to the shock of my life! Standing there in the middle of my bedroom was Elihu, in his white suit and visor looking like a ghost. I nearly screamed. But before I could do so, he placed his gloved fingers across my mouth, whispering, 'it's alright, it's only me, little sister!' And I thought to myself, ONLY you, for God's sake? He's come to kill me as well! He's going to try to tear out my throat, too! But Elihu seemed in a much gentler mood tonight. (Maybe the moon was more favourable!) He said he badly needed my help. (Digging traps perhaps, I thought, no chance!). He said if I loved him at all then I had to help him. They both did! (both of you, I thought. There's more than one of you? Oh, God, they're hunting in packs now! The village is over run! Ring the church bells!) But then he confessed everything, concerning him and Giella. And I lay there listening to him, first with feelings of such joy that all my suspicions about him had been groundless and then, as he went on, with an increasing feeling of such misery and loss, it's hard to put into words. He told me how he'd been meeting Giella. That what had begun as friendship had grown into something much deeper. They were now very much in love and were planning to run away together. My first thought was, no, it was me she loved, not him. Me. Me! Surely? If Giella was going to run away with anyone it would be with me. And then it gradually dawned on me that she had never said she loved me, not in so many words. In fact, the reverse. She had never loved me. All this time, she'd been using me to get closer to Elihu. All the questions she'd asked, which I'd stupidly thought had shown her interest in me, were simply to find out more about my brother, the real object of her passion. I've been so totally stupid! She's loved Elihu all the time and I've never even suspected. As I lay there, I started to cry and I never felt more lonely and betrayed. Before I could prevent him, Elihu, in response to my tears, suddenly raised his visor and kissed me on the forehead and stroked my cheek with his gloved hand. I thought to myself, what is he doing, he's gone mad. I'll infect him! I was sure to infect him! And then he told me excitedly that he and Giella had been meeting unprotected for weeks and that there was not a trace of infection. Which meant he must surely be Immune! Perhaps he was even The Chosen One himself. There was no other explanation. But for the sake of safety they had both decided to meet as little as possible in future. It only needed one person to let something slip to the Monitors! Till further notice, they were going to write to each other. But they were in need of a messenger. A go-between. Before he left he slid an envelope under my pillow, asking me to deliver it to her and guard it with my life! The final indignity! Another night without sleep.

LETTER FROM ELIHU CLAY TO GIELLA TARNESS
2ND DAY OF AUTUMN.

My dearest darling most precious one,

I'm hoping this reaches you safely. I'm going to entrust it to Little Sister when I see her. I will talk to her first, as we agreed, before entrusting it with her, though I'm certain we can rely on her.

It seems very strange to be writing to you and I feel a bit self-conscious doing so as I know my spelling isn't that great and, besides, writing it down like this makes it all look so flat and won't be at all spontaneous, not like talking to you. I just want to say how much I love you and always will love you, my darling, whatever happens to us in the days to come. The future's so uncertain for both of us, isn't it? I realise, as the Man, I'm supposed to make the decisions, or so all the books tell me. All the books I've been given to read have stressed how superior a Man is to a Woman in every way and it's only since knowing you that I realise how wrong that is! But then I expect they give Women books in which they tell you how inferior you are to Men! Don't believe a word you read, my darling! Having known you even for this brief time, I have the growing belief that Men and Women are actually equal partners and we should both make our decisions together. That isn't to say I will shirk my share of the responsibility but I hope we can make our plans together. Do you remember I told you about the Goddess Venus coming out of the sea on her giant seashell? Well, you've replaced her, my darling, and are now my Divine Goddess of Beauty who I will love, worship and adore for ever more.

With all my fondest love,
Your devoted
Elihu. xxxxxxxxx

120 PD

DIARY OF SOWEEN CLAY, 3RD DAY OF AUTUMN
(IN MY SIXTEENTH YEAR)

———————

I delivered the note to Giella this morning. I passed it to her with such ill grace that she must have immediately sensed my displeasure. She took the envelope, covering it with her hand, whispering as she did so, I'm so sorry, I'm so sorry, Soween. And I knew then, sorry or not, she must have been aware of my feelings for her all along. She must have been aware of them, yet continued to use me regardless. Which is so heartless and inconsiderate! People are so disappointing. At the end of the day, she'd found time to write a note of her own, which she passed to me to take back to her beloved Elihu. I felt like stuffing it down the nearest drain. Or down her rotten lying throat! But I didn't because I'm a very, very nice person unlike the rest of this rotten world.

120 PD

LETTER FROM GIELLA TARNESS TO ELIHU CLAY.

3RD DAY OF AUTUMN.

My sweetest, most precious, most darling of Men,

I'm secretly writing this on a page of my exercise book whilst the English class continues round me and Teacher Jollie, assuming I'm taking notes, drones on in the background about Suitable Books for young women to read, as if there ever were such things! Presumably she's referring to books suited to our smaller brains! Yes, they do indeed teach us that!

Thank you for saying we are equal partners. I know in my heart that's true but coming from a Man who must have had it drummed into him from birth what a superior creature he is, coming from you as it does, it reflects on the generosity of spirit which I know you to have. I do so admire you, my darling. You have such integrity, such clarity of soul. Just thinking of you now as I write this, all the love I feel for you wells up inside and brings tears to my eyes, because of the sheer beauty you have both inside and out. You wrote of worshipping me, well, I can tell you that worship is mutual. We must stay strong for each other, mustn't we? And if the worst happens and they find out about us, then we will both face the consequences bravely together. The single glorious fact is, given all the time we've known each other, that I can't possibly have infected you, my darling, and you must surely be an Immune Chosen One. So when the time does come for us to face the world then what the hell can they do about it, eh? In the end, my darling, we must keep telling ourselves we have done nothing WRONG. Whatever they say, what we're doing is RIGHT! RIGHT! RIGHT!

All my undying love,
Your devoted Giella xxxxxxxxxxxxxxxxxxx

DIARY OF SOWEEN CLAY, 3RD DAY OF AUTUMN
(IN MY SIXTEENTH YEAR)

————————

I handed Giella's letter to Elihu this evening and he, in turn, handed me another for her. Dear God, is this going to be the pattern of my life chasing backwards and forwards delivering messages of love whilst feeling totally unloved myself? This has got to stop! What would Jane have done? Probably banged their stupid heads together, knowing her. Love makes me sick!

LETTER FROM ELIHU CLAY TO GIELLA TARNESS.
3RD DAY OF AUTUMN

My sweet exquisite divine precious one,

I dream of you every night now. Although it's been several days, it feels like several years, since we last made love and I felt the soft touch of your skin beneath my hand. Nonetheless in my dreams I am making love to you every night. Are you aware of this, I wonder? Is there something linking us which causes me to appear beside you in your bed so you can feel my arms holding you and my lips brushing across your breasts? In my dreams, you sit astride me as you love to do with me inside you, causing me such exquisite pain of anticipation as you rock to and fro, holding me back, deliberately, teasingly, taking your time and taking my time and causing us to have no time at all. All the while making those little sounds in your throat, those little stifled cries of pleasure.

I sometimes feel we could stay that way forever. They'd find us locked together in years to come in our little cave, fossilised by the water dripping from the roof, which gradually turned us to stone.

I miss you so much. I can't wait till we're reunited on our "wedding day". How advanced are your parents' plans for arranging our escape? I'm longing to see the sea, aren't you? I read in one of my (Men's!) books that the sea is vast and appears endless and vanishes completely over the horizon as if it's overflowing off the edge of the world! But maybe that's not true. After all, as I said, you can't believe everything you read in books! Must stop now and give this to Soween. I think she's taking it in good part, considering she can't enjoy being a go-between for a love affair which she can't be part of. But she's a loyal sister and I have every faith in her.

All my love, my darling one, until I see your precious face again,
Your loving,
Elihu xxxxxxxxxxxxxxxxxxxxxxxxxxxxxxxxxxxxxxxxxxx

DIARY OF SOWEEN CLAY, 4TH DAY OF AUTUMN
(IN MY SIXTEENTH YEAR)

—————

Another note delivered this morning to Giella and another received from her to take home to my brother. Only this time we both got a little careless and when she tried to pass me her note, I'm sure that Axi and Sassa noticed the exchange. That beady eyed little pair don't miss a trick! We will need to be more careful in future. Though to hell with it, it's hardly my problem, is it? I don't care if they find out or not. I'm just the desperately wretched, thoroughly miserable, insignificant little messenger aren't I?

LETTER FROM GIELLA TARNESS TO ELIHU CLAY.
4ᵀᴴ DAY OF AUTUMN

My dearest, sweetest, divine, and most precious Man,

Two of my classmates, Axi and Sassa have been watching me today and I'm afraid they suspect that all the busy writing I've been doing in class over the past couple of days may be less than genuine. Although it certainly fools Teacher Jollie, who never seems to notice anything except the sound of her own voice! But I'll have to keep this letter brief just in case. If those two were to discover what we're up to, it would really be a complete disaster. Axi's the leader of the gang here called the Falcons which consists of half the class including me and Soween (they were the ones who were bullying her). Axi is a seventeen-year-old monster and quick to spot any weakness in anyone which she will then exploit ruthlessly. She can reduce most girls to tears in seconds. Always excluding yours truly, of course. But then I've never allowed her to see any weakness in me to exploit. But I think my writing notes to you might make me a wee bit vulnerable to possible threats and blackmail, were she to find out. So I'm going to be doubly cautious when I pass this one to Soween at the end of the day and if you reply then please tell her to be extra careful, won't you?

All my love as always, my darling one and please excuse the brevity,
Your adoring,
Giella xxxxxxxxxxxxxxxxxxxxxxxxxxxxxxxxxxxxxxxxxxxxxxxxxxxxxxxxxx

DIARY OF SOWEEN CLAY, 6TH DAY OF AUTUMN
(IN MY SIXTEENTH YEAR)

Disaster occurred today! On my way back to school, Axi and the rest of the gang (without Giella, of course) were waiting for me in the road outside. She asked me if I had any messages for her. I hate it when she smiles because it generally means something really nasty is going to happen, as indeed it was. I tried to look very innocent (despite the fact that I knew I was blushing like MAD!) And I said, sorry I'm afraid I didn't have any. Not for her. And then they all crowded round me and, whilst Molwin and Yoteez held my arms, Axi started to search me, running her hands all over my body. It didn't take her long to find Elihu's letter. And then, with cries of glee, they danced away, triumphantly giggling with delight. When I arrived in the classroom Giella looked at me hopefully and I just shrugged. She must have realised what had happened. At the end of the day, she didn't give me a note to take back. It seemed a bit pointless. When I got home, I told Elihu what had happened and he looked very worried. Sorry, I did my best, brother. I'm not risking ten days of Solitude just for your miserable love letters!

EDITED EXCERPT OF MINUTES OF MEETING

SOUTH SARUM VILLAGE COUNCIL, 7 AUTUMN

Present:

Cllr. T. Chilzer (Chair) (Moderate)

Cllr. K. Clay (Orthodox)

Cllr. M. Chalice (Moderate)

Cllr. J. Grosh (Orthodox)

Cllr. F. Harran (Moderate)

Cllr. H. Tarness (Progressive)

Cllr. Doben (Moderate)

Cllr. L. Kriffitt (Progressive)

Cllr. C. Nivess (Progressive)

Cllr. G. Whipple (Progressive)

Apologies: Cllr. L. Marling (Orthodox)

The Orthodox Party members, Cllrs Grosh and Clay, having concluded their private reading in the antechamber, joined the main meeting as usual.

Cllr. Chilzer (M), Chair wished it conveyed to Cllr. Marling best wishes for a swift recovery from her recent attack of food poisoning.

1. Bad behaviour had been xxxxxxxxxxxxxxxxxxxxxxxxxxxxxxx their parents.

2. Further action needed to be xxxxxxxxxxxxxxxxxxxx immediately.

3. Proposal for Day of Colour Fest. Cllr. Tarness
(P) re-introduced The Progressive Party's proposal,
first raised a year ago, to hold a Day of Colour
to be held this time on 17 Autumn. Since it was
last proposed, soundings had been made around
the Village and it appears there is considerable
support for the idea. It would take the form of
a street party held in the Village Square with
trestle tables, loaned by the Chapel, decorated
by Progressive Party volunteers with free food
and refreshments provided by local shopkeepers
and private benefactors. Cllr. Tarness foresaw,
depending on the success of the venture, this could
well become a popular annual event in the Village
calendar. Cllr. Clay (O) said it was outrageous
that Cllr. Tarness should even contemplate
reintroducing this proposal, following the negative
response it received from the Council only a year
ago. She said it then and she would repeat it now,
she felt the idea totally inappropriate especially
with the additional embellishments to the original
proposal from a few colourful clothes into what
she could only interpret as a full blown public
orgy. And, as she understood it, the event would
take place in the very shadow of the Men's Memorial
itself. What greater insult could there be to
their memory? She, along with many others, was
becoming increasingly alarmed at the Progressive
Party's continued covert campaign, aimed at the
erosion of traditional values through the insidious
introduction of so-called minor modifications to
our moral code. Cllr. Whipple (P), amidst laughter,
said she didn't consider a sticky bun and a glass

of orange squash constituted an orgy. Cllr. Clay
told her to shut up. She was sick of the sound of
her whining little schoolgirl's voice. Cllr. Whipple
responded saying not half as much as she was of
listening, meeting after meeting, to Cllr. Clay's
monotonous self righteous pontifications. Cllr.
Chilzer intervened and said if the Councillors were
unable to contain themselves she would ask both of
them to leave the Chamber. She considered it tragic
that this once responsible administrative body,
once looked up to by the entire community, should
be reduced to a level of tawdry petty squabbling.
Both Councillors then apologised to the meeting,
Cllr. Whipple adding that she felt sorry for Cllr.
Clay as she'd clearly never had fun or experienced
any sort of pleasure in her entire life. At which
point, Cllr. Clay struck Cllr. Whipple across the
face. Both Councillors then voluntarily left the
meeting. A vote was then taken by the members
remaining on whether the proposed Day of Colour
Fest should be held on 17 Autumn. The motion was
carried by 8 votes to 1 with 1 abstention. There
being no other business the meeting was concluded.

DIARY OF ELIHU CLAY, 7TH DAY OF AUTUMN
(IN MY SEVENTEENTH YEAR)

Soween told me yesterday of the breakdown of our postal service and how my letter to Giella had been intercepted by members of her wretched gang. Unfortunately, the letter confirmed details of the time and place of our proposed wedding ceremony. We had decided it was to be held at her house in just over a week on my sixteenth birthday at midnight, making it a combined wedding and birthday party. Today, I took something of a risk by going round to her house while she was at school to talk to her parents to see if there was some alternative way I could get in touch with her through them. I asked if I could leave a note for her when she got home. And her Mama, Desollia, suggested why didn't I come back later tonight and give it to her myself? She understood we'd both been sleeping in the Woods lately but the nights were getting too chilly for that surely? And I said, if that was alright with them, then I'd come back later. I must say these Free Spirits are a mass of contradictions. On the one hand planning a full old fashioned wedding for their daughter and on the other, arranging for her to have midnight trysts in her bedroom with her husband-to-be! But the prospect of spending a night in a real bed with her, not any bed but <u>her</u> bed, far outweighed the small risk it entailed. Just as I was leaving, Desollia said she and her partner, Hork, wanted to talk to me about something really important. I suspected from the look in Desollia's eyes, that they wanted to talk politics at me (help!). They usually do, these Progressives. Even Giella, given half the chance, will spout on for hours about Woman's rights which just sends me to sleep quite honestly. I'm all for them in theory, of course I am. But I mean, the fact is the world is the way it is, isn't it? Might as well accept it. Nothing we can do to change things, is there? Just the way we're made.

DIARY OF SOWEEN CLAY, 7TH DAY OF AUTUMN
(IN MY SIXTEENTH YEAR)

This evening, after supper, Elihu came to see me in my room to explain what had happened and that the letter which Axi intercepted had all of the plans for a midnight wedding party they were going to have round at Giella's house. (Midnight wedding? It was the first I'd heard about a midnight wedding!) I asked a bit sniffily if I was invited and he said quickly that of course I was. Giella really wanted me there, too, they both did. It was to be on 16th Autumn, Elihu's seventeenth birthday.

I must be sure to be there.

Great. I can't wait to say goodbye forever to the only two people in my life I really love. And always will do. I'm really looking forward to that, can't wait! Thank you!

When I arrived last night just after midnight at Giella's home, they were all waiting up for me in the living room, her parents Desollia and Councillor Hork Tarness together with Giella herself. I could see the prospect of a glorious night sharing a bed with my beloved was going to have to wait. They all seemed anxious to talk to me, practically before I'd even had time to sit down. Contrary to normal custom, (but when had they ever conformed to normal custom?) they were all without their visors and, as a result, I sat there as their guest, awkwardly wearing my own, listening with a growing sense of dread whilst they told me of their plans for the Wedding. As I listened to them, so enthusiastic, passionate and so fiercely determined, I got the feeling that our wedding was in truth little more than an excuse for something much more than just two people simply exchanging vows. The Tarnesses, it seemed, saw this as a chance to spread their Progressive views and an opportunity to make a number of political points, mostly at Giella's and my expense. The said, after all, we'd been together for so long now that there wasn't the slightest possibility of me being infected. I was almost certainly immune, which was of profound significance for everyone. I said I was worried about making it all too public, but Giella begged me to trust them, please. She obviously did. And she looked at me so imploringly, I just couldn't say no to her but all the time I could hear Mapa's voice in my head warning me never to trust a Woman, especially one who tells you she loves you as she would always be trying to manipulate me for her own wicked ends and she was bound to betray me eventually. But, what the hell, I'm a Man. I can make up my own mind. And so I agreed. And then Giella did the most shocking thing. She lifted my visor clear of my face and kissed me, crying, Thank you, thank you! And there I was, sitting in a room with three barefaced women, entirely unprotected for the first time in years, feeling sort of naked, in a way. And then Desollia came over and kissed me on the cheek, thanking me. And finally her partner, Hork thanked me and kissed me on the other cheek and for a moment we all sat very close together, as if we were communing and the thought passed through my head, well if I'm going to die, this is as good a way to go as any, I suppose! Later on in bed, we made love properly like we used to and after that I felt so much better and all my worries melted away as Giella fell asleep in my arms, still murmuring that I wasn't to worry and to trust them. And she was so soft and warm and smelt so good. How can I ever say no to her? But I woke up thinking, we never really got round to discussing what happens after the wedding, had we?

On the way home today, Giella told me that Axi had read Elihu's letter and had insisted that she and the rest of the Falcons come to the party as well. No arguments! Giella said she'd no option other than to agree. God, with Axi, Sassa and the rest of the gang I can well see it could turn out a recipe for disaster. But Giella seems so excited and happier than I've seen her before and I stopped myself from saying anything which might bring her down from her cloud. She said she had something really important to discuss with me but not there in the road but round at her house, something really important and exciting. She was so glowing and appealing. I couldn't say no to her. How could I ever say no to someone as glorious as Giella? She'll break my heart when she leaves, she will. Maybe she wants to take me to her room and hold me and kiss me, even though it will be the one and only time she does. Before it finally ends between us. I would love to think that she will have kissed me just the once. Dream on!

DIARY OF ELIHU CLAY, 13ᵀᴴ DAY OF AUTUMN
(IN MY SEVENTEENTH YEAR)

Tonight when I got there, they were all waiting for me just as they had been before. We all sat round, none of us visored, whilst Hork poured us all a drink of a potent brown liquid which I suspect was certainly alcoholic. After initially setting fire to my throat though, I admit it did have a most relaxing and soothing effect. So whilst Giella cuddled up by me, her head in my lap, her parents got very excited as they outlined their plans. They were like a couple of kids, really. They were determined to make the news of our wedding as public as possible. That Giella and I were living proof that the current status quo was a total myth. Hork said they wanted everything out in the open. Although the Wedding would, as promised, remain a private affair with just immediate friends and family, people needed to know about Giella and I, how it was possible, once again, for a Woman and a Man to be reunited. That this continuing segregation of the sexes was purely political and now medically groundless. Back in the bad old days of The Plague, separation was a necessity but now it was an irrelevance, an excuse for a small number of the rich and privileged to take advantage as a means of furthering their own selfish personal interests. There were lots of people, she knew for a fact, particularly on the North side of the Divide, she knew on good authority have been exploiting the situation for years. Like they've always done. There's always the few prepared to take advantage of the many. And so, Desollia chimed in excitedly, they were planning to hold a street party the day after the wedding. In the Village Square. The Progressive Party were planning an event, a so-called Colour Fest which they had had passed through Council a week ago. A one day event, all above board and legal. Desollia showed me the leaflet she'd designed which they were distributing to every house in the village, inviting everyone to come along in their brightest clothes for free food and refreshments, music and dancing, everyone was welcome! And I though to myself, you won't get many members of the Orthodox party, I can tell you. I couldn't imagine Mapa dancing in the Village square in bright clothes nor even, to be honest, Mama, though I'm sure she'd have loved to have done so if she ever dared to brave Mapa's wrath. But then, right in the middle of all that, as a so-called special surprise, they would announce our wedding to the world. Show everyone it's possible for a Man and a Woman to be together once again. Giella and I would be living proof! One step nearer to abolishing that awful Divide! We were to think of ourselves as trailblazers, breaking down age-old barriers and thereby allowing others to follow! They got so passionate and excited about the idea, both of them that in the end none of us got to bed till nearly dawn. Giella and I crawled in so exhausted and, though I made a pathetic attempt to initiate lovemaking, I'm afraid I fell asleep almost immediately whispering, sorry, I'm sorry. And Giella whispered back, "It's alright, darling, it's alright, don't worry." It seemed only a few seconds later that her alarm went off. Leaving them all asleep, I hurried back home so I'd be in bed before Mapa got up for work. Heaven knows how much sleep I'm getting these days. An hour here and an hour there. This morning I could barely keep awake through Tutor Morden's droning. He sounds like a bee trapped in a jam jar. After lunch, I fell asleep on my bed and slept for hours until it was practically time for supper. Oh, Giella, I love you so much and I do trust you, I promise. But how's this all going to end?

GET SOME
COLOUR
BACK IN YOUR LIFE !!!!

PEOPLE OF **SOUTH SARUM VILLAGE**, YOU ARE INVITED BY **YOUR COUNCIL** TO JOIN US IN THE **VILLAGE SQUARE** FOR YOUR VERY FIRST

COLOUR
FE(A)ST

Free Food and Refreshment

Live Music and Dancing from Dawn to Dusk!

PLUS AT NOON - A Very Special Surprise!

PLEASE COME DRESSED IN
YOUR BRIGHTEST AND MOST COLOURFUL CLOTHES ✶
AND HELP TO MAKE THIS A
BRILLIANT DAY TO REMEMBER!

—

ANYONE DRESSED IN BLACK REFUSED ADMISSION!

—

✶ Come on, you must have something colourful hidden away somewhere!
If not, please contact our exclusive CLOTHES LINE — Doben's Ironmongers —
in the Village Square and we'll do what we can to help.

—

THIS EVENT
SPONSORED BY

THE
**SOUTH
SARUM
PROGRESSIVE**
PARTY

THE PARTY THAT
WILL BRING COLOUR
BACK INTO YOUR LIFE

DIARY OF SOWEEN CLAY, 13ᵀᴴ DAY OF AUTUMN
(IN MY SIXTEENTH YEAR)

At the end of school today, Giella took my hand and led me home with her. As we walked, she talked endlessly about Elihu. I suppose if I'd really listened to her properly and not been so excited that she was actually taking me home with her, I'd have realised that my dream of some sort of last-minute amorous farewell between us, however brief, was shortly going to be dashed. But that's me, always the optimist! We went straight up to her bedroom, further raising my hopes! She told me to take off my dress and to sit on the bed. So I sat there, so glamorous in my elasticated under vest and my grey baggy over-knickers. I must say, what with my eczema threatening a mass return, I have seldom felt less like an object of desire! But Giella was already taking off her own dress as well, throwing it on the floor. She then disappeared behind an embroidered screen which stood in one corner, saying, "Wait, wait!" Then I heard her struggling into something or perhaps even out of something, who knew? She returned eventually wearing a beautiful high necked, long-sleeved, floor length white dress embroidered with flowers in the same white material, looking so divine and like a goddess, I just stared at her in wonder. What sort of nightdress was that? It certainly seemed far too delicate an outfit in which to seduce me. Like an idiot I continued to hold my breath and sat there expectantly. She explained it was her wedding dress and what did I think, she wanted my opinion. I muttered something along the lines of, "It's beautiful". And then she produced another similar dress and said, "Soween, this one's for you, my darling!" I felt totally confused. Were we both of us getting married? Was she planning to marry me after all, both of us, two Mamas in white? Idiot! She wanted me to be her bridesmaid. She told me excitedly that I was the only person she'd ever wanted and I must agree. This was my dress which she'd had made specially and she wanted me to try it on. I was to take off all that horrid stuff and she'd find me some proper underwear. I let her undress me till I stood before her quite naked like I'd never been with another single living soul before, apart from Mama. And Giella found me a pair of knickers which barely covered anything and then a terribly uncomfortable skimpy bra, which pushed everything I had aggressively forward and unnaturally upward. Finally, I stepped into the dress which echoed her own with its high neck and long sleeves but, unlike hers, came down only as far down as my knees. She then excitedly rifled through her vast collection of shoes until she found me a pair with heels so precarious there was absolutely no chance of me taking more than two steps in them and at which point I firmly called a halt. So in the end, we settled for some little white satin slippers which at least allowed me to walk. Satisfied, she hugged me, overjoyed at the result, finally finishing by kissing me on both cheeks. But that was the extent of our passion. We both got changed again, she still chattering away. She asked me to stay for tea but I made some feeble little excuse and hurried home, bravely only starting to cry once I was clear of her front door and into the Village. But then people there are used to me running through the High Street, crying my eyes out. Oh, it's only her, they probably say to each other, that daft Clay girl at it again!

DIARY OF ELIHU CLAY, 14™ DAY OF AUTUMN
(IN MY SEVENTEENTH YEAR)

Another brief night round at Giella's and I have to confess once again when we finally did get to bed and she started kissing me in an effort to arouse me, somehow or other I still managed to fall asleep in the middle of it. Impossible that could ever have happened a week ago! When I woke up, I was full of apologies but she just laughed saying, it was probably the excitement and there was only forty eight hours to go till the big day and it would all be over. To be honest I'm hardly sleeping because I'm still having terrible doubts about this party in the Square with the entire Village invited. But whenever I mention it she just stares into my eyes, saying fiercely, didn't I want the Woman I loved to be free? To enjoy the same freedoms as a Man has? Didn't I want her to enjoy them, too? And I said, yes, I wanted her to be free, of course I did. But there must be some other way to achieve that, surely, there must? But she said, no, this is the only way. We've been given this opportunity, we mustn't waste it! And I just shut up after that. They've found me a suit from somewhere, too! Not a conventional white protective suit. This one's black and comes in three separate sections which Giella says is traditional for the Man to wear at a wedding. Whereas the Woman would traditionally be expected to wear white. Quite the reverse of normal procedures. Soween's to be her bridesmaid. I wonder what Soween made of that?! They made me try on my suit and I stood there, feeling a bit foolish dressed all in black, just a bit girly.

I'm sure people will start laughing at me. Honestly, I might as well be married in a dress and have done with it! But

in the end I agreed to that as well. Anything for a quiet life.
The priest who's marrying us is, as I suspected, a Free Spirit
from a nearby village who says she's delighted to conduct
what she calls a "proper" wedding. She's left us a printout
of the ceremony together with the text of the vows we'll
be making to each other. All of it's rather sweet in a quaint
sort of way. Giella tells me that tomorrow, being the last
night before we're married, to prevent bad luck, I mustn't
come round, not even to see her, but I'll have to wait till the
ceremony itself before I next set eyes on my beautiful bride.
This whole business is getting crazier and crazier!

DIARY OF SOWEEN CLAY, 14TH DAY OF AUTUMN
(IN MY SIXTEENTH YEAR)

Mapa summoned me to her study this evening to ask me how I was getting on at school. And I told her things were much better than they had been. And she told me she was very proud of me for standing up to the bullies and I was extremely brave. And I thought for one moment she was going to hug me! Heavens, whatever next? Instead, she resisted the urge. But just as I was about to leave, filled with a certain relief that she hadn't wanted to discuss something more serious, she called me back again and gave me one of her looks. The one which made me feel immediately extremely guilty, even when I'd done nothing at all and am completely innocent. A single one of those looks was enough to make my eczema erupt like miniature volcanoes all over my face and turn it the colour of an over-ripe tomato. I think I must be someone whose conscience is in a permanent state of guilt. Did Mapa suspect something was going on? She asked me if I'd been associating with, as she called them, "unsavoury elements", lately? And I tried to look innocent as if I had no idea what she meant (though inside I knew **only too well**!) She said she was referring to those who misguidedly regarded themselves as Free Spirits. But theirs was a misplaced freedom and one I would do well never to be tempted to follow. She sensed I may even have developed a relationship with such people. I couldn't look at her directly but instead I stared at the floor as if suddenly fascinated by the cracks in the floorboards. I'm such a bad liar, muttering that I may have heard of them, in passing. She ended by saying I was not to fall into bad company and that I must surely know how much they both loved me, she and Mama. I was their only child now they'd all but lost Elihu and if anything happened to me it would surely break both their hearts. Blackmail or what??? By the time I left her room, my clothes were soaking, wringing with sheer liquid guilt. I'm pathetic! I didn't have the courage to tell her and stop something happening which I knew, in my heart, was terribly, terribly WRONG. But that would mean betraying Elihu and Giella. My own brother and my best friend. Life gets more and more impossible, it really does. Can it get WORSE than this?

From: Acting Chief Monitor (South Sarum & District)
To: Senior Monitor South West Region
Subject: Request for I&A Operation Tarness Residence.
Date: 14 Autumn 120

I have been advised via undercover source (Informant 63 P) that there is a planned illegal gathering at the home of Councillor H. Tarness in two days' time on 16 Autumn evening. Information suggests that the occasion will be fully Unprotected despite one Vulnerable Male, at least, being present.
The property owner being a prominent serving member of South Sarum Village Council, permission is hereby requested to Intrude and Apprehend (I&A Order KB73/660) where necessary.

Tana Redwitch
(Acting Chief Monitor, South Sarum & District)

DIARY OF ELIHU CLAY, 15TH DAY OF AUTUMN
(IN MY SEVENTEENTH YEAR)

I lay awake most of the night. At Giella's insistence, we're sleeping in our own separate beds tonight. I'd like to think it's for the last time ever. After we're both married tomorrow, with any luck we'll never sleep apart again. I'm still very nervous about tomorrow's Wedding Party at their house. And as for all the public goings-on the following day, I just can't bear to think about all that! I'm constantly on the verge of saying, listen can't we cancel it? The public bit the following morning in the Square, anyway? But they've all gone to so much trouble with their leaflets and secret arrangements, it's taken so much organisation and I couldn't bear to see Giella's disappointment. The thought of letting her down in some way is unbearable. Because I do, I do want her to be free, I really do. I think in my heart all Women should be free, but especially my divine Giella. She's such a pure beautiful spirit and should never be kept in a cage. She should never again need to hide her beauty behind a visor. But this way it's so full of risk and danger for all of us and I couldn't bear it if anything happened to her. I would lay down my life for her, I swear it. I will die with her. We vowed that to each other a long time ago, when there was a real prospect of her infecting me the first time we made love in the cave. Should I die as a result of that, she said, she was ready and willing to die with me. We would die together. God, here I am lying in bed the night before my wedding day and thinking of death! What kind of an omen is that? I hope no one laughs at me in my suit tomorrow, I really do. I'll feel such a great big GIRL, I know I will!

From: Senior Monitor South West
To: Acting Chief Monitor (South Sarum & District)
Subject: Re: Request for I&A Operation Tarness
Residence.
Date: 15 Autumn 120

Request granted.
But proceed in strict accordance with the terms laid
down in I&A Order KB73/660. Councillor H. Tarness
is a Progressive Party member and a popular and
prominent member of the Local Council. Any activity
that exceeds permitted procedures should be avoided.
Please advise your I&A team to observe full C&C*
Regulations at all times.

Dern Teak
(Senior Monitor South West Region)

---

* *Author's note:* C&C = Caution and Courtesy. Monitors were governed by strictly regulated procedures when performing Intrude and Apprehend (I&A) operations. Though in practice these could vary from delicate kid gloves through to downright violence, depending on the rank and importance of the recipient. In this instance, the Senior Monitor is urging caution on account of Cllr. Hork Tarness' rank and popularity. The Monitors, at this period, were gradually becoming less and less popular with the public and were conscious of trying to establish a less provocative image than they had in the past.

DIARY OF SOWEEN CLAY, 17TH DAY OF AUTUMN
(IN MY SIXTEENTH YEAR)

The Wedding (Part one)
Written one day after the event.

    After school, Giella and I went straight to her house and upstairs to change, hours before we needed to but as I soon discovered we needed hours to get ready! After we'd showered and washed our hair, we started getting dressed. She'd found me some tights to go under my short dress which took ages to put on with lots of tugging and heaving from her and wriggling and grunting from me. But the effort was worth it, as they certainly improved the look of my legs. Giella said nearly all Women wore them at one time before the Divide and I said then all I could say was they must have had little time to do anything else. Then she sat me down in front of her table mirror and began to paint my face, working on my eyes and lips especially, showing me the result from time to time. It was like that nightmare I'd had coming true. I couldn't get used to all these mirrors everywhere. Wherever I looked I kept catching sight of myself. I hated it, seeing me everywhere. When she'd finished she showed me the result. And I said, it was great. Though really I thought I looked terrible. I was no longer me. It wasn't me looking back at me. It was another me altogether. A sinful me with a wicked look in her eye. Giella then sat in front of the mirror and started to paint her own face. As I sat watching her gradually transforming into a bright coloured butterfly, looking totally beautiful, I felt this terrible longing to touch her. To touch her entire body with its glowing skin. And I felt a terrible envy of Elihu. She was going to be his! I was full of this mixture of overwhelming love and deep anger. Didn't she realise the pain she was causing me, just allowing me to sit here? And as I watched her, carefully applying paint to her own face, I caught sight of my own reflection in the long mirror. A jealous scowling little creature, crouched there on the bed behind her, with its tight mean mouth and its narrow eyes glinting with anger. I saw what an unlikely couple we would have made. What was I ever thinking? Giella finally slid into her white dress and I helped her with the back fastening. As I stood behind her I was aware she'd sprayed herself with perfume so strong it made my eyes water. She adding earrings, a bracelet and a chain necklace and a ring. Finally, we both put on our shoes, hers with the impossible heels and my own little white satin slippers to which I noticed she'd added some silver sparkly bits. God, I couldn't begin to guess the number of clothing regulations we were breaking. Mapa, if you could see me now! Giella practised one or two tentative steps and I could tell she was unused to wearing them. Then she bravely performed a complete twirl in the middle of the room and looked to me for approval. And she gave me a dazzling smile. It was true. She was beautiful, I had never before in my life seen anyone so beautiful. But the Woman standing there was no longer my Giella. In a weird way, she'd transformed herself and become Elihu's Giella. At that moment, her Mama came to the door and told us the guests were assembled, the groom was now waiting and it was time to come down.

From: Acting Chief Monitor (South Sarum & District)
To: Senior Monitor South West
Date: 17 Autumn 120
Report on I&A Operation Tarness Residence.

Following the departure of Informant 63 P, entry was
effected by a Full 12-member I&A Team (Mixed). Upon
entry, evidence of excessive use of Alcohol and Drugs
Class 2 (Contrary to Regulation P98 & P101b). Several
participants seventeen years or younger including one
male, Elihu Clay, seventeen. All present were without
Protection (Contrary to Regulation U9F&U10M). Many of
those present also dressed in an improper and obscene
manner (contrary to Dress Code D4873F) and brawling due
to drug and drink influence.
Male subsequently removed by North Sarum Sub Team
(M03NS) to a secure residence North of Divide.
Females removed to temporary holding cell in
Village Hall. Where relevant they were collected by
respective parents and taken home to await charges
and trial.
Councillor H. Tarness, Partner D. Tarness and
Daughter G. Tarness, sixteen, held over to await
charges and trial.
Overall outcome: Satisfactory/Good.
Damage to property: Nil/Very Minor.
Damage to individuals: Very Minor (Some self
inflicted)

Tana Redwitch
Acting Chief Monitor (South Sarum & District)

DIARY OF SOWEEN CLAY, 17TH DAY OF AUTUMN
(IN MY SIXTEENTH YEAR)

The Wedding (Part two)
Written one day after the event.

We went downstairs together, Giella leading the way, carefully negotiating every step in her challenging shoes. As we rounded the bend in the stairs, I saw the others assembled below. The Falcons, Axi, Sassa, Molwin, Yoteez and Silje, Giella's parents, the priest visored and in black and finally, looking extremely handsome if a little nervous in his black suit, Elihu. At our appearance there was a burst of whooping and shouting and clapping mostly from the Falcons and we both stopped for a moment whilst Giella acknowledged them. Giella's Mama, Desollia, was in a long green floating dress in the flimsiest material, festooned with necklaces and bangles like a Christmas tree. Her Mapa wore a simple black dress, nothing at all like a normal daytime one, stopping well short of her knees and made up of a shimmery material which caught the light whenever she moved. As for the Falcons, they had a vivid multi-coloured mix of dresses, some short, some shorter still or, I noticed in Sassa's case, virtually non-existent. Typical! All had painted their faces, but, again, Sassa looked, in my opinion, quite grotesque, like an infant's drawing of its Mama with her luminous green eyelids, her mouth a red gash and cheeks painted like a Dutch doll. I felt giddy from the strong smell of all their different perfumes. God knows what it must be doing to poor Elihu! They were all holding glasses I noticed, filled with what I suspected was alcohol (another law broken), some of them clearly on their second or even third drink, causing an artificial excitement and conviviality, much louder than normal. Giella stopped at Elihu's side whilst I remained behind her for the rest of the ceremony. It was simple and traditional. The usual vows. The main difference being it was between a Woman and a Man. Which I must say felt very strange and unnatural. At the end Elihu turned and kissed Giella which was probably the most shocking moment to date, as their mouths met, their lips firmly pressed together, for what seemed like ages. The room became incredibly quiet. When they finally broke apart, there was a positive sigh of relief. Then her Mapa started the music, loud and rhythmic (and definitely forbidden!) More drinks as people milled around, shouting over the music. I noticed the priest had slipped away as soon as the ceremony ended. Elihu and Giella remained close to each other and began dancing together, but dancing like I'd never seen before. Somebody put a glass of clear liquid in my hand, which one sniff of reminded me of Mama's smelling salts, making my head jerk back with shock. I found a shelf and got rid of it. This was fast becoming an orgy! Giella's Mapa and Mama, watching the dancers, were both actually smoking something, passing it backwards and forwards to each other! Giella and Elihu's dance became increasingly private and intimate, the whole room stopped to watch. Both of them very close now, mouths almost brushing again, sharing each other's breath, lost in a world separate from the rest of us. All at once, Sassa shouted out: 'Come on then! Can we all have a go?' Clearly the drinks had affected her. I'd noticed Axi had been fetching her refills. But now Sassa jumped forward and, pulling Giella away from Elihu, grabbed hold of him and thrust her bright red mouth towards his in a manner, I presume, that she thought was seductive. Elihu stood unresisting, a bit embarrassed. Giella angrily seized Sassa by her shoulder pulling her away. The next moment, she and Sassa had tumbled into a heap at Elihu's feet, pulling and tearing at each other. Elihu tried half-heartedly to part them. Others then joined in, taking different sides, trying to pull the two apart. Axi, taking Sassa's side, pulling at Giella, trying to save her drunken friend. Giella's Mapa, then hauling Axi away. All at once, everyone was fighting with everybody. Poor Elihu, now with Giella back safely in the protection of his arms, standing bemused amidst the growing carnage. Just then there was a huge crash from the hall, and the room was filled with Monitors, appearing at the same time from all directions, through every window and doorway. White suited, faceless and frightening, they moved among us swiftly and silently, seizing hold of everyone, pulling them to their feet and driving them, including me, into the hall and out of the front door. It was so quick and unexpected, I think everyone was too shocked and startled to protest. The next minute we found ourselves standing outside the front door in a stunned little group. I'd lost sight of Elihu and then I saw him being led away separately. God knows if, or when, I'd see him next. The rest of us were loaded into a high sided open wagon, the more scantily clad amongst us beginning to feel the cold. We were taken to the Village Hall but instead of entering through the front, we were herded through a small side door and into a small windowless room. The door was locked and all of us stood in the darkness for a while, not daring to speak. At last, someone said in a small voice, what do you think's going to happen to us? Giella's Mapa said, no one was to panic, none of us had done anything seriously wrong. We had merely been enjoying a private party. The only rules we'd broken were minor, out-dated ones involving Improper Dress and Unseemly Demeanour. The most we can look forward to is confiscation of property and possibly a fine. As head of the household, she might possibly face something more serious, but she was ready for that! What about Elihu, Giella whispered, what will they do to him? Her Mapa laughed and said, he's a Man, darling, isn't he? He's not governed by the same rules we are. They'll probably take him across the Divide and give him a stern talking to, that's all. No one's to worry, it'll be fine. Her words reassured most of us. My biggest dread was facing Mapa. I dread to imagine what punishment she'd give me, for having deliberately lied to her. A few moments later the door was unlocked, someone called out my name saying my Mapa was here to collect me. Leaving the others in the cell, Mapa took me home with not a word spoken between us. Mama, too, was grim faced with disapproval. I was sent straight to my room. As I sit on my bed, writing this, I feel like a condemned prisoner waiting for the axe to fall.

From: Senior Monitor South West:
To: Senior Administrator (North), Senior
Administrator (South)
Subject: Result of I&A Order KB73/660/Tarness
Date: 17 Autumn 120

Following I&A Procedure 16 Autumn on home of
Councillor H. Tarness, please find Acting Chief
Monitor's (South Sarum & District) Report attached
and relevant correspondence, subject to the breach
of Infection Protection Protocol Procedures, I am
advising you that the Male, Elihu Clay, due to the
accompanying conditions is, in my view, considered
Vulnerable (High/Critical).
I thought it in the best interests to notify you
immediately of this breach of Quarantine.

Dern Teak
(Senior Monitor South West Region)

DIARY OF SOWEEN CLAY, 18ᵀᴴ DAY OF AUTUMN
(IN MY SIXTEENTH YEAR)

———————

This morning when I awoke, the house was deathly quiet. In the hall I heard Tutor Morden arrive and then his and Mapa's voices and, shortly after, Morden leaving again, having been told, I imagine, that he was not needed. Perhaps no longer needed? Who knows? Presumably Elihu has been taken somewhere North of the Divide. Would he be coming back? Would they even let him come back? Things are SO uncertain at present. After I'd dressed, I wrote up the rest of my diary from yesterday. All of it! I then went to the kitchen to see if I was going to be allowed any breakfast. Mama was there and told me, frowning, that Mapa wanted to see me in her study. When I went in, Mapa gave me one of her don't-say-I-didn't-warn-you looks. She didn't ask me to sit down so I stood in front of her desk, head bowed, suitably meek. She said she realised that I had only played a minor role in the previous night's disgraceful incident, but I had, nonetheless, been involved in a serious breach of basic, decent, acceptable conduct and the authorities were bound to take action against everyone involved, including me! The appalling incident has sent shockwaves through the entire community and I should be thoroughly ashamed of myself. Everyone concerned would in due course appear before the Village Council, where appropriate punishments would be decided. Until such time as I was summoned, I was to remain in the house and was not to leave under any circumstances. As far as school was concerned, I was to consider myself suspended until further notice. She suggested I spent the rest of the day in my room revising my schoolwork. So the rest of today I spent sitting on my bed, wondering what had happened to Elihu!

From: Senior Administrator (North)
To: Senior Monitor South West Region
cc: Senior Administrator (South)
Subject: Result of I&A Order KB73/660/Tarness
Date: 18 Autumn 120

Dear Dern Teak,
Thank you for advising us of the situation regarding
Elihu Clay. I understand his condition is being monitored
at the North Sarum Hospital and I am being kept informed
on an hourly basis by the Chief Medical Officer there.
With thanks,
Sincerely,

S. Jagg
pp Donal Portus
Senior Administrator (North)

CONFIDENTIAL
From: Chief Medical Officer, North Sarum Hospital
To: Senior Administrator (North)
Subject: Elihu Clay: EIS Procedure Request
Date: 18 Autumn 120

Dear Donal,
We've been keeping him under observation continually,
24 hours, and just to let you know Elihu Clay's
condition continues stable and unchanged. In view of
the circumstances, would it be appropriate for me to
authorise an EIS Procedure?
Sorry to ask but it's been some time since this
situation arose and I wanted to check with you whether
such action was still officially sanctioned?
Thanks,

Vint
Vinton Heppinstall,
Chief Medical Officer, North Sarum Hospital

PS. Hope you both had a good holiday. V

CONFIDENTIAL
From: Senior Administrator (North)
To: Chief Medical Officer, North Sarum Hospital
Subject: Elihu Clay: EIS Procedure Request
18 Autumn PD

Dear Vinton,
Re patient Elihu Clay.
You are hereby authorised to proceed with the
requested EIS Procedure as soon as possible.
Yours sincerely,
Donal

Donal Portus
Senior Administrator (North)

PS. We had a great holiday, thank you. Berry
returned looking as brown as his proverbial name! D.

★ *Author's note:* the addition below was scrawled in longhand on the bottom of this
letter, presumably written by Senior Administrator (North):

*Sure go ahead, what the hell, let's make an example
of the little bugger!*

DIARY OF SOWEEN CLAY, 19TH DAY OF AUTUMN
(IN MY SIXTEENTH YEAR)

I spent all yesterday and most of today in my room, apart from mealtimes. The silence in this house is unbearable! I thought school Solitude was bad enough but here at home it's twice as bad. I don't know why Mama is so against me, I really don't. It's like she's blaming me personally for Elihu. Like I've somehow betrayed the family. I should have raised the alarm as soon as I knew about the party. I know I should, but if I had done, wouldn't that equally have been betraying Elihu? Not to mention Giella, my so-called, used-to-be friend? It's like Mama's holding me personally responsible for Elihu prematurely going over the Divide. He was going to have to go anyway in a few month's time, wasn't he, so what difference does it make? I think I'll go mad if someone doesn't talk to me soon. No one says anything except when Mapa tells me to sit up straight or Mama tells me to eat more slowly and not to gobble. My life goes from bad to worse, first no brother, then no friends and now, no parents! I've decided, rather than revise my schoolwork, I'll start reading Wuthering Heights instead, even though it will remind me terribly of Giella. But I need to escape to somewhere, even if it's only into someone else's head. I know it's supposed to be banned and if Mapa catches me reading it, she'll probably beat me half to death. But what the hell, if I'm going to be a criminal, I might as well be a master criminal.

From: Chief Medical Officer, North Sarum Hospital
To: Talyed Chilzer, Chair, South Sarum Village
Council
Subject: Elihu Clay
19 Autumn PD

Dear Talyed Chilzer,
I regret to inform you that having been admitted to
this hospital on 16 Autumn, Elihu Clay is displaying
positive early symptoms of *tertiary femella sepsis* or as
it is more commonly known, The Plague. Since it was first
diagnosed years ago, considerably research has been done
to identify a cure for this most elusive and devastating
illness and with some early success, but sadly, no
certain cure has yet been found. Some small reassurance
might be taken that, thanks to the continuing stringent
Quarantine Regulations still in place, cases of this
sort are these days extremely rare. Not that that should
in any way detract from the present tragic occurrence in
someone quite as young as Elihu.
I must regretfully inform you that his chances of
survival are extremely slim. It is estimated that,
as of today, the disease is entering day 2 of its
normal 10 day cycle. I would be grateful therefore if
you would circulate this information immediately to
whomsoever you consider suitable, most especially to
Elihu's immediate family.
As is customary in such cases, this Hospital will
arrange safe passage for his family, suitably visored,
through the Divide to visit and to say their farewells.
In the light of Elihu's rapidly deteriorating
condition, might I suggest this be arranged sooner
rather than later.

I am sorry to be the bearer of such tragic news and
may I be permitted to add my deepest sympathy to all
concerned,
Yours sincerely,

Vinton Heppinstall,Chief Medical Officer,
North Sarum Hospital

DIARY OF SOWEEN CLAY, 20TH DAY OF AUTUMN
(IN MY SIXTEENTH YEAR)

———————

I was in the middle of reading Wuthering Heights this morning when quite suddenly with only the briefest of knocks, Mapa came into my room looking very serious. In the background I could hear Mama crying in the kitchen. What on earth could have happened? I barely had time to hide Emily's book under my pillow. I'm certain Mapa must've seen me, but she seemed too preoccupied to refer to it. She said they'd just had the most appalling news from North Sarum Hospital that Elihu had been confirmed as infected. The disease was still in its early stages, entering day two of its ten day incubation period. In other words, he had only eight days left. I stood there stunned. How could this have happened? It can't possibly have happened? He told me he was immune, he was certain of it! Mapa said we were allowed a final visit to see him but it had to be very soon as, in a few hours, he would no longer be in a state to recognise us, let alone speak to us. I kept saying over and over to myself, No. Not Elihu, he's Immune. It can't happen to him, it can't. And Mapa said grimly that it seemed it could but she promised that those responsible would be brought to justice! And with that, the three of us left to cross the Divide.

———————

END OF PART III

———————

Part IV
RAISING THE COLOUR

MEMO TO ALL MEMBERS
From: Talyed Chilzer, Chair, South Sarum Village
Council
To: All Members South Sarum Village Council
Subject: Elihu Clay
Date 20 Autumn 120 PD

Dear All,
I am enclosing a copy of the distressing letter I have
just received from the Chief Medical Officer of North
Sarum Hospital regarding Elihu Clay. I think it speaks
for itself. I am personally heartbroken to learn that a
young life should be so needlessly and tragically lost.
I have already notified Councillor Clay. I know all
our thoughts and deepest sympathy go out to Kest at
this time together with her partner Chayza and their
daughter Soween.
In view of the forthcoming trial proceedings arising
from the recent incident at the home of Councillor
Tarness, I feel this tragic development raises a
question as to our level of sentencing. I therefore
intend calling an Emergency Council Meeting as soon as
possible to reconsider our course of action.
This tragic turn of events has now raised this from the
level of mere infringement of a few bylaws, however
serious, to what is tantamount to a possible charge of
wilful murder. It is my hope by discussing this sanely
and sensibly we can, as a committee, avoid any further
tragic consequences than those which already exist.
With good wishes,

Talyed
Chair, South Sarum Village Council

DIARY OF SOWEEN CLAY, 21ST DAY OF AUTUMN
(IN MY SIXTEENTH YEAR)

I had never been North of the Divide before. I'd often wondered what it would be like. I imagined it would be similar to our own village only full of men dressed in white. But I discovered the North to be very different, at least the bit we saw was. Once we were through the linking tunnel and the heavily guarded double Filter Gates and gone through at least three Decontamination Chambers, we found ourselves, visors lowered, in a dark treeless town square surrounded by high buildings on every side. Some of it was in quite bad disrepair. Mapa explained that this was probably the remains of what they used to call the city. Cities were places where, not just hundreds but thousands of people lived together, Men and Women in tiny areas with hardly room to move or breathe. Not like today back home, with our woodlands and fields with only the occasional cluster of homes or the odd farm or factory to interrupt the endless countryside. Mapa said we Women should consider ourselves lucky and that Men had unaccountably chosen to live in such depressing surroundings. I thought to myself, there must be more to it than that surely? Otherwise why are Men so desperate to leave our Village? A Monitor guided us across the square to the entrance of the Hospital. Then through endless corridors to an area marked Quarantine Wing and underneath, No unauthorised personnel beyond this point. We found Elihu in a small room, lying in a transparent tent with tubes and wires attached to him everywhere. He looked deathly pale and, even through the sheeting, we could hear his painful breathing. He seemed to me to be almost dead already. It was all I could do to stop crying and I heard Mama behind her visor starting to weep. At that moment, Elihu opened his eyes and stared at us in alarm, as if we black faceless spectres had come to claim him. The Doctor said we may raise our visors if we wished and we did so. After all, the harm was done. What more could we do to him? So we all raised our visors and looked at Elihu through his protective screen, trying our best to smile, but I'm not sure any of us managed to convincingly. He attempted to lift his arm by way of greeting but clearly even that proved hard for him and his hand dropped back immediately onto the sheet. He seemed in terrible pain. I don't think any of us was quite sure how long we were expected to stay or how long any of us could bear to. Mama asked the Doctor if they were giving him anything for the pain. He assured her they were doing all they could. We stayed a little longer and then, as if by mutual agreement, we all turned to leave without goodbyes as Elihu appeared to have slipped by then into a sort of coma. On the way home we didn't speak a word to each other. We are fast becoming a silent family. I think all of us were remembering our final image of Elihu with love mixed with a terrible pain. When we got home, we all went our separate ways, Mama straight to their bedroom, Mapa to her study and me to my room where, in desperation, I tried to escape to the comparatively untroubled world of Heathcliff and Cathy. But the words on the page were all blurred and I couldn't read a single one.

From: Senior Administrator (North)
To: Senior Administrator (South)
Subject: Elihu Clay
Date 20 Autumn

Dear Senya,
I hope you've been kept up to date with all the
details of this unhappy affair thus far.
The boy, Elihu, has definitely become infected. This
has recently been confirmed by the Chief Medical Officer
of North Sarum Hospital.
Hardly surprising really, seeing he was discovered,
according to the Monitors, in a roomful of semi-naked
women, most of them the worse for wear as a result
of alcohol or drugs! A young man who chose to live
dangerously. Well, sadly, he's now counting the cost
of an all-too-brief misspent youth.
Senya, to the serious point of this letter. I
heard from a source that the Village Committee are
considering upgrading this unhappy affair to a full
murder trial, first degree, wilfully causing the
death etc. I understand that those involved were
mostly kids, some as young as fifteen and it could,
if pursued further, cause a fearful counter-reaction
in certain quarters. You know how passionate these so
called Progressives can get!
I would urge caution, I really would. Could you
possibly bring influence to bear on matters and at
least reduce the charges to accidental infection,
perhaps? Which at least takes the death penalty off the
table. Officially, so I understand to my horror, those
terrifyingly cruel Ten Day Collars are still legal
South of the Divide. I thought they'd been outlawed

long ago. It would be a nightmare if they were all of
them charged and the village streets became awash with
desperate young women counting off their days!
God willing, such barbaric times are behind us.
With all good wishes,

Donal
Senior Administrator (North)

DIARY OF SOWEEN CLAY, 1ST DAY OF WINTER
(IN MY SIXTEENTH YEAR)

The diagnosis of Elihu's infection alters everything, of course. No longer are the guests at Giella's wedding party going to be charged with Improper Dress or Indecent Underwear or Unseemly Demeanour or other minor offences. Now it's become a full-blown murder trial. A life has been sacrificed. And, if justice is to be done, other lives, Mapa says, should be taken as well. She's become so angry. And in a way I understand her reasons. But what good does it do to be so vindictive and vengeful? Nothing will ever bring Elihu back to us, will it? But no, Mapa thunders on. Last night slamming doors and blaming the Tarness family for **everything**. Especially Councillor Tarness who she especially really **hates** with a deep loathing. Deliberate Causing of Infection she says, thumping the table, there's only one penalty for that. Death! She's lost her only son and, as a member of the Council, she's going to demand the death penalty. I'm due to appear before them, presumably I'll be charged with murder as well? I don't care if I am! They can cut my head off or hang me upside down, or drown me, or put me in one of their awful collars which strangle you! I don't care, I don't! My dear darling brother is dying. Two days to go till the trial! The waiting's agony. Oh, God, what's going to happen to us all?

South Sarum Village Council
1 Winter 120 PD

Events arising from an illegal gathering at the Tarness household on 16 Autumn 120 PD. leading to the deliberate Infection and consequent death of Elihu Clay. Hearings scheduled for 7 Winter.

LIST OF ACCUSED AND CHARGES.

Councillor Hork Tarness
Organising an illegal function.
Illegal possession of alcohol
Illegal possession of class 2 drugs
Enticement and subsequent corruption of minors
Knowingly unprotected in the presence of a
vulnerable male (Secondary contact)
Unseemly and improper dress and appearance
Disorderly behaviour under the influence of drugs
and alcohol

Desollia Tarness
Same as the above

Giella Tarness
Knowingly unprotected in the presence of a
vulnerable male (Secondary contact)
Unseemly and improper dress and appearance
Disorderly behaviour under the influence of alcohol

Axi Abatis

Same as the above

Silje Abatis

Same as the above

Molwin Sann

Same as the above

Yoteez Zuni

Same as the above

Sassa Saraveen

Same as the above

Soween Clay

Knowingly unprotected in the presence of a
vulnerable male (Secondary contact)
Unseemly and improper dress and appearance

From: Cllr Kest Clay
To: Talyed Chilzer, Chair, South Sarum Village Council
Cc: All Members
2 Winter

Dear Talyed,
Thank you for sending the copy of the charge sheet
regarding the illegal gathering at the Tarness
household on 16 Autumn, scheduled for 7 Winter.
I note that all the Contact charges are Secondary
ones. I wish to state in the strongest terms that,
following the news that my son Elihu has now officially
been diagnosed as Infected, there is clearly a very
powerful argument for upgrading the charge in one
instance to that of Primary Contact. I believe there
is an overwhelming case to be made against Giella
Tarness who was, by her own admission, on intimate
and unprotected terms with the victim several
days prior to the 16 Autumn Events and was almost
certainly the first point of contact.
I propose that the charge sheet in the case of Giella
Tarness be amended to read "Knowingly unprotected in
the presence of a vulnerable male (Primary Contact)."
Incidentally, as my daughter Soween is due to appear,
I will naturally withdraw during her hearing, as you
suggest in your accompanying note. I was of course
already planning to do so.
I will wait with interest to hear your reaction to my
proposal.

Kest

From: Talyed Chilzer, Chair, South Sarum Village
Council
To: Cllr Kest Clay
Cc: All Members
3 Winter

Dear Kest,
May I first extend every sympathy to you and Chayza
for the distressing news of your son's Infection.
I know how awful this must be for you and I fully
understand your instinct to punish those responsible
in the harshest way. I'm certain that the majority of
the Council Members sympathise with your feelings.
Regarding the reason for the charges against the
defendants being only Secondary, I have been advised
by our Senior Administrator that to pursue anything
stronger than this (for instance a charge of Primary
Infection) would automatically involve the defendants
in facing capital charges. I am sure that many of us,
myself included, will be loathe to pursue that course.
Although the death penalty is still technically on the
statute book, the prospect of us, the Council, passing
the death sentence on a seventeen-year-old girl is
quite repugnant to any right-thinking person.
I'm sorry. In the normal course of events, I do
respect your views and often value your wise opinions
but in this instance I really cannot accede to your
request to modify the charges against Giella Tarness.
I hope you will understand my reasons,
Yours,

Talyed
Chair, South Sarum Village Council

From: Cllr Kest Clay
To: Talyed Chilzer, Chair, South Sarum Village
Council
Cc: All Members
4 Winter

Dear Talyed,
Thank you for your reply.
I must tell you that I feel extremely strongly about
this matter and cannot let it rest.
Understandably I am very angry. You wrote, somewhat
emotively I thought, about the Council sentencing
a seventeen-year-old girl to death. But isn't that
precisely what she has done to my son? The only
difference being that he was condemned without benefit
of a trial. I feel that Giella Tarness is at an
age when she has to face the consequences of her
irresponsible actions.
I realise that this is a personal matter of
conscience and it is up to each individual member to
decide. I propose that the Council assemble early
before the trial to debate my proposal to elevate the
charge against Giella Tarness from a Secondary to a
Primary one.
I must stress I write this not out of reflex
vindictiveness but as a grieving parent determined to
seek justice for the loss of her beloved son.
I hope an emergency meeting of the full Council can
be arranged as speedily as possible.
Yours as ever,

Kest

URGENT
From: Talyed Chilzer, Chair, South Sarum Village Council
To: All Council Members
5 Winter

To let you know, at the request of Councillor Clay, there will be a full Emergency Council meeting this evening at 8pm to discuss the possibility of upgrading the charges against Giella Tarness.
This is potentially an extremely serious issue and I would urge all of you to attend.
Please be punctual.

Talyed Chilzer
Chair, South Sarum Village Council

URGENT

From: Talyed Chilzer, Chair, South Sarum Village Council

To: All Council Members

6 Winter

Following last night's debate in the Council chamber, please find attached the amended list of charges against those involved in the Tarness household incident on 16 Autumn last.

Talyed
Chair, South Sarum Village Council

DIARY OF SOWEEN CLAY, 7TH DAY OF WINTER
(IN MY SIXTEENTH YEAR)

I walked to the courtroom this morning with Mama, who is still not speaking to me. Mapa, being on the Council, had already left and I knew she would be serving on the Interrogation Panel. Our Village is too small to boast a proper courtroom but they plan to use the Council chamber instead. When we arrived at the Hall, we were made to wait in a small room. There was a row of benches along one side, facing the door on which were already seated the rest of the Falcons, Axi, Sassa, Molwin, Yoteez and Silje each with one or both of their respective parents. All of us dressed correctly and well scrubbed with no longer any trace of face paint. On the wall facing us was a large sign, "Silence at all times". From time to time the door opened and one of us was summoned along with their parents. Ominously, I observed, never to return. At last only Mama and I were left. Where had the others gone? Had they all been executed? Or dispatched to some distant, dark, dismal, dungeon? I was beginning to get what I always get when I'm specially nervous, a sort of fluttering in my stomach which Mama calls butterflies. They were fluttering as badly as I'd ever had them. I tried holding my breath because that sometimes cures them and then I tried breathing slowly and deeply but that didn't seem to help either. The trouble is, once you consciously concentrate on breathing deliberately, you're frightened you won't be able to restart it again automatically. Because, though they tell you it's automatic, how can you be sure once you switch it off, you'll ever be able to switch it on again? Maybe you'll just stop breathing and die. Anyway, I was really beginning to panic by the time they came and got us.

My breathing problems were temporarily forgotten as we both followed the Monitor down the passageway, and through the double doors into the Chamber itself. It was the biggest room I'd ever been in. A high ceiling going up forever, with flags and banners and windows, way up in the walls. A big horseshoe shaped table and, sitting there, a dozen or so visored black figures, faceless Women, there to judge me. I was led to a spot at the centre of the horseshoe. At one side sat a clerk, pencil poised. A Woman seated in the centre said, for the record, at this stage Councillor Clay had withdrawn declaring family interest. I saw Mapa's vacant chair. All of a sudden, I felt all my breathing problems coming back, only this time — horrors — in the form of terrible, unstoppable hiccups.

* *Author's note:* At this point, my diary is completely blank. I had written down no record of my trial whatsoever. I can only assume my memory of it was completely blanked and by the time Mama and I got home and I was in a position to write about what had happened I was no longer able to do so. Fortunately, owing to the kindness and generosity of former Councillor Talyed Chilzer, I'm including the formal transcript of my interrogation before the Council. I'm afraid it doesn't show me in a very flattering light. I'd like to have been able to come over as brave and defiant as Giella but, typically, I feel my performance in the face of interrogation can be summed up as pathetic. Below is the formal transcript of my trial. Blush! Blush!

FROM SOUTH SARUM VILLAGE COUNCIL MINUTES
7 WINTER. INTERROGATION OF SOWEEN CLAY

Cllr. Clay at this point withdrew from the
meeting, citing personal interest. The accused,
accompanied by her birth parent Chayza Clay, was
read the list of charges against her, including
the charge of Secondary Contact. She was then
asked if she understood them.

C. CLAY: Yes, she does.
CHILZER: (chair) Mama Chayza, please, be quiet. You
must allow the accused to answer for herself.
C. CLAY: I'm so sorry.
CHILZER: I will repeat the question, do you
understand the charges against you?
S. CLAY: Yes, I do. (Accused hiccups)
CHILZER: Do you admit that on the sixteenth day
of Autumn, along with others, you were knowingly
Unprotected in the presence of a Vulnerable Male,
namely your brother Elihu Clay?
S. CLAY: I do. (Accused hiccups)
CHILZER: And have you at any point before that
date been in the company of your brother in a
similar Unprotected state?
S. CLAY: I have not. (Accused hiccups) I promise.
CHILZER: Why are you making those noises? Is
there something wrong with you?
(Accused hiccups)
C. CLAY: : She's got hiccups.
CHILZER: What?

C. CLAY: She's got hiccups. She gets them when she's nervous.

CHILZER: Chayzer Clay, I will ask you again to remain silent. You must allow the accused to speak for herself.

C. CLAY: Sorry.

CHILZER: Well? What's wrong with you, girl? Are you ill?

(Accused hiccups)

CHILZER: Do you have hiccups, is that what it is?

(Accused hiccups)

CHILZER: Monitor, kindly fetch the accused a glass of water.

Monitor leaves the room at this point.

CHILZER: In the meantime, I'll proceed. Do you also admit that, on sixteenth Autumn, you were improperly dressed and slatternly in appearance?

S. CLAY: I think so.

CHILZER: What do you mean you think so? Either you were or you weren't, which is it?

S. CLAY: I don't know what it means. (Accused hiccups) Slatternly. I don't know what it means. (Accused hiccups)

CHILZER: It means, you were dressed and painted little better than a street prostitute, child. You know what a prostitute is presumably?

S. CLAY: (Accused hiccups)

CHILZER: Oh, this is quite impossible! Where on earth's he gone with that water?

(Accused hiccups)

C. CLAY: Try holding your breath, darling, that sometimes helps – sorry.

CLR. KRIFFIT: Press both your thumbs against your little fingers, that usually does it.
CLR. HARRAN: Swallow air, dear, imagine you're swallowing air...
CLR. DOBEN: I find sucking a lemon usually does the trick...

Monitor returns with glass of water for the accused.

CHILZER: Alright! That'll do, please! Now, drink that, girl. This has been a long day for all of us and we want to get home.

Accused sips water.

CHILZER: Is that better?
S. CLAY: Thank you.
CHILZER: Then, let's get on. Are you ready? Had you any prior knowledge of this assembly at the Tarness home on 16 Autumn?

Accused does not respond.

CHILZER: I will repeat that question. Had you any prior knowledge of that event on 16 Autumn?

Accused does not respond.

CHILZER: Had you or hadn't you? Yes or no?
S. CLAY: (Hiccups)
CHILZER: I will take that as a yes.
CLERK: The Council briefly conferred at this point. Accused continues to hiccup.

CLR. HARRAN: Try drinking from the wrong side of the glass.

C. CLAY: Just hold your breath, Soween, darling, that's the only way.

Accused holds breath.

CHILZER: Very well. We have considered. Soween Clay, we feel you have played a comparatively minor role in all this and have decided to deal leniently with you. You should be aware, though, that you have been guilty of a serious crime. You admit to being knowingly Unprotected in the presence of a Vulnerable Male. You also admit foreknowledge of this event and your failure to raise the alarm and possibly prevent it has led to the needless and painful death of your own brother. In view of your age and the distress you have already undergone, we are sentencing you to the minimum permitted under The Preacher's law. Tomorrow morning, you will report to – Oh, for heaven's sake! Catch her, someone!

Cllr. Chilzer then adjourned the meeting.

FROM SOUTH SARUM VILLAGE COUNCIL MINUTES
7 WINTER. INTERROGATION OF GIELLA TARNESS
(PART 1)

The accused was read the list of charges against her, including the charge of Primary Contact. She was then asked if she understood them.

TARNESS: Yes.

CHILZER: (Chair) Are you prepared to tell us the whole truth?

TARNESS: Yes.

CHILZER: And are you willing to swear on The Book of Certitude so to do?

TARNESS: No, I am not. I don't recognise that stupid book! It's total nonsense and pernicious rubbish and every copy should be burnt –

CHILZER: I should warn you, young woman, if you continue in that vein, you will not be helping your case one little bit. Any more of that and you will be facing an additional charge of Blasphemy.

TARNESS: I don't care –

CHILZER: Giella, I should advise you that you are currently facing a charge of Primary Contact which, should you be found guilty, carries the death penalty.

TARNESS: I don't care! If Elihu is dying then I'm ready to die, too. You can kill me, as well, as far as I'm concerned! I don't care any more. I've no further reason for living, if he's gone, let me die too! I loved Elihu more than my own life. So go ahead, you can take it! Take it!

CHILZER: Will you be quiet or I'll have you removed
from the Chamber!

TARNESS: I want to see my parents! I demand to see
my parents! I refuse to talk to you until I've seen
my parents! What have you done with them? Where
have you taken them?

CHILZER: Monitors! Please remove the accused from
the Chamber, immediately!

TARNESS: I refuse to say anything until I've seen
my parents! I want to see my parents, do you hear?

The meeting was temporarily adjourned at this
point.

Part Two of the same day.

As I say, I can remember little of my trial but I recall waking up in the hallway outside the Chamber on a bench with Mama beside me anxiously holding my hand and rubbing my wrist. I'd fainted apparently during proceedings. On the way home Mama actually held me by the hand. Progress, anyway! I think she actually felt sorry for me a little. We actually spoke to each other just like the old days and later I helped her prepare supper for the three of us. When Mapa returned, the atmosphere cooled slightly as she handed me the official court leaflet, detailing the terms and conditions of my punishment. She advised me to read it and to thoroughly digest it before I went to sleep because at dawn I had to report to the Village Square. Supper was almost back to normal, though, over all of us, was a reminder that Elihu was no longer eating next door in the living room. Nor ever would again. Later, I sat in my room and read through the details and terms of my punishment. I had to learn the first fifty names on the Men's Memorial, consecutively and accurately. At the end of the first day, I'd be expected to recite the fifty faultlessly in the presence of two Monitors. If I made a mistake or seriously hesitated, I'd be sent home and would have to start the process over again the following day. After three successive days of failure, I would be beaten and then have to continue the following day. As soon as I'd committed the first fifty names to memory, I'd then need to start on the second fifty names with the same rules and regulations applying. Only, this time, at the end of the day I would be expected to recite the full hundred I'd learnt so far. Three failures and—whack! And so on and so on, till on the last day, the full three hundred!. What had seemed a fairly daunting task suddenly looked impossible. Thank you, kind Gentlewomen of the Council, for choosing to deal with me so leniently!

FROM SOUTH SARUM VILLAGE COUNCIL MINUTES
8 WINTER. INTERROGATION OF GIELLA TARNESS
(PART 2)

The meeting was re-convened and the accused re-cautioned.

CHILZER: (Chair) Having met and talked with your parents are you prepared to answer questions regarding your part in the infection of Elihu Clay?
TARNESS: Yes.
CHILZER: Then, let's proceed immediately. We've already lost far too much time, as it is. Let the record show I am now handing over further questioning to Cllr. Grosh. Councillor, please proceed.
GROSH: Thank you, Chair. Ms Tarness, how long had you known Elihu Clay?
TARNESS: All my life. Ever since Infant School.
GROSH: I meant more recently than that. How long, would you say, from the time he was removed from school and taken into private Tutorage? When do you first recall seeing him after that?
TARNESS: I first saw him when he was swimming in the pool in the Woods with his Tutor.
GROSH: How old would you have been at that time?
TARNESS: Me? Not sure. About twelve, I suppose.
GROSH: And how old would he have been at that time?
TARNESS: About eleven or twelve, I think.
GROSH: You say you saw him? How did you happen to see him? Were you just passing by whilst he was swimming?

TARNESS: No, we spied on him.

GROSH: You spied on him, you say? Were you alone when you did this?

TARNESS: No, there were several of us there.

GROSH: How many is several?

TARNESS: About three or four of us. I'm not naming anyone, if that's what you're getting at.

GROSH: So there were three or four of you spying on him as he was swimming with his Tutor? Is that correct? And how were they swimming?

TARNESS: I don't know. Breaststroke? Dog paddle? I really can't remember –

GROSH: That was not the point of my question, Ms Tarness! I must warn you not to be facetious and to answer my questions seriously.

TARNESS: Sorry, I've no idea what you mean, how were they swimming?

GROSH: I'll rephrase the question. How were they dressed while they were swimming?

TARNESS: They weren't dressed at all, they were both naked.

GROSH: And how did that make you feel, seeing them both naked?

TARNESS: Well, it made me feel a bit randy, really. Especially Elihu. He had a gorgeous body, for a twelve-year-old. It would have got most women cooking, I reckon. Even you, possibly.

CHILZER: Ms Tarness, I won't tell you again about insubordination –

GROSH: Thank you, Chairman. Ms Tarness, your attitude is not helping your case one little bit.

TARNESS: Well, you asked me how I felt, I told you.

GROSH: And when was the next time you saw Elihu

Clay, do you recall?

TARNESS: It must have been two or three years later. It was certainly after he'd been Suited. He must have been about sixteen or so.

GROSH: Which would have made you about the same age?

TARNESS: Roughly, I'm slightly older than him. But only a bit. He'd taken to swimming alone, after he'd lost his first Tutor. He used to go down to the Pool on his own and, when he thought no one was looking, he'd take off his suit and swim for a bit.

GROSH: Again, he would have been swimming completely naked.

TARNESS: Yes, of course, why the hell do you think I went?

CHILZER: Ms Tarness!

GROSH: But he wasn't swimming alone, was he? You were spying on him again, weren't you? How long did this go on with you secretly watching him?

TARNESS: Until I let him know I was there. He got out of the Pool one day and saw me, across the other side.

GROSH: So you deliberately showed yourself to him? Were you fully dressed?

TARNESS: Yes, of course I was. And then we both got talking.

GROSH: And visored? Were you wearing your visor, during this?

TARNESS: No. As I say, I was on the other side of the Pool, well away from him.

GROSH: And this continued for how long? With him one side of the Pool and you the other?

TARNESS: Well, he wanted to draw me, he was a brilliant artist, and he wanted to do a sketch of me. So I sat on the other side of the Pool, posing for him for a bit. But I was too far away for him to draw me properly, so I moved a bit closer.

GROSH: How much closer?

TARNESS: About halfway round the Pool, I suppose. I was still a good safe distance from him.

GROSH: And you kept all your clothes on during this period?

TARNESS: Yes, of course. Well, I may have loosened a few bits and pieces.

GROSH: Can you clarify what you mean by "bits and pieces"?

TARNESS: I may have exposed the odd shoulder.

GROSH: In other words, you presented yourself to him in a state of semi-dress?

TARNESS: If you want to call showing a shoulder, semi-dress.

GROSH: I believe most of us in this room would call it that, apart from you, Ms Tarness.

TARNESS: Then you're a bunch of prudes, aren't you!

CHILZER: Ms Tarness! This is positively your final warning!

GROSH: Go on, Ms Tarness. What happened next?

TARNESS: Well, it was a very hot summer and the closer I got to him, the hotter Elihu seemed to get. I can't think why that could have been! He'd taken to interrupting his drawing and jumping into the pool to cool down. Finally, it looked so tempting I decided to do the same. So I jumped in with him.

GROSH: Fully clothed? Were you fully clothed?

TARNESS: Of course not, I had this great heavy dress on! I took that off first.

GROSH: So you were both of you naked in this pool?

And then what happened?

TARNESS: Well, we kissed.

GROSH: You kissed? Do you recall who initiated this kiss? I would advise you to think very carefully before you answer that, Ms Tarness.

TARNESS: (after a pause) I suppose I did.

GROSH: You did? You admit then to initiating the first kiss between you? Even though you knew he was bound to become infected?

TARNESS: But that was the point. He didn't become infected, did he? That's the whole point!

GROSH: Not then he didn't, Ms Tarness, but what about later on? You recklessly continued this relationship for your own selfish personal gratification, multiplying the risks of him becoming infected, without regard for his safety, in pursuit of pure sexual greed? You appreciate, Ms Tarness, that that is tantamount to an admission of guilt?

TARNESS: Well, one of us had to. It certainly wasn't going to be him, poor darling. He'd have just carried on gawping at me with his mouth open, bless him.

GROSH: So then what happened?

TARNESS: What the hell do you think happened? We ****** each other, of course!

CHILZER: Have that deleted from the record!

GROSH: You mean you both indulged in sexual congress?

TARNESS: Putting it politely.

GROSH: Which you freely admit to initiating and encouraging?

TARNESS: Yes, of course I did! Not that he needed

much encouragement, not once we got going. He
stood there with an ******** the size of the Men's
Memorial and I lay down and spread my legs and
then we ***** and we ***** each other till we were
both senseless.

Uproar as several Councillors interject at this
point.
CHILZER: Order! Order! Order! Monitors please
remove the accused from the Chamber! This session
is adjourned until further notice.

End of court record.

DIARY OF SOWEEN CLAY, 8TH DAY OF WINTER
(IN MY SIXTEENTH YEAR)

Well I did it! I had to get up at **dawn**, as soon as it was light enough to be able to even see The Memorial, let alone read the names and I joined the others in the Square and we started memorising the names starting with the A's. During the course of the day I realised that I had been fortunate. Probably due to my age, along with Sassa and Silje, suddenly three hundred seemed a reasonable target. Whereas for Molwin, Yoteez and Axi (ha! ha! hooray!), being a year or so older, they were expected to learn five hundred, fifty a day over ten days. God help them! Of Giella, there was no sign. Molwin told me she'd heard rumours that Giella's trial had been extended into today. And that her parents had both been sentenced to be publicly flogged and do compulsory hard labour. On top of that, their home had been searched and all illegal items (most of the contents in fact!) had been confiscated and the place generally trashed by the Monitors. I thought of Giella's secret shelf and all those books I had yet to read and thought that they too had probably been destroyed. What could there be left of their beautiful home? Practically nothing, poor things. I feel very sad for them. What on earth's happening to Giella? Why have they extended her trial? It doesn't sound good for her. At dusk, the Monitors arrived and made each of us, one by one, recite our daily lesson. Amazingly I got through it, all fifty names, without a single hesitation! As did Axi and most of the others. Only Sassa failed, losing her concentration and pulling up after only ten names and then wailing pathetically that she couldn't do it, at which point she was sent home. Tomorrow she has to start again, one out of her three chances gone, only two to go, kid. I walked home in the dusk, with a slight feeling of triumph but still worrying a little bit about Giella. But, on the brighter side, I had survived the first day. I knew it would get harder, though, as the days went by, with tomorrow having to learn the next fifty and, at the end of the day, the prospect of reciting the full hundred I'd learnt so far. Mind you, if I just take it one day at a time, I tell myself I can easily do it. (But I don't think even I believe me!)

OPEN LETTER FROM CLLR HORK TARNESS TO
ALL MEMBERS OF SOUTH SARUM VILLAGE COUNCIL.
DATED 7 WINTER

Fellow Councillors,

If I may so address you for I realise I have already, technically at least, ceased to be one of you, though I have yet to receive the official letter confirming my disbarment from the South Sarum Council. However, after nearly six years service to the Village, I feel I am still very much one of you. I am writing this from a prison cell in North Sarum. My partner, Desollia, is in a separate cell along the passage from me. As you already know, my membership of South Sarum Council requires that we both be tried not by you my colleagues and peers but by the Wiltshire Regional Court. We have recently been tried and have both spoken separately and together in our own and each other's defence and now await confirmation of our sentences. In my personal case, I anticipate it will be rigorously punitive, although I pleaded on behalf of Desollia that her role in all this was a comparatively minor one. After all she did no more than any birth mother would in support of her partner's public career. I want it to be known that all blame for this rests entirely with me. I have been guilty of unpardonable errors of judgement throughout my dealings as a Councillor engaging, on numerous occasions, in disreputable tactics to secure votes to further my own materialistic pet causes, many of them in strict contradiction to Preacher's Law. Fellow Councillors, I wish to apologise wholeheartedly to every one of you, most especially to those members of the Orthodox Party who have borne the brunt of my frequent, wholly unjustified attacks. I beg you all to find it in your hearts to forgive me, if you can. In the light of our past history and of my own indefensible behaviour, I realise the enormity of such a plea. I understand, though, that forgiveness is at the core of Orthodox belief especially afforded to one who is as truly penitent as I am. Finally, although our respective fates, Desollia's and mine, have already been decided, I am aware that the future of our beloved daughter, Giella, rests with you. Following the terrible tragic death of Elihu Clay, I understand she is facing a charge of Primary Contact. I beseech you to look upon her case with as much leniency as you can. I know she loved Elihu more than her own life and I assure you his loss has drained all joy and hope from her young heart. None of us can truly know what degree of pain this 17-year-old girl must be suffering at this time. It is simply beyond imagining. The evidence against her is surely circumstantial and to punish her further for an act of love, however misguided, is surely wrong. I beg you to have mercy on my child.

Your friend and colleague,
Hork Tarness

FROM SOUTH SARUM VILLAGE COUNCIL MINUTES
9 WINTER. INTERROGATION OF GIELLA TARNESS
(PART 3)

The full Council having reassembled, the accused,
Giella Tarness was brought before them for sentencing.

CHILZER: Giella Tarness, I want you to know that
this has been one of the most difficult decisions
any of us has ever had to make. There is not a
single member of this Council who has not needed
to search deep in her heart before deciding this.
The most serious charge laid against you is that
of Deliberate and Wilful Primary Contact with a
Vulnerable Male, with the deliberate intention of
causing his Infection and death. It is our feeling
that you have said nothing in your defence which
would serve to mitigate this charge. Indeed, it
could be argued that you have virtually confessed
your full guilt. By your own admission, you did
with an almost cold-blooded calculation, plot and
scheme over a period of several years, to ensnare
a young, Vulnerable Male whom subsequently you
then ruthlessly seduced, employing every wile and
stratagem at your disposal in the knowledge that
the end result would surely end a young Man's
promising life. All this to satisfy your selfish,
sexually driven desires –
TARNESS: That's a ******* lie!
CHILZER: Be quiet –!
TARNESS: – you're making it all sound cheap and

sordid! It wasn't like that!
CHILZER: I said, be quiet –!
TARNESS: – we were in love, really in love!
Something none of you can understand, you dried
up, frustrated bunch of finger *******
CHILZER: Ms Tarness, if you refuse to be quiet, I
shall ask the Monitors to gag you! Now be quiet! BE
QUIET!

Accused is silent, clearly overcome and distressed.

CHILZER: It is now my duty to pass sentence upon
you. Giella Tarness you have been found guilty
of Deliberate and Wilful Primary Contact with a
Vulnerable Male sufficient to cause his Infection
and death. You were advised at the start of these
proceedings that this still merited the death
sentence which I am now bound to carry out upon
you. You will forthwith be taken from here to be
fitted with a Ten Day Collar. During the days you
wear it, you will do well to remember with remorse
the ten final agonising days of suffering that
your heartless behaviour has caused your victim.
You are dismissed.

DIARY OF SOWEEN CLAY, 9TH DAY OF WINTER
(IN MY SIXTEENTH YEAR)

As soon as it was daylight, I was back in the Square at the Memorial with the others to learn my next fifty names to add to the fifty I'd learnt yesterday. We all stood each of us apart and separate, as we had done yesterday, each of us muttering over and over under our breath our ever increasing lists attempting to drum them into our heads. We needed to stand during our learning since the few seats in the Square were too far away for us to read the inscriptions properly. So it became a question of standing close enough to read them and then, when your legs gave out, to go and sit and repeat what you'd learnt so far. The weather was turning colder, too. All in all, these were turning out to be the most miserable of days. I only hope I get through it in the six days allocated and didn't have to endure repeats, as Sassa was having to do today. Pale and tearful, she clings to an increasingly irritated Axi for support. At this rate, I doubt Sassa will fare much better with her second attempt. I'm beginning to feel almost sorry for her! But at dusk, when the Monitors arrived to test us, instead it was me I should have been feeling sorry for. I stumbled midway through the first fifty before I'd even reached the new names I'd learnt today. Somewhere between Abberford and Atkins, for heaven's sake! My mind went a complete blank. Probably the result of not sufficiently revising the previous day's work. As a result, I was sent home and will have to relive today all over again. The others, so far as I know, seemed to get through their second fifty without a problem. Apart from Sassa who again failed midway through and was sent home to try again tomorrow which of course will be her third and final chance.

At the rate she's deteriorating, I'm concerned she'll ever make it. What will happen then? They can't beat her to death surely, can they? Not even Sassa deserves that! As I was walking home I passed the edge of the Woods and I saw someone standing on the grass just inside the trees, like a pale ghost. It was Giella looking so desperate and sad and staring at me in a terrible way, shaking her head as if saying, I'm sorry, I'm so sorry. But my attention was drawn to the narrow steel collar she was wearing around her neck. Shining from the front of it, were ten tiny sharp points of light. Instinctively, I moved towards her making as if to embrace and comfort her but, the moment she saw me approaching, she turned and ran off into the trees. Search as I did, I was unable to find her. When I got home, I told Mama what I'd just seen. She nodded in satisfaction, muttering that it served the little minx right, it was what she deserved. At supper, I didn't dare mention it to Mapa, knowing exactly what she'd say. After all, she'd been in large part responsible for persuading The Council to pass such a sentence, presumably. Upset as I was at losing my darling Elihu, I couldn't see the logic in taking another life as well, especially not one as beautiful as Giella's. Last night I hardly slept, unable to get out of my mind the memory of that terrible image. Those ten little lights, gleaming in the darkness, as her life ticked away inside that wicked collar, second by second. Oh God how can I sleep? I must sleep or I'll end up like Sassa.

From: Senior Administrator (South)
To: Senior Administrator (North)
Subject: South Sarum Village Council
Date: 10th Day of Winter

Dear Donal,
The attached letter from Talyed Chilzer, Chair of
the South Sarum Village Council, I feel, speaks for
itself. As you will see, despite my best efforts to
dissuade them (and, believe me, I really did try)
the South Sarum Council have voted to go ahead
and yesterday passed the death sentence on Giella
Tarness. She was apparently fitted with a Ten Day
Collar (yes, they do still exist) on 9 Winter, that
same day. The Collar is not due to finally close until
dawn on 19 Winter and, provided the girl doesn't
choose to do away with herself before, we still have
some leeway.
Although of course, as Senior Administrator, I am
empowered ultimately to override such matters, I'm
normally reluctant to intercede in individual Council
decisions. Traditionally the Villages here in the
South jealously maintain their independence from
federal authority. If necessary, of course I will
intercede but I need to know first whether you would
approve such an action. I am loath to take such a
decision unilaterally.
The situation is further complicated in that it
appears to be politically loaded, as well. The girl's
parents, former Councillor Hork and Desollia Tarness,
are both leading members of the local Progressive
Party. Currently they are both in prison, having been
found guilty of all manner of offences and, following

the confiscation of their property, are currently
awaiting public flogging and two years' hard labour.
One of Elihu Clay's parents, Kest Clay, is also a
Councillor but with extreme Orthodox views.
I fear this is potentially a powder keg. The severity
of the Tarness family's sentencing smacks strongly of
an impending vendetta. If their sentences are allowed
to stand, especially in the case of the girl's, it
could well promote a serious Progressive backlash.
That Party, as you are aware, has been gaining
strength over the past year or so and this situation,
were it to be exploited by them, could well upset the
current delicate balance between the two extremes.
In my view, the Progressives would welcome such an
opportunity.
As always, Donal, I welcome your wisdom and advice on
this matter.
With all good wishes as ever,

Senya
Senya Wahl
Senior Administrator (South)

DIARY OF SOWEEN CLAY, 10TH DAY OF WINTER
(IN MY SIXTEENTH YEAR)

Another dawn, another day in the Square. My second chance to deliver my first hundred names. I decided, learning from my lesson yesterday, to start by recapping the first, then revising my more recently learnt second fifty. By mid-afternoon, I felt confident I could master the challenge by the end of the day. Nonetheless I was nervous that, when standing isolated under the faceless gaze of the Monitors, I might fail again. Behind them each evening, I've noticed a small crowd has been starting to gather, cheering each success and jeering our failures. We are fast becoming, as I'm sure was intended, a source of free public entertainment. At midday, my prayers of the previous night were answered when unexpectedly the wraith-like figure of Giella appeared some distance away in a far corner of the Square. So intent were we on our learning, that it was some time before any of us noticed her. I'd no idea how long she'd been standing there. She looked even thinner and paler than when I'd seen her last night, with a deathly white face and dark rings under her eyes, as if she'd not slept. She was shivering slightly from the cold and I was sure she can't have eaten. Significantly, on her metal collar only nine lights were now shining. How much longer can she endure this torture, before she does something drastic? Eight whole days to go. Eight days with that thing ticking away round her neck, waiting for death. Surely they'd stop things before then? No one can be so cruel. I turned again to look for her but she'd gone. Despite my worries, I achieved my hundred names and went home with a great feeling of relief. But not before I'd seen Sassa fail again for the third time and be led away for punishment. Both Axi and Molwin achieved their hundred and fifty's but Yoteez and Silje failed and will need to return tomorrow for their second attempt. This evening, before I went home, I made a quick detour to Giella's house in the hope of finding her there. But the place was all shuttered up with Monitor's official tape sealing the doors and no one appeared to be home. Pressing my face to the windows I tried to see inside. Even in the gloom, I could make out the damage that had been done to their beautiful home. The furniture stripped of its bright covers, the patterned rugs removed from the floors, together with most of their decorations and Desollia's sculptures. Their once rich wall coverings had been painted over, crudely daubed with white paint. It was as if every attempt had been made to remove any trace of the soul of this once warm welcoming home. I know the family were guilty but this could hardly be right, could it? Such gleeful devastation couldn't be the answer, surely? People can be so spiteful and small!

From: Senior Administrator (North)
To: Senior Administrator (South)
Subject: South Sarum Village Council
Date: 11 Winter

Dear Senya,
This is fast developing, as we would say North of the
Divide, into a prize cock-up! For God's sake, Senya,
what the hell gets into these piddling little Village
Councils over your side?
The situation is somewhat more serious than you
realise and I will need to take matters to the very
top, to The Preacher's Office itself. Played wrongly,
this could easily bring the whole effing card house
crashing round our ears in which case the effluent
could well hit the air conditioning system.
Yes, by all means be ready to intercede but, please,
in view of the time we have left, leave me to consult
with Higher Authority first.
I'm sorry if I offend your sensibilities here, Senya,
but honestly, bloody Women!
Your somewhat pissed-off opposite number,

Donal
Senior Administrator (North)

DIARY OF SOWEEN CLAY, 11TH DAY OF WINTER
(IN MY SIXTEENTH YEAR)

———————

Another good day for me in the Square! I got through my hundred and fifty without a single pause or hesitation! I felt very pleased with myself and only came down to earth by remembering I was now only halfway through! I still have another hundred and fifty to go. Mustn't get too smug, Soween! Poor Sassa, though (she now has my every sympathy and all is forgiven) arrived late this morning, obviously shaken from her punishment yesterday, walking quite stiffly and awkwardly. But again, despite attempts from Axi and others (including myself!) to coach her, she's continuing to struggle. She's either unable to cope with the pressure or she's a memory like a sieve! She was never the brightest of buttons in the box, dear Sassa! Today she can still barely remember the first ten names, let alone the first fifty she's still trying to master. I think one of her problems, too, is the crowd that continues to gather in greater and greater numbers each evening. They've begun to single her out as some sort of fall girl, treating her as a particular source of amusement, one they can goad and taunt and make fun of. Under the circumstances, it's amazing she can concentrate at all, since her faltering recitation can hardly be heard over the din from the audience. The Monitors, of course, remain impassive and do nothing to help her. What's more, Sassa's plight is proving a distraction for the others and, for the first time, first Axi and then Molwin failed on their first attempt to reach two hundred. All in all, I think I've escaped quite lightly so far. When I got home this evening, Mama greeted me with the news that 'that girl' had turned up at the front door as soon as I'd left. Mama had found her shivering on the doorstep. I presumed by 'that girl' she was referring to Giella. I asked if Mama had let her into the warm. Mama replied, no, she'd shut the door in the trollop's face! I was horrified. How could she? I told Mama if Giella called again to let her in and what was she thinking of, leaving her out there in the cold?

Rather wickedly, during the past couple of days, underneath my black dress, I've taken to wearing my white bridesmaid's outfit! The full works—minus tights and shoes or the killer bra, of course. Apart from giving me a good feeling of thumbing my nose at the Monitors and helping to keep me warm, too, also in some way it brings me closer to Giella in her time of need. Pathetic gesture, but what the hell? What must she be going through, poor darling. I think I may even risk staying home tomorrow to wait and see if she calls again. On the other hand, I'd miss a whole day in the Square and get badly behind with my learning and risk a beating. Am I brave enough to risk the wrath of the Monitors? Tomorrow will tell.

HANDWRITTEN LETTER FROM CHAYZA CLAY
TO RUDGRIN OBOLOS, DATED 11 WINTER

———————

Dear Mr Rudgrin,
forgive me writing to you and I know it must seem impurtinint after the way you were got rid of from our house. My partner as you know is very orthodox and strict and believes everything has to be done by the book of certitude which is right and proper but it is difficult to live that way all the time. I wanted you to know that if I had my way you would still be here teaching my darling Elihu who we all miss very much. I know from your time here that you and he were friendly and the three of us had some happy times together and I hope good meals as well. But now he is in North Sarum hospitol with the Plague and he has only a few days to live as he was infected by a wicked girl from the village Giella Tarness who I shall never never forgive the trolop for doing that to him. She has been sentenced today and serve her right, I say. But as his friend if you have time and he only has a few days left to live if you could go in see him in the hospitol and stand near to him so he feels he has a friend with him it will help his passing a little. I would be very grateful if you could do me this favour as I know like me you love him very much and would not want to see him suffer any more than he has to. I would go to the hospitol myself only I am not allowed to though I have begged them to let me lots of times. I miss him so much and think of him every minute of the day.
Thank you and please forgive my spelling but I was never properly educated like my partner was.

Yours in friendship,
Elihu's Mama, Chayza Clay

PS: I found your adress among his things when I was cleaning out his room after he'd gone. I hope you don't mind me writing. CC.

CONFIDENTIAL
From: Senior Administrator (North)
To: Chief Medical Officer, North Sarum Hospital
Subject: Enquiry re Elihu Clay
9 Winter

Dear Vint,
Just an enquiry re the condition of Elihu Clay. How's he doing?
Regards,

Donal

PS are you coming to Marcus's bash next week? Sounds like it's going to be quite something! Berry and I would love to see you both.

DIARY OF SOWEEN CLAY, 12TH DAY OF WINTER
(IN MY SIXTEENTH YEAR)

I didn't have the courage to stay at home. When I woke this morning, the prospect of facing two hundred names by the end of the day, made me hurry out again to the Square. I don't know why I hurried, really. I failed again! I was so angry with myself. How would I forget Cobham, E. S. Cobham. Cobham! Cobham! Cobham! Write it out a hundred times, idiot! Now I've lost another day. Axi completely lost her temper this afternoon. At the end of the session, she was midway through her recitation and hesitated slightly. The crowd jeered at her, of course, and Axi in a sudden fit of fury charged at them, fists flying. As they all scattered, the Monitors restrained Axi and held her until she'd recovered and then sent her home. God knows what's in store for her tomorrow, I dread to think. When I got home Mama told me Giella had called again only this time she came round to the back door and Mama apparently this time spoke to her and told her she wasn't welcome but still didn't let her into the house! Even though I'd told her to. Giella just stood there on the back step saying over and over again that she was sorry, forgive her, she was sorry. Mama said she drove her mad with her whining and that she was about to send for the Monitors and the next thing Giella was being sick and throwing up all over the clean doorstep which was the final straw as far as Mama was concerned and so she went straight to fetch Mapa from her surgery, to deal with the wretched girl herself. And Giella and Mapa had a long talk together outside and then Mapa took Giella back to the surgery but Mama couldn't for the life of her think why she'd bothered, the sooner the girl died, the better! A little later, Mapa came home looking extremely grim and distracted. But, despite all my questions concerning Giella and her condition, all Mapa would say is that there'd been a worrying development. By tomorrow morning Giella will have only six lights remaining on her collar. As usual, before falling asleep, instead of sheep, I ran through the first hundred and fifty names in preparation for my second attempt at the two hundred.

From: Chief Medical Officer, North Sarum Hospital
To: Senior Administrator (North)
Subject: Enquiry re Elihu Clay
Date 12 Winter

Dear Donal,
Thanks for yours. Sorry not to get back to you
sooner but yesterday was Passing Out Day here at
the Hospital when all our young probationary nurses
finally get their qualifications. It's always a moving
ceremony and this year we've had a particularly
bright bunch of chaps.
As to your enquiry, Young Elihu is doing fine. He's
now, though still a little weak, sitting up and
taking nourishment and is rapidly recovering from the
after-effects of the EIS Procedure. Considering it's
classed as a so-called simulation and classified as
harmless, it's still a hell of an ordeal for someone
to go through even for a young man as fit as he is.
Almost, but not quite, as bad as the real thing,
though God spare us from ever going through that
again.
Still, he's fine and he'll be more than ready, in a
day or two, to go where ever you want to send him.
Presumably straight into an apprenticeship of some
kind, since we can hardly send him home again, can
we?
As is customary in these cases, and you'll appreciate
in recent years there have been precious few of them,
he's going to need a spot of counselling to get him
over the shock of finding himself still alive! Equally
he'll need to get over the trauma of his unusually
abrupt departure and the realisation that he will

never see friends and family again. It's always
more disturbing when you don't get the chance for
prolonged farewells and fond goodbyes. One minute
you're there, the next you're gone.
Not going to be able to make Marcus's bash, alas,
either of us. As from tomorrow we're off on holiday
for a month. You're not the only ones who have
holidays! Not before time, I may add. Zig, in
particular, has been working his butt off, rushing to
deliver the plans for his new mega building. Who'd be
an architect, eh?
Kind regards as always,

Vint
Vinton Heppinstall
Chief Medical Officer, North Sarum Hospital

DIARY OF SOWEEN CLAY, 13TH DAY OF WINTER
(IN MY SIXTEENTH YEAR)

Today, the worst happened and it started to rain, not heavily but that awful incessant drizzle which gradually soaks through you till you're reduced to a sodden, miserable lump. Axi arrived late and, as a result of her actions yesterday, was wearing restraints. Both her hands were fastened by a chain to a wide belt round her waist whilst her feet were shackled by a short metal bar attached to both her ankles, forcing her to take short steps and waddle a bit like a duck. It took several minutes for her even to reach the Memorial. I hope they hadn't made her walk all the way from home like that or she'd have had to have set out at midnight! Thankfully, various parents soon arrived, supportively with umbrellas and a few, including Mama bless her, with mugs of soup. They stayed with us as long as they dared but, fearful of breaking our concentration, they soon left us alone to continue with our repetitions. Mama promised to return at the end of the day to support my second attempt to reach two hundred. I didn't know whether that would make me even more nervous, but I appreciated her gesture, anyway. She told me Mapa never went to work today (which was extraordinary!) but cancelled all her appointments and stayed home, locked away in her study. Worrying about something, apparently. I thought perhaps it was as a result of her meeting with Giella yesterday. What could possibly have happened? Later on, would you believe it! I went and failed my two hundred! I was called up first to recite today and got stuck, this time by jumping from Cairns to Corcoran and missing out twelve whole names, idiot! I walked home with Mama, damp and dejected. I was doing so well, too! I didn't wait to see how the others got on after me but I'm pretty certain Sassa will have failed again. I thought again this evening about Giella. Tomorrow morning she would wake up, if she'd slept at all, with only five of her collar lights still lit. God knows where she's living these days. I heard earlier, before the rain came, that someone had deliberately set fire to the remains of their poor house and that it's now a charred ruin. People are so spiteful and vengeful! After all, it's us who've lost a son, a brother, not them. We haven't gone round setting fire to things, have we? We're civilised. I think it takes something like this to bring out the worst in our society. How could they do such a thing? More important, where are Giella's Mama and Mapa living now? They were sentenced to be flogged. And presumably they have been and are now doing their hard labour. I've no idea. I've been too busy in the Square over the past few days trying to avoid a flogging of my own. I hope they're alright. I guess, wherever they are, they must be as worried about Giella as I am, if not more so.

From: Senior Administrator (North)
To: The Preacher
Subject: A potential problem - South Sarum Village
Date: 14 Winter

I apologise for troubling you with a seemingly
trivial matter but I feel it is best to do so before
matters become more serious. I am attaching all
relevant correspondence regarding the matter to date
but briefly to summarise: -
A sixteen-year-old South Sarum boy, Elihu Clay, began
a clandestine relationship with a local girl, Giella
Tarness, of similar age. This was intercepted by the
local South Sarum Monitors on 16 Autumn. The Male
was immediately moved North of the Divide, the other
Female miscreants being left to be dealt with by the
local South Sarum Council.
As is customary with cases of suspected Wilful
Infection, North Sarum hospital initiated a standard
EIS procedure on the boy by way of sounding a
cautionary warning to all the Women concerned.
South Sarum Village Council, on the assumption that the
condition of Elihu Clay was critical, initiated capital
charges against Giella Tarness who was subsequently
found guilty on 9 Winter and placed in a Ten Day
Collar. She is currently entering her fifth day.
You will appreciate we face the dilemma of either
taking measures to halt the process and spare the
girl's life or of allowing it to continue and cause
her death by strangulation. Interrupting the Collar
might arouse suspicion but this we can allay somewhat
under the guise of exercising clemency.
There are also strong opposing factions involved

here, the Boy has devoutly Orthodox parents, whilst
the Girl's are radically Progressive. The latter are
already facing stringent punishment for their part in
the incident and the tension could well be worsened,
if the sentence on Giella Tarness is completed.
Senior Administrator (South) advises me that there is
a danger of a serious backlash, especially from the
Progressive Party who are currently strongly active
in that region.
I would respectfully request your guidance as to how
best to proceed.
I remain as ever your obedient servant,

Donal Portus
Senior Administrator (North)

DIARY OF SOWEEN CLAY, 14TH DAY OF WINTER
(IN MY SIXTEENTH YEAR)

Again, a day of mixed blessings! The good news is that I sailed through my two hundred this time, effortlessly! Well, apparently effortlessly – in fact, I put so much effort into it, I think, once all this is over, I shall need to lie down for two months, my brain is buzzing so much with names of men, long dead but who will, certainly in the case of this person anyway, never be forgotten! Is there a limit I wonder to how much the brain can hold during a lifetime? If it's finite, then I'm using up valuable space with all this. Don't they realise they could possibly be blunting the intellect of a major novelist? I bet Emily and Charlotte never had to go through this. Which reminds me, I must get back to Wuthering Heights as soon as I'm able to. I badly want to know what happens to Cathy. I hope she ends up happily like dear Jane did. But I have a nasty feeling she doesn't! Emily's got an altogether darker streak in her nature, I suspect. Mapa continues to be secretive and silent and has been ever since her meeting two days ago with Giella. She's never told us what happened between them. Why does no one ever let me in on secrets? I said this to Mama. But she said, typically of course that there were certain things best left to Mapa and that I should be grateful. I'm not sure now, when I'm older, that I want to be a Mama anymore. I'd prefer to be a Mapa and then I can at least be let in on what is going on. Mind you, if I'm ever going to become a Mapa, I've yet to find myself a Mama, haven't I? Some hope of that! Now I'm standing out there every day in the Square, exposed to public ridicule, that probably classifies me as soiled goods! Tomorrow, I will wake up and try for two hundred and fifty names, whilst Giella will wake up with only four lights left shining. I know which I'd prefer.

From: Cllr Kest Clay
To: Talyed Chilzer, Chair, South Sarum Village Council
Cc: All Members
Subject: Important discovery regarding Giella Tarness
Date 14 Winter

Dear Talyed,
I am sorry to raise this unfortunate matter again
but, in my capacity as a doctor, I had cause to
examine Giella Tarness on 12 Winter, resulting from
which I have made a serious discovery. Giella Tarness
is pregnant. A fact that, until I advised her of
it, she was completely unaware of, although the
foetus is I estimate at least six weeks' developed.
The repercussions arising from this are, naturally,
very serious. Not least because, were her sentence
allowed to run its full term, we would be guilty of
terminating not only the girl's life, but that of her
unborn child.
On these grounds alone, I urge you to repeal the
death sentence recently passed on Giella Tarness. Due
to the relatively advanced state of her pregnancy it
would also seem extremely unlikely that the Infection
of my son Elihu occurred at the time of their first
contact. It would strongly suggest, on the contrary,
that he was infected later probably at the time of
the gathering on 16 Autumn at the Tarness home when,
by all accounts, he was unprotected and in close
proximity to at least eight unvisored women.
Logically therefore, it follows we should be passing
death sentences on all the females involved at that
event (apart of course from Giella Tarness, herself)
since the supposition that Infection occurred on

16 Autumn is considerably more probable, given the comparatively recent date when his illness was diagnosed.

Since it is clearly futile, at this stage, to attempt to ascertain which other person or persons might have infected Elihu, I would strongly urge you to abandon the hope of finding an alternative culprit but straightaway release Giella Tarness who is palpably not guilty.

I appreciate the irony that, only a few days ago, I was the most vociferous among you in calling for Giella Tarness to face the maximum penalty for her actions but, in the light of recent events, I urgently request that the Council reverses its decision as soon as is humanly possible.

Yours sincerely,

Kest Clay
Councillor

From: Talyed Chilzer, Chair, South Sarum Village
Council
To: Cllr Kest Clay
Cc: All Members
Subject Important discovery regarding Giella Tarness
Date 15 Winter

Dear Kest,

Thank you for your letter. You realise, of course,
that were I to accede to your request, this would
place the Council in a most invidious position.
You will fully appreciate the anguish and general
searching of consciences that went on during the
recent debate before reluctantly finding Giella Tarness
guilty. Passing the death sentence upon her was no
easy decision for any of us and, as I'm sure you're
only too aware, was contrary to many Councillors'
strong beliefs regarding the sanctity of life. Indeed
it was largely due to the passion and eloquency with
which you personally (along with Cllr Grosh) presented
the case for the maximum penalty arising from your own
tragic personal involvement which persuaded many of us
to vote in favour.

One of the most telling points you made was that
inflicting such a deterrent sentence would serve to
prevent future similar tragedies, as happened to your
own son Elihu, from occurring again.

I have taken a sounding amongst the majority of
Council members and there is an overwhelming feeling,
distressing though this is, that there is little
to be gained by reversing our original sentence on
Giella Tarness. On the contrary, any going back at
this stage may well be interpreted on our part, in

these uncertain political times, as a display of
vacillation and weakness.
I am sorry to disappoint you, but the sentence must,
in my view, be upheld.
Yours sincerely,

Talyed
Chair
South Sarum Village Council

DIARY OF SOWEEN CLAY, 15ᵀᴴ DAY OF WINTER
(IN MY SIXTEENTH YEAR)

So much has happened today, that sitting here this evening, I don't really know where to start. From complaining yesterday that I was never let in on things, today I feel I've been let in on far too much, thank you! First, the news that I reached two fifty! I am now left with fifty names to go till the end of my punishment. But judging from the events that occurred later, I've no idea whether I'll be made to finish it or not. Sassa managed her first fifty (at long last!) But today she failed to do her hundred. Axi again arrived waddling in her shackles. She seemed very subdued as if it was all starting to get to her. Midway through the day, I noticed a stream of liquid flowing out from under her dress and I realised, shackled as she was, she'd been unable to make it to the public toilets, even if she'd managed to do anything about it when she got there! At the end of the day, I saw her actually crying. Axi, crying! That must surely be a first! Naturally she failed again. I feel almost sorry for her. Almost, but not quite! First Giella, then Axi, they're breaking all our spirits, one by one. But not mine! Jane Eyre lives! As far as I can tell, the others are all doing fine with Molwin well on her way to her five hundred. When I got home, Mapa gathered Mama and me in the kitchen and we sat round whilst she told us what had been concerning her over the past two days. After she'd taken Giella back to her surgery three days ago, she'd discovered Giella was six weeks pregnant. So whoever had infected Elihu, it hadn't been her. We'd assumed all along it was Elihu who was Immune but clearly that wasn't the case. He'd been infected like any ordinary man. Historically, the rapid rate with which the Plague symptoms developed suggested he was almost certainly infected on the night of the party. Besides Giella, there were eight other women present, any single one of whom could have infected him. Mapa looked at me and said that included me and that I might have been responsible for killing my own brother. Oh God, I'm a possible murderer now, guilty of fratricide (I had to look that up!) By this time tomorrow I could find myself wearing a Collar, perhaps even two Collars, who knows? Watching their lights slowly being extinguished! Another sleepless night!

FROM THE OFFICE OF THE PREACHER
From: Marzin Deffling, Chief Secretary to the Preacher
To: Donal Portus, Senior Administrator (North)
Subject: Re: A potential problem - South Sarum
Village
Date: 15 Winter

Dear Donal Portus,
I am instructed by the Preacher to reply to your
communication of 14 Winter. The Preacher wishes it to be
known that they are more than a little disturbed by your
communication and wonder why stronger action was not taken
earlier to avert this crisis.
Since the Girl in question, Giella Tarness, has only
days left to live, assuming she has not by this time
already taken her own life, she has the makings,
certainly seen through the eyes of dissident members
of the community, of becoming a martyr to their
unsettling cause unless immediate action is taken.
Two things must be done at once: -
1. Giella Tarness must be pardoned immediately. To
facilitate this, you are instructed to use the phrase
"due to the Preacher's merciful intervention" in all
public announcements.
2. It is felt that Elihu Clay will continue to
prove an embarrassment. The Preacher considers in
his case the premature decision for the use of EIS
procedure was ill-judged. The Preacher has thus
decided, reluctant as they are to lose a young Male
in his prime, that his life should be immediately
terminated. You will please instruct those
responsible at North Sarum Hospital to proceed with
this course of action. Since the assumption already

exists, certainly on the South side, that Clay is
deceased, the Preacher anticipates that this will
provoke the minimum social disruption.
Nonetheless, their feeling is that this whole
affair has been handled with a considerable lack
of forethought. You are instructed to initiate
straightaway the actions detailed in paragraphs 1 and
2, above, pending a full enquiry by this Office in due
course.
Yours sincerely,

Marzin Deffling
Chief Secretary to the Preacher

From: Donal Portus, Senior Administrator (North)
To: Talyed Chilzer, Chair, South Sarum Village
Council
Cc: All Members
Subject: Giella Tarness
15 Winter

Dear Talyed Chilzer,
The Office of the Preacher has instructed me to
inform you that, as of now, the capital sentence
recently passed by you on Giella Tarness, due to the
Preacher's merciful intervention, is to be rescinded.
Please ensure such action is taken immediately.
Sincerely,

Donal Portus
Senior Administrator (North)

From: Donal Portus, Senior Administrator (North)
To: Chief Medical Officer, North Sarum Hospital
Subject: Elihu Clay
15 Winter

Dear Vint,
God Almighty, the S has certainly hit the F and if
we're not very careful we're going to be covered in the
stuff for ever! Just had a very shirty letter from the
Preacher's office (attached), telling us we've effed up
big time.
I don't know who's running things up there these
days, that Preacher Committee rotates every few
months of course, but they're certainly a pretty
ruthless bunch of lads and lassies, if this is
anything to go by.
I enclose a copy of Marzin Deffling's letter to me.
Please note the instructions contained in paragraph
2, regarding the termination of Elihu Clay. Hope you
can facilitate this without causing too much pain to
the poor little bugger. I'm sure you will, but then
you medical chaps have a way with drugs, don't you!
In haste, best regards,

Donal
Senior Administrator (North)

PS Have you yet breached your case of the 112 yet?
If you haven't, you're in for a treat. It's drinking
superbly. D

DIARY OF SOWEEN CLAY, 16TH DAY OF WINTER
(IN MY SIXTEENTH YEAR)

At noon today, the Monitors came into the Square and told us to stop our learning and to report to the Village Hall immediately. Presumably the result of Mapa's emergency meeting earlier. Axi had her shackles removed and most of us, relieved but a little bit mystified, were trying to guess what had happened. Only I knew the truth or at least a small part of it. The six of us took our places in the centre of the Chamber, facing the committee of faceless women. WE were asked if we knew the whereabouts of Giella Tarness. But none of us had seen her for two days. We were told our punishments were suspended until further notice and that we were all to return to our homes immediately. But instead, we all milled around rather aimlessly in the Square, feeling a bit lost. Whilst none of us had actually enjoyed our recent ordeal, all that remorseless name-learning, day after day, now it had stopped so abruptly, I think we all rather missed it. Having conditioned ourselves to complete the task, it was more than a little frustrating! At least, that's the way it felt to me. So we stood like sheep, who'd unexpectedly been let out of our pen, waiting for someone to herd us, wondering what to do next. Someone suggested we should maybe start a search for Giella. But with her home completely destroyed, we had no idea where to start. Better left to the Monitors. With the Monitors, as my parents were fond of saying when we were little, there is nowhere to hide! So I went home early and surprised Mama who wasn't expecting me till later. I told her what had happened and how Giella had gone missing. Mama said grimly that it was her guilty conscience, that's why she was hiding. I don't think Mama will ever forgive Giella, somehow. She'll always hold her responsible. Mapa sent word that she was delayed at the Village Hall and wouldn't be home until late. So Mama and I sat alone eating in silence. There seems so little to say to each other, these days, until all this business has been resolved. Tonight, with no more names to learn for the time being, I tried to read a little more of Wuthering Heights. But I couldn't concentrate. I thought of Giella somewhere out there all alone, waking up tomorrow with just the three lights still glowing. I felt a little sick at the thought of it. God knows how she must be facing death with the knowledge there's a baby inside her. So I did something I haven't done since I was five. I prayed for her. I put my hands together, knelt down beside my bed and I prayed for sweet, innocent Giella.

To: Senior Administrator (North)
From: Walby Tibbifer, Acting Chief Medical Officer,
North Sarum Hospital
Subject: Elihu Clay
16 Winter

Dear Donal Portus,
Sorry not to have got back to you sooner regarding
your letter of 15 Winter, but I am standing in for
Vinton Heppinstall who is currently enjoying a well
earned holiday with his family.
As Vint's Acting Deputy, I read your instructions and
prepared to act upon them immediately, as per The
Preacher's instructions, regarding our patient, Elihu
Clay.
However, I am informed by the nursing staff that Mr
Clay is no longer on the premises. He apparently
left late yesterday together with his tutor, Rudgrin
Obolos, with the intention, so he informed our staff,
of resuming his interrupted studies.
All our best efforts to date, including alerting the
local Monitors, have as yet yielded no results as to
his location. I hope this is not in any way causing
you too much inconvenience.
If there's any other way in which I can assist you,
please don't hesitate to get in touch again.
Yours sincerely,

Walby Tibbifer,
Acting Chief Medical Officer, North Sarum Hospital

120 PD

UNDELIVERED. INTERCEPTED BY
STATION N5 NORTH DIVIDE TUNNEL.
HANDWRITTEN LETTER FROM RUDGRIN OBOLOS
TO CHAYZA CLAY, DATED 15TH WINTER

Dear Chayza,

Thank you for your letter of 1 Winter which I'm afraid I received rather late, hence my tardiness in replying. I fear the Monitors are intercepting most of my mail but, in the case of your letter, they evidently deemed it innocuous enough to allow it through. I was deeply touched by your sentiments and, of course, went straight away to North Sarum Hospital to visit Elihu, passing myself off as his Tutor (discreetly leaving off the 'ex' part!)

Anyway, imagine my surprise when I found him fit and well! Sitting on the side of his bed, reading every book he could lay his hands on, bored to tears. He'd clearly made a miraculous recovery from that terrible disease, so the doctors had told him. He certainly looked as good as ever. I told him all I knew about everything that had been happening in South Sarum since his absence (well as much as I could gather from your letter) including the awful accusation against poor Giella, blaming her for his apparent "death".

At this, he became very disturbed and urged me to help him leave the Hospital immediately. Despite my initial attempts to prevent him we finally made our way out via a series of service elevators and back corridors. I took him straight to my flat warning him it was certainly under observation and it wasn't safe for him to stay there for any length of time. He continued to insist on returning to the Village as soon as possible. I finally lent him one of my old Tutor's uniforms which I hoped would serve to get him safely through the Tunnel, providing the Monitors on duty weren't too alert.

Heaven knows if you'll even get this letter, dear Chayza. It's full of the most incriminating things and I'm sure the Monitors will confiscate *it, declaring it scurrilous and seditious! In which case, if you're reading this, enjoy it, you nosy bastards!*

I do hope things work out happily and satisfactorily for you all. I do miss you and think about you often. My love to Soween and of course to Kest, who I know never much approved of me but do tell her, I intended nothing but good for Elihu whom I'd grown to love very much, too, over the years.

> *With every good wish,*
> *Your good friend,*
> *Rudgrin*

DIARY OF SOWEEN CLAY, 18TH DAY OF WINTER
(IN MY SIXTEENTH YEAR)

Not having to get up quite so early again, I lay in bed late today spending the morning mooching about the house. Mid-morning two Monitors called and searched the house from top to bottom, every cupboard, under every bed, looking for Giella, I presume. They're probably doing this throughout the whole Village, house by house. They asked us again if we'd seen her but neither Mama nor I could enlighten them. Mama said she needed to go shopping but wouldn't be long. I considered offering to come with her but I decided, in her present depressed mood, she'd sooner I didn't. I think, in some way, I remind her too much of Elihu, the dead son she would have preferred to be still alive, as opposed to the irritating daughter she probably wished would drop dead. But perhaps I'm just being over-sensitive! Alone in the silent house, I was conscious of the clock as it ticked away Giella's remaining minutes. Oh please, find her! Somebody find her in time, please! I heard the front door opening and presumed it was Mama returning. But then I heard footsteps running along the passage and, a moment later, Elihu's bedroom door being flung open. I knew that could never be Mama! Then my own door burst open and I sat up, rather alarmed clasping the book to me, in a vain attempt to conceal the title for I assumed for a second that the white suited, visored figure standing in the doorway was a Monitor. Perhaps bringing news of Giella, who knew? But then he pushed back his visor to reveal his face. To my amazement, it was Elihu, shouting excitedly, "Where is she? Where's Giella?" I just stared at him. Speechless. But then it isn't every day you're confronted with the ghost of your dead brother dressed in a Tutor's uniform! A moment later,

I forgot any idea of him being a spectre, as he ran forward, seized me firmly by the shoulders and shook me to the roots of my wisdom teeth, all the time continually screaming at me, "Where is she? Where is she? Where is she?", over and over again till I had to scream back at him, "Stop it! Will you please stop doing that!"

Whereupon, he let go of me and stood in the middle of the room, as if trying to gather his thoughts. He was still panting and had obviously been running the length and breadth of the village. I had so many questions I wanted to ask him. Not least of all, How come you're still alive? But, just then, an idea seemed to occur to him and he turned sharply and rushed out of the front door before I could ask him anything. I ran after him, calling. But he was sprinting so fast he quickly left me far behind. I saw him running towards the Woods and soon he'd disappeared amongst the trees and, by the time I got there, he'd gone. And then it occurred to me where he must be heading. The cave! Of course, the hidden cave! Where Giella caught her first sight of Elihu, swimming with Rudgrin. That must have been the lovers' own secret hiding place, surely? It was growing darker as I began running in the direction of the Pool. When I reached it, there were several others grouped around the edges, Monitors, Villagers, including one or two of The Falcons. They were all standing staring at the water. Giella and Elihu, hand-in-hand were wading steadily and deliberately towards the centre of the Pool. Both of them were naked apart from Giella's collar on which one solitary light still shone. They reached the centre and turned to face each other. Elihu took Giella's face in his hands, drew her to him and then they kissed. Deeply. Passionately. Endlessly ... They both slowly stopped paddling with their feet as, continuing to embrace, they gradually sank beneath the surface until they were swallowed by the water. Then just a few bubbles and

THE DIVIDE

they were gone. Gone from all our lives for ever. There was a silence for several moments. I don't really know who started it. It might have been some sort of spontaneous mass reaction, that overcame us all at that moment. Silently, several of the Women, me included, removed our bonnets, allowing our hair to run free. Then several of them shrugged off their heavy black dresses, revealing their clothes they'd been wearing underneath, much of it brightly coloured. The rest of us began to join in and I finally got to show off my creased, slightly grubby bridesmaid's dress to the world — hooray! In the end, everywhere you looked it had become a festival of colour, reflecting in the Pool and lighting up the twilight. It was a moving sight! Lastly, wonder of wonders, the Monitors themselves, many of them Men, also raised their visors and threw back their hoods. Some of them were even quite good-looking! It was as if a miracle had occurred this evening around our Secret Pool. One which nobody who was there will ever forget.

END OF PART IV

Part V
AFTERMATH

REPORT BY CHIEF DIVER, SUB AQUA MONITOR TEAM,
S 46/D. 20 WINTER

My team assembled at first light to begin the search for the bodies of Giella Tarness and Elihu Clay. After several hours of continuous underwater activity, just before noon, the operation was abandoned. The pool has, at 6 metres depth, at approximately dead centre, a sinkhole into which excess water from the waterfall above is funnelled, this presumably in turn feeding into an underground stream below. The force of the current around the edge of this funnel is sufficiently powerful to drag down even the most powerful swimmer. Indeed, this was nearly the fate of one of our search team but for his safety line. It is therefore concluded, without further information as to the direction or path of the underground stream or river, both bodies must be presumed missing.

Recommended action: The fitting of a permanent grill over the sinkhole in order to prevent further accidents of a similar nature, whilst allowing free flow of the naturally accumulating excess water to continue.

JDW
Chief Diver

---

* *Author's note:* As the Chief Diver recommended, a fixed grill was fitted over the sinkhole in the Secret Pool which, of course, was no longer secret any more but became quite a famous pool. It was renamed Lovers' Pool and became, traditionally, over the years, a popular place for lovers of all types, Male and Male, Female and Female and yes, even Male and Female (!) to swim and pledge their love for each other. Very few of them bother with the niceties of costumes and thankfully, to date, no one has actually drowned!

There has incidentally, in recent years, arisen a charming if slightly fanciful legend, popular with children, that Giella and Elihu, having been drawn through the sinkhole and dropped into the river below, were then carried along the river's path, still locked in their embrace, till they reached the sea at Bournemouth Village. There they met the god Neptune who took pity on them and turned them into a merman and merwoman, complete with their merbaby. At nights, if you're very lucky, you may catch a glimpse of Giella as she sits on a rock, her tail tucked under, combing her hair and, round her neck, a collar with ten lights brightly shining.

CONFIDENTIAL

From: Mondrian L. Cazabeedis, Monitor 2nd Grade, SW Region

To: Dern Teak, Senior Monitor South West Region

Subject: Report on Discovery of Body of Doctor K Clay

Date: 20 Winter 120 PD

At 0820 this morning I received a call from the surgery of Doctors Clay and Zubin from Ms F Hakenfelt, receptionist. Apparently, the door to Doctor Clay's office was locked from the inside which was highly unusual and Ms Hakenfelt, having knocked and called through the door, had become alarmed at receiving no reply. Having arrived with my team and, under instruction from Ms Hakenfelt, the door of the office was forced open. Upon entering we discovered the body of Doctor Clay, seated at her desk, whom we ascertained had been dead for some hours. This was confirmed a few minutes later by Doctor Clay's colleague, Doctor J Zubin who suggested, so far as she could tell, death had been the result of poisoning or overdose by a substance or substances unknown. On the desk was a note written presumably by the deceased and addressed to her family. With further permission from Ms Hakenfelt, this was opened and read in order to ascertain if it provided further clues as to Doctor Clay's death. As a result of reading it, this would appear at first sight to be a case of suicide. The note is of a personal nature, expressing regret for actions taken recently by the deceased. Upon the arrival of Monitor Forensic Team Sw87341S at 0915 hours, the initial hypothesis of Dr Zubin was tentatively confirmed. Following a thorough

examination of the room and immediate surrounding
areas, no other suspicious findings were discovered by
the team. The body of Doctor Clay was then removed
to the Mortuary at 1045 approximately for further
examination. Doctor Clay's family were subsequently
informed and the note from the deceased, having been
copied, was handed over to them.

Mondrian L. Cazabeedis
Monitor 2nd Grade, SW Region

DIARY OF SOWEEN CLAY, 20ᵀᴴ DAY OF WINTER
(IN MY SIXTEENTH YEAR)

———————

They came to break the news to us regarding Mapa's death and handed Mama a copy of her suicide note (though they retained the original for some unaccountable reason). Mapa's body was taken away to the mortuary where they presumably took it apart and reassembled it again before returning her to us, along with her sad bundle of personal belongings and the clothes she'd been wearing, neatly folded. I noticed, not without some irony, that Mapa's clothes, unlike practically everyone else's around the Pool yesterday, were strictly correct down to her regulation elasticated vest and baggy grey bloomers. Orthodox to the last my dear Mapa, down to her very skin! Mama and I sat down at the table while I read her the note. She couldn't bear to read it herself.

My dearest Chayza and Soween,
Forgive me. I have done terrible wrong. Through my selfish actions, I have harmed so many people, my worst crime of all to be the cause of the deaths of an innocent girl and her unborn child and, indirectly, of my own beloved son. I want you to know I am solely to blame and no one else. Contrary to the rulings of The Preacher, I blindly allowed hatred to enter my heart where it drove out all compassion as He predicted it would. When I first set out in this world I was filled with love and determination to do only good. I felt equally loved by you all, my dearest family, and for that I will always be grateful. But I leave now with the feeling that all love has been drained out of me, as a result of my actions. I am, in turn, no longer worthy to receive love from anyone.
I hope maybe one day you will find it in your hearts to forgive me.
Your devoted, Mapa

When I finished reading, Mama and I cried together for the longest time. We clung on long after all our tears had dried up and the sounds of our grief had been reduced to a sort of rusty wheezing. It's moments like those that bring you closer, of course. Right now, Mama and I are the only people we have left in the world. I believe I have in me the resilience to continue. After all, I have the rest of my life ahead of me. But what on earth's going to happen to Mama? She seems quite lost now, staring about her as if she doesn't know where she is or even who she is any more. Help, someone! If there's anyone out there, please help us! I know one thing. It's definitely not worth looking in that stupid Book of Certitude for any answers. My copy's the first thing that's going on the bonfire, I can tell you, along with our dreary black dresses and bonnets, including Mapa's drawers!

* *Author's note:* At this point my diary, with its diligent and conscientious daily entries by my younger self, comes virtually to a halt, for which I must apologise. My excuse is that both Mama and I spent a long time at this stage of our lives, trying to come to terms with our respective futures. I confess I was tempted at one point to join many of my contemporaries and seek fame and fortune by crossing North through the recently abolished Divide. But Mama was reluctant to move or indeed express any inclination to go anywhere and I felt honour bound to stay with her. I owed her so much and could never leave her entirely on her own. She'd been so brave in the face of such a lot, it was the least I could do. Actually staying with her was no sacrifice for me, as it turned out. Mama and I got on fine as we largely shared the same pathetically passionate interest in constantly trying to keep the house clean and tidy. Even with only the two of us living there, the place still managed to accumulate a mountain of dirt and dust. After a few months, I persuaded her to go back to work, at least part-time, and I did the same. Unsurprisingly, Mapa had left us well provided for. She had stored a tidy little nest egg for us which, on top of her pension meant we were comfortable enough financially. But going to work at least meant getting

out of the house which was a lot healthier than being constantly cooped up together. Mama got her old job back at the factory on a part-time basis, whilst I volunteered my services three days a week to help out at my old infant school where, miraculously, Silla Kluth was still teaching. I say miraculously but she was still only in her early 40s and must have been, at the time she taught me, in her 20s, but back then, viewed through my child's eyes, she seemed ancient! The other major reason for abandoning my diary was the introduction, or perhaps I should say re-introduction to general access to the Internet and the opportunity for us all to communicate swiftly and immediately, initially at least, through the novelty of e-mail. It is through this, that the remainder of our remaining story, such as it is, will mainly be told from now on...

JUST OVER TWO YEARS LATER...

Still getting used to this new diary. Having been brought up on the PD system of dating, it's difficult to get my head round the previous old-style AD dating. It's very confusing. I used to celebrate my birthday regularly on 5 Spring but now it turns out I have to celebrate it today on 12th April. It's not a particularly special birthday this one and I told Mama not to go mad and start baking a cake or anything. After all, there's only the two of us here and it would look a bit sad and pathetic, me blowing out candles with just her watching. With the fall of the Divide, well over a year ago now, the Village has become unrecognisable. A lot of the Women, once they were free to do so, began drifting North across the former barrier into those once forbidden Male areas. These refugees were referred to locally as the triple H brigade (Hopeful Husband Hunters) or by the few remaining Orthodox diehards, more simply, Whores. Amongst the ones who left were Molwin and Yoteez. Happy hunting, girls! Axi and her sister Silje still live and work on their farm together. Sassa's there with them too although, so rumour has it, heaven knows for how much longer. She and Axi are, by all accounts, at each other's throats day and night. From the North as well, Men began drifting South, probably driven by similar motives as their North bound sisters. Significantly, within a few months of their arrival here, local rape statistics increased for the first time in 20 years by 300%! But starting from a base rate of zero, that totalled three in all. But it was enough to panic many local residents who, acting on the principle that if there are wolves prowling about outside, better marry a dog for protection, hurried into all manner of hasty, ill judged unions, many of which foundered within weeks. Never a sound basis for a long-term relationship, I felt. And so it proved when, after a few months, cases of marital abuse and domestic violence increased alarmingly. I'm sure things will settle down eventually but so far Mapa's dire warnings about Men's generally violent behaviour towards Women have been borne out. For all her fierceness, to my knowledge Mapa never raised a finger to Mama, although in the early years she certainly walloped the hell out of us two! Significantly, Mama and I now choose to go shopping together rather than individually, particularly around dusk. And as for solitary walks in the Woods, they're certainly a thing of the past, I fear. Ironic, considering we have such freedom these days in our dress, we still tend to cover ourselves strategically so as not to cause any passing Male to misinterpret a glimpse of a shoulder or an ankle as some sort of covert invitation. Men are quite extraordinary. Catch their eye in the Street and they seem to interpret it as an open sexual summons! But things can only improve, I hope. There are one or two signs already with genuinely happy marriages occurring and both partners, Man and Woman, sharing responsibilities in the normal way. Me, I try to avoid Men whenever possible. I prefer to wait till Mapa Right comes knocking on our door. Ha ha! Don't wait up, Soween! I'm now competing with a whole load of Men for her as well! I had the most extraordinary and unexpected email today. Almost the very first I have ever had and I got quite excited. But when I opened it, I discovered it was from Elihu's old school friend Fergo Flyn of all people! How on earth he got my address is a mystery. Why he should want to write to me to wish me a happy birthday, I can't imagine. I don't remember, back then, particularly ever liking him very much. I think he was one of the reasons I went off boys for life! He made my life a complete misery. Forever pinching and teasing me, when he wasn't pulling my hair. A loathsome little boy. Still I suppose he may have improved over the years. Though I somehow doubt it!

From: Fergo Flyn
To: Soween Clay
Subject: Birthday Greetings!

Hi! I don't know if you'll remember me but I was
a friend of your brother's at one time back in the
early days, though we both sadly lost touch when
I came of age and moved north of the Divide. Now
things have all changed (to my mind very much for
the better) I am back on the south side and about to
take up a post as a PE teacher at the newly formed
Tarness co-educational college. I hope you don't mind
my writing to you but you have recently been in my
thoughts a lot for some reason.
If you feel like writing back, I would very much like
to hear from you.

Your one time junior school companion,
Fergo Flyn

From: Rudgrin Obolos
To: Fergo Flyn
Subject: Well done.

Dear Fergo,
Well, the first step is the hardest, they say, and at least you've made that first bold move and actually written to her. I'm not surprised you found her response slightly 'cool' as you put it. She is, when all's said and done, a Woman and after all the years of enforced separation and with the traumatic recent events that followed, she is likely to remain a little suspicious of the male sex!
I am flattered you consider me, as you so kindly put it, 'an expert in Women'. I am, dear chap, so far as that beautiful, dizzying, unpredictable sex is concerned, as much in the dark as you are, I fear! Nonetheless I am very flattered that you chose to write to me.
Incidentally, talking of which, I have met (though whisper it not abroad) what I will refer to as A Special Someone. Though I won't reveal her name yet as it may all come to nothing. Call it superstition on my part!
Please don't hesitate to contact me again to let me know how you get on in your pursuit of your own Special Someone! From what I learnt about her from her dear brother, she is indeed very special!

Your comrade in the search,
Rudgrin

From: Soween Clay
To: Fergo Flyn
Subject: Replying to your last

Dear Fergo,
I was, as I said in my previous email, extremely
flattered that you remembered my birthday, though how
on earth you did that when I scarcely remember it
myself these days, was a miracle. And no, I can't say
I recall us ever being particular friends at Junior
School.
Besides, it would in those days have been highly
improper for me, a girl, to have harboured any
thoughts of a fond nature, let alone amorous ones,
towards a member of the opposite sex, albeit we
were both six years old! My young heart back then
was entirely given to my classmate Sassa Saraveen,
as I recall, for whom I carried a torch for several
years, until finally, of course, she took up with the
terrifying Axi.
On the subject of Sassa, I heard the other day that
she and Axi are no longer together and that Axi
finally lost all patience with her and chased her
off their farm at gunpoint! To be fair, Axi had some
justification, having recently warded off a horrific
attack by an itinerant male farm worker which must
have left her very shaken, poor woman, and then,
added to that, if Sassa as usual was behaving true to
type …
I believe, though, that the lesson for us all is
that we must not linger in the past, especially a
misremembered, rose tinted one like yours appears to
be, dear Fergo.

After all, we both have our futures to look forward
to now which inevitably will take us on our separate
ways. Farewell and goodbye.

Yours sincerely,
Soween

From: Rudgrin Obolos
To: Fergo Flyn
Subject: Lack of progress

Dear Fergo,
So sorry to hear your latest news. How very
frustrating it all must be for you. I do sympathise,
really I do. I wish I could be of more use. Do you
think it would be helpful to meet up with her face
to face, perhaps? I don't mean a formal meeting
which she clearly would decline, but something more
'accidental', perhaps, a chance encounter in the
village square (there are plenty of good new cafes
springing up there on almost a daily basis). Or maybe
just take the bull by the horns and why not simply
knock on her door unannounced. She can hardly slam
the door in your face, can she?

e bold, dear friend, is my advice,
Rudgrin

Thank you for asking. My own relationship with my
Special Someone grows day by day! Ironically, I have
the reverse problem to yours. Mine is moving things
forward so fast, she's practically taking my breath
away! Women! What can you do???

From: Soween Clay
To: Sassa Saraveen
Subject: Greetings to you!

Dear Sassa,
How lovely (not to say unexpected) to hear from you!
Yes, I heard all about your break up with Axi and I
was sorry but, if I'm to be truly honest, I'm not too
surprised by that turn of events! I think it was for
the best, Sassa, I really do, for both of you in the
long run. I was also sorry to hear, of course, about
Axi's frightening encounter. I hope she was not too
shaken by it. It could, perhaps, explain her extreme
behaviour towards you, to some extent. Poor Axi.
Despite her treatment of me in the past, I almost
feel sorry for her. Almost but not quite!
What I didn't know, of course, and was fascinated
to hear about, were your subsequent adventures north
of the Divide. How brave of you to join the triple H
brigade. It sounds such a lottery, I could never be
brave enough to try it myself. But Sassa, darling,
selling yourself for money, how could you?! I admit I
wept at the thought of that perfect, beautiful body
up for sale to the highest bidder. Oh, how sordid
and awful things have become for us! We have our
new freedom, true, but is it worth the price we have
to pay for it? How fortunate you met such a gentle,
understanding man on your very first outing. And in a
bar of all places! That little devil is still lurking
in you somewhere, isn't it? You make me feel so
timid, by comparison.
I am also being pursued. Yes, me! And guess who by
of all people? Fergo Flyn. That horrid boy from

our Junior School, do you remember him? Used to be
a close friend of Elihu's, for some inexplicable
reason. Well, I suppose you could call it 'pursuing'
me. After sending me a stream of increasing friendly,
not to say forward, emails (to which I replied with
due frostiness, I may add) he then turns up on my
doorstep, would you believe? Quite blatantly with
nary a blush! Mama, needless to say, invited him in
and plied him with tea and biscuits. Whereas I felt
like slamming the door in the wretched man's face, I
can tell you! Dear heaven, what do you make of these
creatures called Men, Sassa? They simply won't take
the hint! Please advise.

Mind you, having said that, I have to admit that,
over the years, he's grown into something quite
presentable, almost personable. Sort of handsome,
if you care for that sort of look. And being a PE
teacher he appears to be, from what I could gather,
what they term 'well muscled'!

Glad your own relationship is progressing smoothly,
but do beware my reckless darling, won't you? As my
beloved Mapa used constantly to warn me, "Men only
want ONE THING from you, Soween!". Mind you, knowing
you, you wicked imp, that's probably all you want
from them, too, isn't it?

All my love as always,
Soween xxx

From: Desollia Tarness
To: Soween Clay
Subject: A Special Request

Dear Soween,
I've been approached by members of the Village
Council asking whether I'd do them a sculpture to
stand by the Pool to commemorate Giella and Elihu. As
you know, it's become quite a visitor attraction of
late and the Council feels it needs a special feature
to mark it. But before I go any further, I wanted to
clear it with you and your mother before I said yes
to them, to see if, in theory, you both approved.
Perhaps we could meet somewhere to talk about it
further?
I was so terribly sorry to hear about Kest Clay.
I know she and Hork had their differences in the
Council Chamber over the years but I always respected
the unswerving conviction with which she held her
Orthodox beliefs even though I personally did not
agree with them.
I look forward to hearing from you,

With very good wishes to you and your mother.
Desollia Tarness

From: Soween Clay
To: Sassa Saraveen
Subject: News update from South Sarum

Dearest Sassa,
Thanks for all your latest news. Though I don't feel
you really needed to impart, in quite such lurid
detail, your nocturnal encounters with your beloved.
You are making this particular old maid feel quite
jealous!
On a more mundane, if more salubrious level, here
is my news. A couple of days ago, out of the blue, I
received a request from Desollia Tarness. Not someone
I imagined I would ever hear from again, given Mama's
continued and understandable aversion to all things
Tarness!
Anyway, on my way home from the school this
afternoon, I met her in a chic new cafe which has
recently opened in the Square. I don't think it would
have met with my Mapa's approval, somehow! I hadn't
seen Desollia since Elihu and Giella's wedding.
I remembered her as a tall, slim, slightly floaty
figure, as if carried on air. She's very different now.
Haggard, pale, hesitant with a slight tremble in her
voice. She looks a good ten years older, too. She
brought me up-to-date with what had happened to her
and her partner, former Councillor Hork Tarness. She
told me they had both been sentenced to a flogging
and hard labour but, after the tragedy of Elihu and
Giella, they both got a last minute compassionate
reprieve and instead only served a few months in
prison. But as soon as they were released, Hork
turned round and told her she couldn't continue their

relationship, blaming it on Giella's death, saying she couldn't face Desollia any more. Desollia would always be there to remind Hork of Giella. Desollia said sourly that, despite her overwhelming grief, that hadn't stopped Hork from running off with her Progressive Party protégée, Lebelia Whipple, who had, from all accounts, been making eyes at Hork across the Council Chamber for ages. Desollia said she'd felt totally betrayed! She then asked me about the proposed sculpture of Elihu and Giella and how I felt about it. And I said that, as far as I was concerned, it was a lovely idea but the final decision as to whether she went ahead entirely rested with Mama. Desollia would have to talk to her personally. So let her meet up with Mama, if the dares, and just watch the sparks fly!
More news anon,

All my love,
Soween

He keeps 'dropping in' for tea, by the way! It's becoming practically a daily occurrence. There must be some sort of spray you can buy to keep them away, mustn't there? Help!
Another thing! He confessed to me that when we were both at Junior School together he actually had "a thing" about me and on one occasion stole my new pencil case (which I got blamed for losing, naturally, and punished by Mapa, I might add!). He said he'd slept with it under his pillow for weeks afterwards because it made him dream of me. How utterly pathetic!

From: Fergo Flyn
To: Rudgrin Obolos
Subject: What now?

Dear Rudgrin,
I think I'm going out of my head with frustration. I
know people are subject to moods, can sometimes blow
hot and cold but she does it regularly within the
same sentence. Yesterday I got as far as to actually
hold her hand. A major step forward, you might think!
I certainly thought it did. But when I tried the same
thing today she snatched her hand away as if I had
leprosy! What does she want? Does she want to be left
alone, as her mouth is telling me, or to be kissed
passionately as her lips appear to be implying? Why
do women need to be so complicated???
I sometimes think the Preacher was right and we're
better off apart. I'll just find a good man and settle
down and live happily and uncomplicatedly ever after!
The problem is I don't want to settle down with a
man, good or otherwise!
One thing, though. We can't carry on sitting in
her kitchen, day after day, drinking tea and eating
biscuits and cake. We'll both grow as fat as pigs and
then no one will want either of us!
Help me, font of all wisdom on things female!

Yours in desperation,
Fergo

From: Soween Clay
To: Sassa Saraveen
Subject: More news from South Sarum

Dearest Sassa,
Listen you really mustn't keep sending me these
TERRIBLE SEXY emails, you really mustn't! What are
you doing to me, you sinful, wicked creature? I
wake up in the night with these FEELINGS. You know.
Feelings my Mapa, had she known, she'd have cut my
fingers off! Seriously, Sassa, it has to stop, please!
What's even worse is I'm starting to dream about him.
The demon biscuit eater!
Went to see Desollia's sculpture today, the one
she's doing to commemorate Elihu and Giella, I have
to say it's really beautiful and far better and more
tasteful than I expected. Simple and yet it says
'love' somehow. Quite moved, Mama and me and I had
a little cry, too. God I'm such an emotional gooey
mess!
All thanks to you, little Miss Hotpants!

Fondest love,
Soween xxxx

From: Rudgrin Obolos
To: Fergo Flyn
Subject: Go for it

Dear Fergo,
Sorry, I can do no more. You are evidently one of
love's lost causes, dear boy.
Here's my final, last ditch, make or break advice.
Take hold of the wretched girl firmly by the shoulders
and kiss her on the mouth. When she opens it in
protest, stick your tongue deep inside and wreak
havoc with her tonsils.
At least, that's what my beloved tells me you should
do. And, believe me, she knows about these things!
I speak as one who has had his tonsils "wreaked" on
numerous enjoyable occasions.
Incidentally, my Special Someone also says she has it
on good authority, though don't tell me how on earth
she knows this, that she is absolutely certain that
this is all that your own precious object of desire
dreams of secretly every night.
Go to it, lad or as they used to say in the days of
yore, have at it!

Your true friend in matters of the heart,
Rudgrin

I am eighteen years old today and the day when Desollia's statue will finally be unveiled. What a day it turned out to be, too! Virtually the entire Village turned out to watch. Since that dreadful time when Elihu and Giella had finally vanished beneath the waters, there can hardly have been more people gathered round the Pool than there were today. Everyone was there. The statue, now concealed beneath a cloth awaiting its unveiling, was sited just to the right of the waterfall on the slightly higher ground. Desollia and the current Council Chair, Feena Harran, stood either side of it and, just behind them, Mama. The rest of us milled around, churning up the damp grass around the banks, trying to avoid getting jostled into the Pool. I knew Mama, up there alone, had been asked to say a few words but of course she'd declined. At the other side of the Pool I caught a fleeting glimpse of Fergo and, anxious in case he saw me, I quickly turned away. A voice on my other side greeted me and I saw it was Sassa. She was wearing a brightly coloured, rather unseasonal summer dress and had on so much make-up that at first I scarcely recognised her. She was clinging to the arm of a long, tall, lean figure which I guessed must be her Most Perfect Man. To my surprise when he turned towards me I saw it was Elihu's former Tutor, Tutor Rudgrin. Not that miserable, overweight fanatic who'd replaced him. I must say Rudgrin and Sassa seemed a happy enough couple although, even in her absurd shoes, she barely came up to his belt buckle. But presumably, she added cattily, that was the area of her Most Perfect Man that she was most interested in. Silence was called for by the Councillor who then said a few formal words of welcome. She was followed by Desollia who spoke more personally about Giella and Elihu and the real love there was between them. A love like theirs, Desollia believed, was something immortal. When we die, she said, all that remains of us is the love we leave behind. Nothing else we leave is of any consequence. She said she hoped her sculpture, which she had named The First Kiss, would remind us of this and she urged us all to try to copy it, each in our own way whoever we were and of whatever persuasion, religious, political or sexual. Then Mama was called upon to officially unveil the statue. I sensed round me sounds of those struggling unsuccessfully to hold back tears. Including Rudgrin, who appeared especially moved but that may also have been the result of Sassa's claw like fingernails drilling into his arm. The statue really did look wonderful. Since we had last seen it in the barn in its rough state, the sculpture had taken on a sort of—not quite a shine, nothing as obvious as that—what I can only describe as a glow. It glowed. In the watery afternoon sunlight, it was truly moving to behold. A few of the crowd clustered forward to take a closer look at the statue and then, randomly, a few couples began to mirror it, clasping each other in an echo of the stone figures, pressing their mouths together in intimate and prolonged kisses. Men and Men. Women and Women. Men and Women until there was scarcely an individual figure to be seen anywhere. I saw Sassa reach up and pull Rudgrin down to her and devour him with a massive kiss of her own. And as I stood there feeling just the tiniest bit spare, there he was at my elbow. But before I could open my mouth to say anything he'd grasped my head and I'd grabbed his head and we held each other so fiercely before entering into the longest, deepest, most satisfying kiss of my whole life. I don't know if Fergo yet qualifies as my Most Perfect Man but on the strength of that, I'm prepared to risk it. Thank you, Giella, thank you, Elihu. Thank you for the gift of your love. It will live in this heart for ever. The end.

AFTERTHOUGHT...

* *Author's note:* It turned out that I did, after all, find The Most Perfect Man (for me at any rate!). A few days ago, Fergo and I celebrated our Golden Wedding Anniversary. Fifty years and counting!

> *Soween Clay-Flyn*
> *April 2154*

Bratton

Westbury

Imber

Chapmanslade

g

4

1

2 2

mf

Corsley Heath

Warminster

ne

4 2

Heytesbury

e

120

18 18 92 90

n/d

97

16

Codfo

ne

2

St Peter

(c

Long

Bridge

Walker Bourne

14

Maiden Bradley

Deverell

Bradley

4

Chicklade

Will

Ho.

New

Kilmington

6

Fonthill

Inn

103

100

The Hutt

92

3

98

Stour Head

96

8

14

12

Ho. Mere

Hindon

100

98

Zeals Ho.

10

16

Chilma

E

Fonthill Ho.

Kneyle

Nadder

12

Wardour

Castle

9

14

Ludwell

98

D

Fern

O

100

R

Shaftsbury

108 b

Ashcom

Rushm

S

E

L

Painell
Pa.
12

Tidworth
Nth

Shrewton
82
84
6
Mere
18
Stone Henge
10
Winterton
Stoke
80
Amesbury
Pa.
78
76
74
Amesbury
Malb

Deptford
8
6
6
Avon R.
Bourne R.
Lapca
Corne
the
Hutt

Grovely
Lo
8
4
4
2
Old Sarum
89
82
78
W
Ha

Barford
8
6
Wilton
2
S A L I S B U R Y
Clarendon
Park & Ho.

92
99
Wilton Ho.
86
Longton Ho.
88
Longford
W. Grimsteed
4

Hovent
Hutt
Ho.
Standlynch Ho.
Barford
New Ho.
6

S a l i s b u r y   Plain
4

ernditch Chace
6
Downton
Tippet
8
Tussuner Pa.
Brea
Bramsh

ALAN AYCKBOURN is an Olivier, Tony and Molière Award winning playwright. He lives in Scarborough, North Yorkshire, and has written more than 80 plays, many of which have been produced in London, in New York and throughout the world. As an acclaimed director, he has worked extensively in the West End and at the National Theatre. He was Artistic Director of the Stephen Joseph Theatre, Scarborough, from 1972 to 2009, where the majority of his work is premiered. Previously, he has written a best-selling guide to writing and directing, *The Crafty Art of Playmaking*. *The Divide* is his first work of fiction. He was knighted in 1997 for services to the theatre.